.... Shara raised her hand and let it fall. "The mercenaries hold the center of the land. But they have had no further help from off-world since our raiding parties destroyed the call tower at Three Ports two years ago. They have already had to abandon many of their weapons for lack of ammunition or repairs.

"Also there was the choking death, and they died from it, more of them than us. It is even said that the choking death was one of their weapons that was misused, since it spread out of Zohair after they occupied it. There are other ills, though, that Kadaya has loosed—the night crawlers—"

Andas shivered. "But those are only legends—to frighten children. Sensible men—"

"Sensible men believed not—and died!"

ANDROID
AT
ARMS

by
Andre Norton

ace books
A Division of Charter Communications Inc.
1120 Avenue of the Americas
New York, N.Y. 10036

1

It was a sere wasteland, riven by stark gashes, as if some intolerant and sadistic god had lashed it with a flail of lightning. There was no vegetation, whether gray, green, purple, or blue, nothing but the broken rock that sometimes reflected the heat of sun blaze, sometimes lay grimly dark under a thick massing of clouds—which was true now.

The building clinging to the rock tenaciously was so squat that it might be crouched awaiting some annihilating blow. It was uglier than the wasteland, for it had been built, not wrought by pitiless wind and weather.

Not that the prisoner, huddled by the narrow window slit that gave him so small a view of the world, could see the building. That he was a prisoner in a prison he understood. Why he had come here—who he was—

Sometimes he dreamed, and in those dreams he thought he knew. But though he tried to hold on to even a scrap of such a dream, he never succeeded. Upon waking, all he carried into the next stultifying day was a discontent, a dim belief that there *was* a different life he had once known.

There was food for his body and clothing, and now and then that discontent set him to force his sluggish mind to work—not to uncover lost memories, but to look through the slit, to wonder a little at the bare and blasted landscape. Yet never in all the time he had so watched had he seen any movement of lift there.

Cloud shadows reached out, spread, dwindled—nothing else, save when the storms came in their wild fury and torrents of rain ran in the gullies cut by earlier

7

floods and hail fell in great chunks to lie melting in the hollows.

One thing he could remember—why he did not know. He had a name—Andas Kastor. Was it really his name? He frowned now as his lips shaped that name, which was all he had.

There must be a different life out there somewhere, but what had he done to be exiled from it? How long had he been here? Once he had tried to count the days by scratching on the wall, but he had been sick and lost count. After that it had not mattered. There were the robots that brought food at intervals, that had tended him when he was sick—faceless things that he hated with what emotion had not been wrung out of him, but that were impervious to any attack or rebellion on his part. Twice he had tried that, only to have sleep gas flood his cell.

It was going to storm again. A faint flicker of interest stirred him. That was out of the normal pattern, and any thing that broke the pattern was to be treasured. They had had one of the bad storms only two days ago. The pools it had filled out there among the rocks had not yet entirely drained. To have a second so soon was most un-usual.

The clouds were gathering so fast that it was as dark as night. The lights in the corners of his cell came on, though they usually did not in storm time.

He stayed by the window slit, though the aspect out-side was threatening. Somehow the fear it caused sharp-ened his mind. There had been many storms. Wind, hail, pouring rain had done no harm to the building. Why should he feel apprehensive this time?

Night darkness and the howling of the wind—he could hear it even through these sound-deadening walls. He put his hands flat against the windowpane and felt a vibration of force. Solid and secure as the building was, the storm was striking at it with no ordinary power.

Now the lightning began, and the flashes were such that he was driven from his viewpoint, his hands over his eyes. He stumbled to his bed, crouched there, his head down on his upthrust knees, his hands over his ears. He was afraid as he could not remember having been before. This storm was such fury unleashed that he could only cower.

There was a great burst of light—then nothing.

Imperial Prince Andas sat up to stare about him dazedly. His head spun. He felt more than a little sick. But he steadied himself with one hand against the wall and looked about in desperate disbelief. He could *not* be seeing this! A dream—surely a dream!

Where was his own bed? There should have been four posts of Caldroden golden marble, each carven into a losketh with wings outstretched, and over his head the Imperial demi-crown of precious darmerian wood interset with the five gems. The walls—these gray walls? Where were the proper hangings of painted lamn skin, bronze-green, with here and there a tinge of faded red? There were no rugs—no—

Where *was* he?

Andas shut his eyes firmly to this nightmare and tried to think, to fight panic, which was a sour, foul taste in his mouth, a shaking throughout his body.

Anakue! This was Anakue's doing! But how—how had that half-crazed rebel—whom none took seriously—done this?

Andas kept his eyes closed. The how—that was something he could discover later. The now was more important. Grisly events from past history crowded into his mind, a montage of all the horror tapes one could imagine. Palace intrigues—he had heard of those—but only in the past. Such things did not happen nowadays—they could not! Why, no one with any sense listened to Anakue's ravings. His right to the throne was nonexistent, coming as he did from the illegitimate lines both long discounted.

Cautiously Andas opened his eyes again and forced himself to study what lay about him. This was not his bedroom, this gray box with its very simple furniture, lacking all the color and beauty he had always known. Now he looked down at himself, running his hands along his body to assure himself by touch that his eyes reported the truth.

No silken nightrobe—no, a coarse one-piece coverall such as laborers wore, gray as the walls. His hands—their natural brownness had a yellow tinge, as if they had not felt sun for a long time. He missed the rings he had always worn as his status insignia, just as his two wristbands were gone when he hurriedly pushed up his sleeves to make sure.

Now he began to explore his face, his head, by touch. His thick hair was not as long as it should be. It was clipped closer to his skull.

Shakily Andas got to his feet. Out—he had to get out, to discover where he was. But, this must be a prison—only, when he looked to the far wall, he saw a half-open door, though that part of the room was very dim, for the only light came from a slit of window.

Wary yet of the door, Andas went to the window and looked out on a scene that was a new and sharp shock. This was not Inyanga. Nor Benin, nor Darfor—he had visited both of those sister worlds in the Dinganian system. He braced himself by one hand on either side of the window and stared out at the forbidding wilderness of twisted and broken rock now running with streams of water. This was nowhere in the world he knew! Which meant—how could it be Anakue's doing?

Swaying, Andas edged along the wall, steadying himself with one hand. He had to find somebody, to learn— He had to *know!*

But when he came to that half-open door, Andas hesitated. It was even darker beyond, and what might lie in wait? His hand went to a belt he no longer wore. He had not even that ceremonial long knife which was seldom drawn from its elaborate sheath. He had nothing but his two hands. But the need for knowing drove him on, to sidle around the door and stand in a dark corridor.

There were one or two faint beams of half-light, as if they issued from other rooms. He slipped on, keeping to the wall, heading toward the nearest of those.

This was like combat training at Pav. He was suddenly fiercely glad that he had argued his grandfather into letting him have that experience. Of course, he had been then only third in line for the seat of the Lion, and it did not matter that he wanted to see life beyond the Triple Towers.

He reached the doorway and froze. The faint scrape of sound was from within. The room was not empty. Andas flexed his hands. He had learned a lot in combat training, and now he felt, rising above his bewilderment and fear, that cold and deadly anger that was the heritage of his house. Someone had done this to him, and he was ready to make the first comer among the enemy account in return.

"Please—is there anyone—anyone at all?"

A woman. But this was not too strange. Many times in the past a throne had toppled from intrigue begun in the Flower Courts of the Women, though he knew none favoring Anakue.

"Anyone—" The voice was a low wail.

Andas read fear in it, and that brought him into action. He rounded another half-open door to confront the occupant of a cell exactly like his own. She stared at him, and her mouth worked. In another moment she would scream. He did not know how he guessed that, but it was true. He moved with trained speed to catch her, holding his hand over her mouth.

But she was no palace woman, nor even of the Dinganian system—he would take knife oath on that. Her skin was very light against his own, and it was covered with tiny pearly scales, which felt rough to his touch. Her hair was green, and she had odd lumpy growths on either side of her slender neck.

"Be quiet!" he whispered.

After her first instinctive recoil when he had caught her, she ceased to struggle. Now she nodded, and somehow he trusted her enough to take away his hand. It was plain as he looked about that cell that she, too, must have been a prisoner, though her race and home planet he could not guess.

"Who are you?" Her voice was steadier than it had been earlier when she had cried for help. It was as if by seeing him she had gained assurance.

"Andas of Inyanga, Imperial prince of the Dinganian Empire," he told her, wondering if she would believe him. "And you?"

"Elys of Posedonia." There was that in her tone which made that name as proud a title as the one he had voiced. "What is this place?"

Andas shook his head. "You may guess that as quickly as I. I awoke and found myself here. By rights I should be in the Triple Towers at Ictio."

"And I in Islewaith. This—this is a prison, is it not? But—why—?"

He nodded again. "There are a number of 'whys' for

12

us, lady. And the sooner we get some answers, the better."

She spoke Basic as well as he, Andas noted, which meant that she was from some planet within the general sphere of influence of the Terran outflow in the past. But since no man recently had attempted to number those worlds, there was no reason why she should know his home system, any more than he hers.

"Do not leave me!" She caught his sleeve as he turned back to the door.

"Come quietly then," he ordered.

But an instant later they heard a footfall in the dark corridor that made them both tense. A shadowy form appeared in the doorway. Andas half crouched, his hands ready to deliver the blows he had been drilled in.

"Peace!" The newcomer held up a hand, palm out in a gesture of good will as old as time in the galaxy. He was a little taller than Andas, but this time his race was known to the prince.

Salariki! From his point-tipped ears to his sandaled feet, their claws retracted now, he was unmistakably of that feline ancestry. The fur on his head and outer arms and down his shoulders and spine was blue-gray, his skin a shade or so darker. And the slanted eyes in his broad face were a brilliant blue-green. He did not wear a coverall like the other two, but a kilt of the same coarse material. Now he stood with his hands on his hips, surveying the two of them.

"Two more fish in the net," he commented, his Basic slightly slurred with the hissing inflection of his species.

"And you?" Andas demanded. He found the Salariki's stare irritating.

"And I," agreed the other readily enough. "Though how I got here from Framware—"

"Framware?" Somewhere Andas had heard that name.

Then he put memory to good use. "Framware, the trading station of the Growanian Six Worlds!"

The Salariki showed his fangs in a grin, which Andas thought did not denote much humor.

"Just so. In fact, I was the head of our trade mission—I am Lord Yolyos."

Andas introduced himself, as did his companion. The Salariki rubbed a forefinger across his chest, the long, dangerous-looking claw at its tip extended to the fullest.

"It would seem," he remarked, "that someone has been collecting notables. You are an Imperial prince of somewhere—which doubtless has a weighty meaning in the right time and place. And you, lady"—he turned to the girl—"are you perhaps a ruler, or ruler to be?"

"I am the rightful Demizonda, yes." There was pride in her swift reply.

"We have other companions in misfortune," Lord Yolyos continued. "There is one, Hison Grasty, who assures us, and continues to do so regularly, that he is Chief Councilor of some place called Thrisk. And an Iylas Tsiwon, Arch Chief of Naul, and also one called Turpyn, who so far has not seen fit to supply us with more than his name. Now, what do you remember?" He shot that at Andas in an entirely different tone of voice, a sharp demand for information that the prince found himself supplying before he had a chance to resent such inquisition.

"Nothing. To the best of my memory, I went to bed in my own chamber—and woke up here. And you?"

"The same. Where *here* may be none of us seems able to supply. You, lady?"

The girl shook her head. "No more. A familiar room—then this!"

"There are indications," Lord Yolyos continued, "that there has been a power failure in this building."

"Power failure—" Andas repeated. "Inhibitor! They

14

may have had an inhibitor on us!"

"Inhibitor?" Apparently Elys did not understand.

"A mental block—to keep us from remembering. If none of us can, that must have been it!"

"Possible, yes. There is another point," the Salariki said. "We seem to be alone here. To all purposes, this prison was run by robots only."

"But that is impossible!" Andas protested.

"I shall be most happy to have the opposite proved true." Lord Yolyos held up his hand, extending all his finger claws, armament that Andas eyed with respect. He would not like to meet the Salariki in unarmed combat, not even with his own training. "I would like," the other continued, "to have an interview with the lord of this place. I do not think he would deny me any answers I desired."

Search the place they did, thoroughly. But when the band of prisoners gathered once more in the central space, they pushed among robots halted statue-like, sure that there were no other humans but themselves under this roof.

Of their company Iylas Tsiwon was clearly the eldest, though with all the rejuvenating methods now generally in use, plus the fact that there were great differences in the aging speed of various races, they could not be sure of that. But he was clearly the least strong, a small man, close to the Terran norm physically. His hair was thin and white, his face a pallid wedge with deeply graven lines on either side of his beak of a nose. His coverall seemed too large for his shrunken frame, and he pressed his hands tightly together to still the tremor in them.

Hison Grasty loomed over Tsiwon as if to make two of the frail Arch Chief. But it was mostly blubber that made up his bulk, Andas decided with inner aversion. His round face was rendered doubly unattractive by a dull red flush about his nose and mottled dewlaps. His obese body strained the seams of his clothing with every ponderous movement.

Turpyn, who had impressed Andas with his skill at seeking out every possible hiding place in the prison, was in great contrast to the other two. He, also, was probably Terran, but there were certain subtle modifications of the original that hinted at planetary mutation.

His hair was cut very short and looked almost as thick and plushy as that on the Salariki, but it was white, though not with age. In addition, he had a thick tuft of it jutting from the point of his chin. And his eyes were very curious indeed, showing no whites at all, only a wide disc expanse of silver. He spoke seldom and then only in monosyllables, nor had he made any other statement concerning his past than his name.

But he was the first to speak now. "No one here—robot controlled."

"We must get away," broke in Elys eagerly. "Get away before someone comes to start the machines again."

Turpyn turned those cold discs of eyes upon her. "How? We are in desert country. There are no transports here. And we don't even eat unless we can activate the food section again."

"And if an attempt to activate that starts everything—even the guards?" Andas demanded.

Turpyn shrugged. "I don't know if you can live without food. I know I can't."

Andas realized that he himself was hungry. So Turpyn was right—they had to have food.

Yolyos spoke first. "What chance have we of getting at the food supplies? I freely admit my people seldom deal with robotic equipment, and I am totally ignorant of the field. Have we an expert among us?"

Tsiwon shook his head, and a moment later Grasty's

16

jowls wobbled in the same gesture. Elys spoke aloud.

"My people are of the sea. We do not use such off-world machines."

Andas was angry that he must also deny any useful knowledge. But when the Salariki looked to Turpyn, there was a faintly different expression on his face.

"But you, I believe, do know. Is that not true?"

Andas wondered if the Salariki was purposely extending his finger claws as he asked that question, or if it was an unconscious reaction brought out by that hostility Andas, too, was sure lay beneath the surface of Turpyn's attitude.

"Enough—maybe—" The man turned and went to the far side of the room, being closely trailed by the rest. There was a control board there, and he walked along it slowly, now and then extending a hand as if to push some button or lever, but never quite completing that movement.

Was he a tech, Andas wondered, an engineer of such standing as would make him equal in rank to the rest of their prisoner band? Yet he did not have the manner of the techs Andas knew. He had, rather, the self-confidence of a man well used to giving orders. But unless he was playing a part now, he was not very familiar with these controls.

At length he appeared to make up his mind and returned along the wall installation, pausing only a second now and then to flip up a switch. When he reached the opposite end, he stopped and glanced over his shoulder at them.

"This is the test," he said. "I will switch on to an alternate power source. That may or may not work. I hope I have turned off the guard robots—perhaps I haven't. It's stars across the board, risking all comets." He reduced their chances to that of the galaxy-wide gambling game.

Tsiwon put out one trembling hand as if in protest, but if that was what he had in mind, he thought better of it and said nothing. Grasty backed to one side, into a position from which he could better see both the board and the robots. The Salariki did not move. Andas felt Elys's light touch on his arm, as if she thus sought some reassurance.

Turpyn pulled a last switch. Lights went on. They blinked against the brightness. Andas thought that those lights were a concrete argument that this room must sometime be used by humans—robots did not need them.

He was watching those robots with the same apprehension that held the others tense. Only one moved, and as it trundled doorward, he saw that it was a servo. It passed them at a steady pace and came to the wall at the end of the room, where it flashed a beam code against what seemed solid surface. A panel opened.

"So far, so good." Even Turpyn appeared to relax visibly. "But if we are going to eat, I would suggest that we get back to our rooms. That thing is programed to deliver the food there." And he started for the ramp leading to the cell corridor.

A little hesitantly the others followed. Tsiwon and Grasty first, the other three behind. As they started up, Yolyos made a small signal for caution.

"He knows more than he admits." There was no need for the Salariki to indicate who "he" was. Suddenly Andas had an idea. What if their jailer now posed as one of them? What better way to conceal himself than to claim to be another prisoner?

"He might be one of them you think?"

Yolyos again displayed his fangs. "An idea clever enough to be born from the mind of Yared himself! But not to be overlooked. I will not say that he is our enemy, but I would not hail him as cup-brother with any speed. We must discover the purpose for our being here, because only then can we bring our true enemies into the open. Think about that while you eat—"

"Need we eat apart?" Elys cut in quickly. "I confess freely to you, my lords, I have little liking for entering that room again, less for sitting there on my own. Can we not take the food when it comes and bring it to some common place?"

"Of course!" Though he would not have mentioned it, Andas knew the same uneasiness. To enter that cell and wait gave him the feeling that once more the doors might lock.

"Your room is between mine and the prince's." Yolyos fell in with her suggestion at once. "Let us collect our food and come to you."

Andas did not even go in his cell, but waited outside until the robot came rumbling down the corridor, pushed into the empty room, slid two covered containers and a lidded mug on the table, and went out. Then he collected all quickly and went to Elys's cell, from the doorway of which the robot was just emerging.

When he entered, she stood away from the wall. Andas pulled the upper covering from her bed and rolled it into a tight ball, which he pushed down to keep the door from closing automatically.

"Well thought on." As the prince got to his feet, the Salariki arrived with his own dishes.

It was when they opened all the containers that they had a new surprise.

"This," announced Yolyos, "cannot be prison food. Smalk legs stewed in sauce, roast guan—" He now flipped up the lid of the mug to sniff its contents. "Vormilk well aged, if I can believe my nose."

Since the Salariki sense of smell was famous, Andas

19

thought he could. But he was bemused at his own supplies. This was food such as might reasonably have come from the first table at the Triple Towers, except it was not ceremoniously served on gold platters and he was not wearing a dining robe of state.

"They put us in cells, dress us so"—disdainfully Elys flicked the stuff of her coverall—"and then feed us richly. Why?"

"Food of our own worlds, too." Andas looked at the girl's main platter. He did not recognize the round white balls resting on a mat of green resembling boiled leaves.

"Yes." The Salariki raised a spoon to suck noisily at its contents. And the prince remembered that the aliens made a practice of eating with sound effects, so that the host might be sure of the enjoyment of his guests.

Just another question to have answered, he thought. Then he fell to eating with full appetite.

2

Whether their fellow prisoners had been moved to dine together, Andas did not know or care. But once his hunger was satisfied, he realized that their party seemed to have divided in two. He, Yolyos, and Elys—the other three (unless Turpyn walked alone) in the other group. He commented on this.

The Salariki replaced the lid on his mug, having drained the last drop of its contents with relish.

"Of Naul I know something," he said. "It is close to the Nebula, a collection of three systems, ten planets. We have trading stations on three. One exports the Tear Drops of Lur—"

He must have noticed Elys's baffled expression, for he explained.

"Perfume, my lady, and a very rare one. It is distilled from an exudation that gathers on certain stones set like pillars among native vegetation—but it is not traders' information you seek now. It remains that I have heard of Naul, and if this Tsiwon is who he says he is, then in him you see one of equal power perhaps with your emperor, Prince. Incidentally, where lies this empire?"

"From here—who knows? We of Inyanga hold the five planets of the system of Dingange—Terran rooted. Our First Ships came with the Afro outspread," he said proudly, and then knew that this history meant nothing to these aliens and hurriedly added, "That was a very first outspread."

But since that appeared to mean nothing either, he elaborated no further. Instead, he waited for Elys to add her bit to their pooled information.

"I am Demizonda of Islewaith. We have spread to no

23

other planet, since our sun has but three, and two are near waterless. But I have heard of Thrisk where this Grasty must rule. They control the Metallic Weed Combine."

"Naul, Inyanga, Thrisk, Posedonia, Sargol—" Andas began when the Salariki corrected him.

"Not Sargol—if you mean from where I was snatched. As I have said, I was on Framware then. I wonder how the trade treaty advanced after my disappearance." He flexed his claws, eying that display absently.

"Time!" Andas got swiftly to his feet, for the first time sharply aware of what might have been for him a disastrous passage of planet days—even weeks. "What day—month can it be now? How long have we been here?"

Elys gave a little cry. Her hands, with the delicate webbing halfway up the fingers, flew to her mouth. "Time!" she repeated. "The full tide of Qinguam! If that is past—"

"So." That word in Basic became the hiss of a feline in Yolyos's mouth. "May I guess that each of you also were faced with a situation in which time had importance?"

Andas caught the significance of that at once. "You think that is why we are here?" And he followed that question quickly with an answer to Yolyos. "Yes, time has importance for me. I am not in direct line to the throne. Among my people it is not as on some worlds; the crown does not pass from father to son. Rather, since my ancestors had a number of wives—officially one from each of certain noble families—the Emperor designates his choice from among those of the royal clan houses who are of suitable age. Though such multiple marriages are no longer common, yet the choice still lies among all the males of the royal line.

"It is my grandfather who rules the Triple Towers now, and he had three possible heirs of my generation—four if one counts Anakue. But when he summoned me to his presence, it was thought he had chosen. Only to make it final, I must appear on the day of Chaka and be crowned by his own hands in the presence of all the houses of a Hundred Names. If I am not there—"

"You lose the throne?" Yolyos prompted as Andas's voice trailed away. For the first time he realized just how deeply disaster might have struck.

"Yes." He sat down on the edge of Elys's bed.

"Now I have a treaty instead of a throne to protect. But if I am not at Framware to argue it through, then it is not only that I shall have my name and clan blackened, but also Sargol loses." Once more the Salariki flexed his claws, and his voice dropped to a low throated growl.

"I must sing the full tide in, I must!" Elys clenched her hands into fists. "If I do not, the charm passes from the blood of Elden to Ewauna. And that must not be so!"

"Three of us, and perhaps them also." Andas nodded to the door to signify the others. "But why? Those who might wish us elsewhere are widely scattered and have nothing in common. Who would collect us here?"

"Well asked, young man." The voice might have had the tremor of age, but the words came forcibly. They looked up to see Tsiwon within the door. "I, too, can add to your list of people who have reason to want to know the present date. If I have not been present to speak against the proposed alliance with the Upshars—" He shook his head. "I fear for Naul. Now"—he rounded on Andas—"on what day do you remember being last in your proper place?"

"It was the fifth day past the feast of Itubi. Oh, you mean in galactic reckoning—wait." Andas did a sum in his head—planet time was for planet life only, and from world to world the length of days and years varied. "As far as I can make it—but it would be the year only—2230 A.F."

"You are wrong!" Elys shook her head emphatically. She had been tapping fingers on the table top as if counting off some numbers. "It was 2195. I know that's true," she continued triumphantly, "because I had reason to consult the overdating just the day before—the day—"

"You say 2230, this young lady 2195," Tsiwon repeated. "Now I have good reason, very good reason, to know the proper date, since I had contact with the Central Control commissioner and thumb-signed two documents. And the date on those was 2246."

"I shall add the final confusion." Yolyos broke across the assurance of that statement. "My last date was 2200."

Andas glanced from one to another. There was indignation plain to read on Tsiwon's age-seamed face and Elys's youthful countenance. Only the Salariki appeared unruffled by what must certainly be the most inaccurate working out of galactic dating he had ever heard.

In his head the prince did some adding and subtracting. Between his date and Elys's lay thirty-five galactic years, between Yolyos's and his thirty years, while he differed sixteen years from Tsiwon.

"Do you now begin to wonder"—Yolyos broke the silence of their dissent—"just *how* long we have severally been here and whether it is possible we did not all come at the same time?"

But Andas did not want to consider that. If Tsiwon's reckoning was correct—why, then, long since had his chance slipped from him! Who ruled now—Jassar, Yuor, even Anakue? How long had he been here? He looked at his smooth brown arms and what he could see of his body. He did not seem any older. He could not be so—he would not!

"First, how do we get away?" Elys demanded. "What

matters speaking of time until we do? We have been under a mind lock here—we must have been, or we would remember how we came to these holes!" She glanced about with disdain. "So perhaps we do not remember clearly even now. But get away—I must!"

Andas had gone to the window slit. The scene outside was almost exactly what he saw from his own cell, save that the water which had been there earlier was drying, leaving pools and threads of streams where there had been small lakes and rivers. But the bleakness promised nothing in the way of escape.

"I think we should ask Turpyn," Yolyos said.

Andas looked back. "Do you think then that he might be a guard, pretending to be one of us?" He repeated his earlier thought.

"Ingenious and possible. Though I believe on our first meeting I detected in him some of the same reactions to awaking here in the unknown. But he either knows this place better than we do, or else he is aware of its purpose and that of our being here, for his first reaction was outrage."

"As if some trap of his own had sprung on him?" Tsiwon interrupted. "You are right, Lord Yolyos. I had a similar impression when we first gathered. So, let us ask questions of Turpyn and this time receive straight answers." The old man's face had not looked benign before, and now his straight-lipped mouth and the expression in his eyes made Andas shift from one foot to the other.

The history of Inyanga was bloody enough. There had been rebellion, the rise and fall of dynasties accompanied by blood spilling, much his people had to feel shame for. But that they did today feel shame for such acts was hailed as a definite step toward another civilization. In Tsiwon's face he read recourse to older and darker ways.

But there was nothing to say until they found their

man and he either refused to talk or otherwise opposed them. He followed the Arch Chief of Naul and the Salariki out the room, Elys behind him.

Neither Turpyn nor Grasty was in his cell, and once more the others descended the ramp. The standing robots made it difficult to see the whole of this room. It was a perfect place for an ambush. Andas motioned the girl behind him. He wished he had even a knife of ceremony. One man with a stunner or blaster could master them all.

"Over there—" The prince started at that hiss from his left. The Salariki was pointing to the far right where a door stood half open.

They took the long way around, not weaving among the stalled robots, but keeping to open spaces along the walls, a precaution Andas heartily endorsed. He had not trusted Turpyn from the first, and whether there might be others here they had not located in their search was a question that continued to plague him. Somehow the idea of a prison run only by robots did not seem possible.

"—no better than the rest. So don't try it! My offer is the only one worth taking."

Grasty's voice, thick and throaty, reached them. There was a muttered answer they were too far away to hear. Once more Grasty spoke, his tone one of exasperation and rising anger.

"You will do it because you are no better situated than we are, Veep!"

Veep! That title was one which almost every civilized planet in the galaxy knew to its sorrow. Thieves' Guild boss! It fitted this situation exactly! Kidnaping on the scale their presence here represented could only have been carried out by the Guild. In that case, they were being held for ransom, and Turpyn *was* the one left in charge—

Andas caught the Salariki's eye. The alien made a quick gesture of assent. Tsiwon and the girl—Andas motioned them to stay where they were. Shoulder to shoulder with Yolyos, he moved toward the door, aiming a kick that sent it flying fully open. The alien entered with an effortless leap, and Andas followed. Grasty was standing over Turpyn, the Veep, who was sitting before a small control board.

Both swung around at the entrance of the other two. Grasty fell back a step or so, which in that narrow space brought him against a cabinet for tapes. Andas crowded him, hands coming up to deliver the blows that would render this man helpless before he could move his flabby bulk. The Salariki had gone for Turpyn, hooking his claws in the other's coverall at the shoulders, dragging him up and out of his seat.

"What—" began Grasty.

"Close your mouth!" Andas scowled at him. "Or I'll close it for you. What deal were you making with this Veep?"

"Ask at the source," Yolyos said. He gave his captive a deceptively gentle shake, and the man's pallid face twisted, though whether in pain or apprehension of what might happen to him, Andas could not guess.

"Now, little man," Yolyos continued, "tell us what you know that we should be aware of." With apparently little or no effort, he held his captive so that Turpyn's feet no longer touched the floor. Though the man writhed and fought, he could not break free. His face smoothed, then, as if he had come to some decision, and he stopped his useless struggles.

"I will tell you what I know," he agreed in a flat tone. "It is little enough, though there may be that here which will inform us." He pointed with his chin to the wall facing him.

Andas saw then that the cabinet against which Grasty leaned was not the only record depository. Three of the four walls were so furnished, and behind the control desk where Turpyn had been seated, there was a visa-screen, now blank.

"Speak." Yolyos lowered him into the chair, but he did not release his hold. He stood behind Turpyn, those claw points visibly piercing the fabric, at some places marked with small red stains.

"I don't know much." Turpyn's face was now expressionless. "And a lot is guessing—from things I once heard—"

"Spare us time waste," ordered Yolyos. "Begin with what you do know and let us judge whether it be small or large."

"Mind you—I have only bits and pieces," he still insisted. "But what I have heard is this—that there is a place where, for a price, one could exchange a man for his android double. And that double could be programed to do what the buyer desired, while the real man was kept in storage, to be disposed of later if wished."

"A likely story!" Andas burst out.

"Be not so quick, young man." That was Tsiwon now inside the door. "Never say anything is impossible. And this service"—he advanced to the other side of the desk and leaned across to better meet Turpyn eye to eye—"was run by whom? The Guild?"

Turpyn shook his head. "None of ours. Would I be here if it was?"

Grasty snickered. "You might, if there was a power struggle on. Promotion in the Guild changes often by force."

Turpyn's mouth drew tight, but he neither looked at the councilor nor answered that taunt. "The Mengians were responsible—according to what I heard."

Andas was bewildered. That name was new to him. But he saw the change on three other faces. Grasty speedily lost that malicious grin, and both Tsiwon and Elys looked startled. There was a shadow of what could only have been fear on all three.

"Enlighten us," Yolyos ordered. "Do not complicate matters. Who—or what—are the Mengians?"

"The heirs of the Psychocrats." Tsiwon spoke before Turpyn. "It is not generally known, but those were not totally wiped out when their oligarchy fell. There have always been tales that a handful escaped, withdrew to some hidden place to carry on their experiment, the code name for their headquarters being Mengia. Now and then legends have a remarkable core of reality."

Andas shivered. Psychocrats had not meddled in Dingane's system. But they had heard tales. If their sort still existed, it would be dark knowledge to set at least a quarter of the galaxy having nightmares.

"This—this could be so." Grasty had lost his arrogance. "It is the sort of plan they would make, this introducing rulers of their own. And, by all accounts, their techs had the skills to make undetectable androids. Why, they could reconquer all they had lost, without discovery until too late! Back—I must get back to Thrisk—warn—"

"It may already be far too late," Tsiwon said slowly. "We do not know how long we have been here. Our replicas could well have turned our rulerships into holdings for the Mengians."

That first chill Andas had felt was nothing to the cold encasing him now. If they had been prisoners of some remnant of the Psychocrats, why, then even the weird difference in time they had worked out earlier could also be true! They could have been kept here in some state resembling stass-freeze. And that had been known to last for centuries of planet time!

It was Yolyos who spoke. "You mentioned earlier, Turpyn, that this service was run for sale. Then you speak of it being a Mengian plot to regain their control. Which was it—transactions with those who had good reason to wish us personally out of the way, or a plot aimed at us simply because we held the positions that we did?"

Turpyn shook his head. "That is one of the things I can't answer, and it is 'can't' and not 'won't,' I assure you. I heard of this setup as a straight transaction. On payment, anyone selected would be taken, his android double substituted. Then there was a second rumor that the buyer himself was double-crossed. How true I can't tell."

"But to fashion such an android, implant it with the proper memories—how could they do it?" Elys wondered. "They would have to be almost flawless to deceive those who know us well. Such a process would take time. And if we did not lend ourselves to memory taping, how *could* they do it?"

"If the Mengians are the Psychocrats and they are responsible," Andas said, though he shrank from what seemed the truth, "then they could do it, somehow. They did stranger things with men's bodies and minds when they ruled."

"All the more reason"—Grasty pushed forward—"for us to get back as quickly as possible and see what has happened, repair the damage—"

He must not have considered time lapse, Andas decided. But to get away from here, yes, that was their first concern. Only how? Yolyos was already on that track.

"You know something of such installations as this." He addressed Turpyn. "How do they get supplies? I do not believe that the food we have just eaten was grown from proto cells."

"Behind you is a ship call, but the setting suggests a

robot autocontrol," the Veep answered. "If any supply ship comes, it must also be robot, locked on a single course. In order to use it for escape, we shall have to substitute tapes, and where will you get another? Unless the ship has a collection—which is not always the equipment of a locked course transport."

"What is this room? There are records of some sort stored here." Andas tried to fit his thumb into the release on the nearest cabinet and found it impossible.

"Locked—on some personna lock."

"Since when has such a thing as a personna lock," inquired Grasty, "kept a barrier intact when faced by a Guild tech? You can open these."

"Given time and tools, yes," Turpyn admitted.

"You'll have both," the Salariki promised. "Suppose we start looking for tools now."

Though Turpyn grumbled and swore that he probably could not find the delicate instruments he needed, he went to the smaller section of the outer room where one of the robots, halted like the rest in mid-section, had been engaged in repairing one of its fellows whose outer casing sat to one side. The main parts of its inner works were spread out on a bench.

There the Veep picked and chose until he had a handful of small tools Andas could not identify. They had all trailed along to watch him, as if their united wills could spur him to greater efforts.

With his possible pick-locks he went to the record room and set to work. That he was an artist in his field was clearly to be seen. Andas wondered at his dexterity. If he were a Veep, surely he would not be one of the general workmen of the Guild—unless there were criminal actions that fell to the upper class alone. At any rate, he knew what he was doing.

It took a long time. Tsiwon pleaded fatigue and went

back to his cell. Sometime later a drooping Elys followed him, seeming to have lost her fear of being alone.

Grasty had taken the chair before the visa-screen, fitting his flabby bulk into it with difficulty. Andas watched for a while, but was too restless to stay on in that narrow room, choosing to prowl about the larger chamber, moving less warily now among the stalled robots.

Beside the repair alcove was the room into which the food robot had gone, but he could not open that door. However, there was another, which yielded.

A burning hot wind blew into his face. His eyes squinted against a glare as he took one step into the outer world, his hand keeping the door ready for retreat from this heat, light, and smell, for the air had an acrid odor that set him coughing. He feared to remain outside long. He had had time enough to sight the burn-scarred, slag-frosted surface of a landing field. How long had it been since the last ship set down there?

Coughing, he retreated, sealing out that atmosphere. One thing was plain. Without some form of body protection, probably also breathing masks and eye goggles, none of them could last long planet-side here.

There were no other openings. He made the circuit of the walls, returning to the room where Turpyn still worked. And he arrived just in time to see the Veep stand back and give a jerk with a tool he had set point-deep in one of those depressed locks. There was a splintering sound, and the drawer opened.

His guess was right. Orderly rows of taped records faced them. Grasty was still trying to pry himself out of the chair, but Yolyos elbowed Turpyn aside and raked out the nearest tape case.

Where there should have been a title there was only a code—as they might have expected.

"A reader—where is a reader?" Grasty hammered on

34

the desk top with the puffy palm of his hand as if that would make the necessary device rise out of its surface.

But it seemed that Turpyn knew something more of the room. He snatched the tape from the Salariki, shook it from its case, and snapped it into a slot topping a small bank of controls that took up more than half of the desk surface.

"Out of the way, you tub of sogweed!" He pushed at Grasty, sending the big man away from the desk.

Turpyn paid him no more attention, turning instead to thumb a lever. The visa-screen rippled alive, and a clear picture showed there in tri-dee detail. It was the body of an alien, totally naked.

"Zacathan." Andas did not know he had made that identification aloud until he heard his own voice. But that was speedily drowned out by a precise voice, human in timbre, reciting a series of code sounds that had no meaning. The picture changed from the whole body to sections, each enlarged, and always accompanied by the code.

They watched to the end of the tape, learning nothing more than the exact details of the unknown Zacathan's body. Then both the pictures and the voice were gone.

"I think," Yolyos remarked, "that that was a pattern for the making of an android. Some other unfortunate who was meant to join our company, but he did not. Suppose we try another."

The second tape was poised in his hand to be inserted in the reader when the visa-screen flashed a new image. But now the code symbols running across it meant something to Turpyn.

"Ship planeting," he announced.

At the same time there was a clanking noise from the outer room, and Andas, nearest to the door, moved to look out.

Three of the largest robots, which had been in one line against the far wall, were moving forward as if the arrival of the ship activated them when it was still off-world. They were cargo carriers, and they were rumbling on toward that door through which Andas had looked out into the waste.

3

"That is the present situation." Yolyos had their full attention as he stood with one hand resting on the broad back of a carrier robot. "We have managed—or rather Turpyn has—to halt the unloading. And until the ship is emptied, it will remain finned down out there. It is not a passenger ship, but there is a life-unit section in it for emergencies, though we shall find those quarters very crowded if we can retape the ship and take off."

Andas considered all the ifs, ands, and buts that now faced them. It would be easy enough to stow aboard in that life section and allow the ship to transport them back. Only that would land them in the hands of the enemy. They must reset the ship with another trip tape. But so far all the cabinets had offered them were broadcasts of code and series of pictures in detail of men and aliens.

Watching those as they tested tape after tape, Andas wondered if they would turn up those pertaining to any member of their own small company. So far that had not happened. And Turpyn was raiding more compartments than the first he had opened, now choosing samples in a random fashion.

They ate again and, driven by fatigue, slept. And they continued to split into two parties, though Tsiwon at present stayed closer to Andas and his companions. While they kept together, neither Grasty nor the Veep appeared very friendly.

It was on the second day that Turpyn admitted defeat. He stood surrounded by gaping drawers, a full tide of discarded tapes rising almost ankle-deep on the floor.

"Nothing." He announced failure in a flat voice. "Nothing we can use."

Andas spoke up. "We have not tried the ship."

"Getting into her will be the problem," but there was a trace of animation in Turpyn's tone. "I have some tech knowledge, but I am no spacer. What of you?" He swung his head slowly, giving each a searching stare.

Andas's own experience went no farther than that of a passenger. And he believed no one here could say more, unless Turpyn, in spite of his denial, was holding out on them. To their surprise, Elys spoke first.

"I know that the entrance ramps are controlled from within. But certainly this is a problem that must have arisen somewhere, sometime before. Are there no emergency ways to enter a ship?"

It was as if her words turned a key deep in Andas's memory. He had a fleeting picture of a ship finned down on a landing strip, a figure climbing by handholds on the outer edge of the fin itself, something he had seen in passing. He had asked an idle question at the time.

"The service hatch!"

He was not even aware they were all watching him. Surely all ships were general in some points of construction. If so, this one should have the same hatch.

"Above the fins." He cut his explanation. "A repair hatch for techs. There's a chance that might open."

"Any chance is worth taking now." Tsiwon's usual quaver disappeared in an excitement that strengthened his voice.

"At night or at twilight anyway," Yolyos said. When Andas, eager to try to prove his memory right, would have objected, the Salariki pointed out the obvious.

"We have no protective clothing. To go out in the glare of that sun and perhaps have to remain in the open working—"

He was right. To none of them, different in race and species as they were, did this world hold welcome beyond the door of their prison.

And Andas, impatient as he was, was aware of another problem. Once within the repair hatch, if they could find and open that, was there access to the rest of the interior of the ship or only to a confined section for techs? If he, if any one of them, only knew more! The education of an Imperial prince was certainly lacking in survival training. Not that they would speedily die here if they could not find a way out, but perhaps quick death would be better than lingering stagnation.

The party attempting to invade the ship narrowed to three—Andas. Yolyos, and Turpyn, whose tech knowledge was indispensable. After the harsh sun that blistered this unknown world set and its glare was gone, they headed for the field.

Whatever remote controls triggered the landing of the cargo had not functioned. It was as hatch-sealed as if in space. But they wasted no time in heading directly for the fins. Luckily the winds, with their torturing dryness, had died away, though it still hurt to breathe too deeply, and Andas wondered what long exposure to this atmosphere might do to their bodies.

The hand and foot holds were there. Though they did not want to, they must let Turpyn make the first climb, since if the hatch was to be forced, only he could deal with it. Andas swung up close on his heels. He had no trust in the Veep.

Clinging to the holds below Turpyn, whom he heard now and then spitting an oath in a tongue not Basic, Andas tried not to breathe too deeply and to ignore the stinging of his nose and the way his eyes teared.

Turpyn gave a louder grunt and humped up, Andas quick to follow, with Yolyos behind him. As he pulled within the shell of the ship, he found himself in a narrow passage, so narrow that it was difficult to squeeze through. There was a second hatch Turpyn's torch showed, but the Veep had started to climb again, using more handholds to ascend to the upper levels.

So they won through the narrow ways meant only for techs, on major repairs, into the living quarters. After a quick inspection Turpyn gave a sigh of relief.

"This has been in use and not too long ago—perhaps on the last trip of the ship. It can be activated with some work. But we shall have to see about the controls. It will do us no good otherwise."

They followed him up to the control cabin. There were signs that at times this drone did carry a crew, for webbing seats were slung for both pilot and astrogator before the proper controls.

Turpyn pushed past those to stand before the pilot's board, studying the array of buttons and levers. Then he pressed one, and there was an audible click as a trip tape arose from a slot.

"If there is a file of these—" He weighed the useless one in his hand. Andas had already started searching by the astrogator's seat. And his prying and pulling at a snug thumbhole paid off. A compartment opened to show in its well-cushioned interior four more tape casings. He clawed the first out to look at the symbol on its side. But he did not recognize it. In fact, they might be entirely off any galactic map he was familiar with. He dropped it to the web seat and picked a second.

Again disappointment. No longer did he expect any luck, but perhaps some other of their company would know more. Only—the third! At first he could not believe the report of his eyes, running his finger back and forth to feel the slight roughness of that raised design, assuring himself that it *was* there.

"Inyanga—it is Inyanga!"

Yolyos had scooped up the two discarded ones. "And that one—" He pointed to the last in the compartment.

"It does not matter!" The prince treasured his find in his two hands lest someone snatch it from him. He had his key to home. "Don't you understand? This will take us to Inyanga—and from there you can reach your own worlds."

"Still I am interested." Yolyos secured the last one.

"Naul—"

Andas held to his tape with a jealous grip. All right, so there was one for Naul. But they would go first to Inyanga.

"I think"—the Salariki might have been reading his mind—"that you will find some slight opposition to such a plan, Prince. And we do not know where we are, so that Naul may well be the best and safest choice after all."

Yolyos shoved the two unknowns back into the compartment. He kept the one for Naul. But Andas had no intention of surrendering the one he held until he himself dropped it into the right slot and knew the ship was heading for home.

Oddly enough, Turpyn paid little attention to their exchange. He was moving around the control cabin testing this lever, pressing that button, as if to assure himself that the ship could be switched from drone to active status. Finally he spoke.

"It will do. Cramped quarters for all, and no knowing how long a flight. There ought to be E-rations on board. But we had better see to supplies."

They went down into the living space again. As the Veep had pointed out, that section was never meant to house more than four at a time. But to get away from their prison was worth any amount of crowding.

There were stored rations, and the air plant was in action, though if their voyage was too long—*Was* Naul nearer? Perhaps their best chance lay with one of the strange tapes. Yet why would Naul or Inyanga be stored at all unless they were both within easy cruising distance? Only a First-In Scout or a Patrol cruiser carried tapes on long voyages.

So reassured, Andas was ready to do battle for his choice as they returned to the prison, this time down the ramp they could lower from within. They found the others waiting eagerly.

"Naul, of course," Tsiwon said as if there could be no possible question. "We have excellent transshipping from our ports, and you will have no difficulty in reaching your homes. Also we have a Patrol Sector office. This offence must be reported at once. To discover how deeply this conspiracy has taken root needs expert investigation."

"Inyanga's ports are also Sector centers," Andas stuck in, determined to hold his ground. "I see no reason for choosing Naul."

"The two of you," Elys said wearily, "can doubtless continue to argue for days. I, for one, have no wish to waste time sitting here listening to you. To my mind, Naul has no advantage over this Inyanga as far as I am concerned, and perhaps that is also true for Chief Councilor Grasty and Lord Yolyos, as well as Veep Turpyn. After all, on my own world I had never heard of either, which means I may have half the galaxy to cover before I reach home. Since we cannot guess where we are at present or in what relation we lie to either of your two worlds, it will be largely a matter of chance as it is."

"Naul!"

"Inyanga!"

Almost in one voice Andas and Tsiwon answered.

Yolyos made a sound not far from a growl. "The lady is right. We have two tapes and six of us who may be bound in directly opposite directions. Neither of the ports you urge upon us has any great appeal as far as we are concerned. Therefore, let us let chance decide. Here—" He picked up one of the lidded basins in which their last meal had been delivered. Taking up the cloth that had served as a napkin, he wiped the basin out thoroughly.

"Now"—he offered it to Tsiwon, who held to the Naul tape as tightly as Andas did his—"drop it in, Arch Chief. You, too, Prince. We shall have a drawing—"

"And who shall do the drawing?" Tsiwon demanded before Andas could. "The lady has been with you, and you—you have been his constant companion." He stabbed a finger at the Salariki and then at Andas.

"True enough." Yolyos put the lid back on the basin. "Turpyn, can that robot doing the repairs be activated enough to pick up one of these? We cannot accuse it of any favoritism."

"Yes, it can." The Veep sounded almost eager, as if he had despaired of their ever coming to a decision. "Come—"

With all of them watching, Yolyos placed the basin, uncovered once more, where the robot stood. Andas and Tsiwon dropped in the tapes. One of the tentacle arms that had been so long raised in the air dropped the small tool it held and descended to the basin after Turpyn had made the adjustments he thought necessary. It raised jerkily again, one of the tapes gripped fast. The Veep hastened to kill the power, and Yolyos pried the selection loose.

"Inyanga," he informed them.

Tsiwon could not say that the choice had not been fair. But his expression was sour, and he took the rejected tape, holding it as if with it in his possession he might still have a chance to use it.

They had no luggage, but they raided the food room, bringing with them all that was container-stored. The harsh dawn was breaking when they finally climbed the ramp into the ship and somehow fitted themselves into the life section. There was some relief from the crowding when Turpyn, Yolyos, and Andas went to the control cabin. Though he was no astrogator, the tall Salariki settled in that seat, while Andas took the stand-by officer's seat just behind. Turpyn was in the pilot's place. The prince watched the Veep slip in the tape and set the auto-pilot to take off.

The warning sounded, and they strapped in, ready for the force of the blast. When that came, Andas found the strain to be far worse than he expected. There was less cushioning that eased the passengers through this ordeal than on the usual flight.

He aroused groggily only to discover another difference between this and the transportation he had been used to. There was no artificial gravity in the drone, and he had to adjust to weightlessness. The ensuing period of time was a new form of torment.

Among the others, Yolyos, though he admitted he had not met this before, was the first to learn to handle himself in space. Tsiwon, Grasty, and Elys felt it the most. They had no drugs such as were normally issued, nor voyage-sleep, which was the final refuge of those who could not stand the physical discomfort.

The monotony itself was hard. Elys and Tsiwon stayed mostly in their bunks. The other four, though Grasty grunted and groaned and was as uncooperative as he dared be, took turns sharing the other two sleeping places. Time had no meaning. There was no ship's timer to cut the crawling period into night and day. There was sleep, but one could only do so much of that, and Andas found it harder and harder.

Grasty's eternal grumbling was so much a source of tension that at times Andas found himself having to use all his control not to turn on the man with a blow across his whining mouth. Turpyn, once he had taken them into space, said little or nothing. If he had the use of a bunk, he slept; if not, he slouched in one of the webbed seats of the control cabin, his eyes still closed for most of the time. Andas suspected that the Veep was engaged in thoughts he had no intentions of sharing with his ill-assorted companions.

There remained Yolyos, though the Salariki had his periods of deep silence also, and Andas respected them. But when he was willing to talk, he described a new way of life with barbed humor. Andas found himself babbling away on the state of an Imperial prince, with a tongue loose enough to shame him now and then. He had never believed that talkativeness was one of his faults, but now it seemed a major one.

"Have you thought"—the Salariki advanced a thorny question—"of what might have occurred during your absence, always supposing that our time differences are true?"

Andas had, though he did not want to. Suppose he had just vanished? Then they would have selected one of the other princes as heir. But what if there had been an android in his place—then he must prove substitution. There was a way. He glanced around, for they were in the control cabin. Neither Turpyn nor Grasty was present. He could not conceive of the Chief Councilor ever successfully playing eavesdropper. His wheezing at the slightest movement in free fall heralded his presence in a way that could not be concealed. Turpyn was another matter, but by swinging his web seat around a little,

Andas could be sure that the Veep could not come swimming into the cabin without his knowledge.

As for Yolyos, somehow, with the alien Andas had not the least fear of being frank. The Salariki had no ties with the empire, and the more Andas saw of him, the more he found him the most congenial of this company. Also there was some pressure in Andas himself driving him to talk, as if by discussing a few concrete plans aloud, he could ensure their success.

"There is more to the Triple Towers than most of those who live within their walls know. Building has spread far beyond the original towers—like throwing a stone in a pool and watching the ripples run out. Only those ripples are walls, pavilions, gardens, halls, audience chambers beyond number. No one, I am certain, knows them in entirety. There would be surprises even for the Emperor. Parts have been closed from use for generations. There have been ill doings in the past, and portions have been shunned because of the tales of slayings and worse, for the royal clans have warred among themselves for generations. Some parts of our history have been deliberately suppressed or altered, so the truth is lost.

"But fragments are rediscovered. We do not inherit from father to son as in some monarchies, which is the simpler and more direct fashion. The son of an emperor's sister, always providing that her marriage has been within a defined circle of the royal clans, may have first consideration. However, the sister of the present emperor has no sons, so the choice has reverted to the second line of sons. But it is the Emperor's duty to select his heir in good time and see him crowned as throne-son before the families of the Hundred Names. Once that is done, to dispute his right is treason.

"I am one of three—four if you count Anakue, even though his line is illegitimate. It was a surprise to all when Akrama the Light-Holder summoned me. The Emperor waited a long time before he announced he would name his heir. There have been many urging a need on him—especially with Anakue leading what is close to rebel forces. Three years ago there was an uprising in Anakue's name on Benin. It took four regiments of the Inner Guard to put that down. But he denied all knowledge of it, and there was no one, even among the Eyes and the Ears, to tie him to it.

"If I just disappeared, then it may be that Jassar or Yuor is now the Imperial Prince. That I must discover before I make myself known. Which means I shall make use of the secret ways to learn what has happened."

"Secret ways? You know such?"

"By luck I do. It is almost as if I have been prepared by fortune for what has happened. My father was a recluse. Shortly after my birth, within two years of his marriage to his cousin, the Princess Anneta, the daughter of a former emperor, he was injured in an explosion of his private flitter. He was one of the unfortunate few who cannot tolerate plasta-flesh transplants, and his face was terribly scarred without hope of recovery. My mother was very young and of such a nature that she had accepted her marriage as a duty that she took no joy in. Also she found disfigurement in others made her ill. Realizing this, my father forswore her with honor and withdrew to one of the remote and half-forgotten portions of the palace, such as I mentioned.

"His one pleasure in life became history, first of the empire, and then of the Triple Towers and the intrigues and secrets of the royal clans. Since he was second son to the Emperor, his position was secure, and he lived undisturbed.

"In fact, he was largely forgotten as the years passed, keeping his own small court apart from the general life of the Triple Towers. And I lived in that solitude, with nurses and then with tutors he selected, until I was of an age to be sent to Pav for warrior training. I never saw my father without a mask fashioned by one of the great artists of the court, which gave him a semblance of the handsome face he had once had. But I learned to know him as well as he would allow anyone to penetrate to his private world.

"Part of his training for me was the rediscovery of palace secrets. There were hidden ways within the walls, spy holes through which one might watch, even chambers with secret doors in which were stacked weapons of another time, or treasure. And he made me memorize each new one he discovered. I do not know how his passion for the strange research developed, but he was certain that such knowledge would be of benefit to him who knew it. And it finally brought about his own death."

Andas no longer saw the Salariki's face, the searching brilliant eyes. His attention was for a mind picture that had mercifully begun to dull a little now, but that he would never forget.

"How?" Yolyos asked. "Or is that something you do not wish to speak of?"

"For a time I could not. I know it, and one other—Hamnaki, who was my father's personal servant. We—I had come back on leave from Pav—missed him all through one day. So at last we took torches and started hunting the ways. We found him in a newly discovered section, but it had been designed by some builder who was more suspicious of mind or had a greater and darker secret to hide, for there was a man trap set within. There was only the belief that he died instantly to comfort us. We got him out and said that he had died of a fever. Since no one any longer cared or remembered him much,

50

there was no question. They gave him a funeral of state as was his right and a lesser name-carving in the temple. Do you know, until I saw that in place, I had not even known my father had the right to wear the two plumes. He had won that during the pirate invasion of Darfur—but no one had ever told me.

"What he gave me—and he was right that it may be of the greatest importance now—was his knowledge of the ways. Let me get to Inyanga, to even the outermost wall of the Triple Towers, and I shall be able to discover what has happened."

"And if Turpyn's suspicions are true and an android is acting out your role?"

"Then I will learn enough to be able to present the Emperor with the truth."

"Let us hope so."

There sounded a sharp signal they could not mistake. The ship was about to pass out of hyper. They were that near to their journey's end. Andas's hands shook a little as he made fast his safety belt. Inyanga—they were home!

4

They landed. Andas aroused from the effects of a hard fin-in to see the visa-screen providing a view of what lay beyond the ship walls. But—

Not Inyanga!

At first he could not believe what he saw pictured there. They had not set down in any port. As the screen slowly changed to give them bit by bit a view of the surrounding land, he saw that there were the scars of deter rockets, yes, but old—no recent burns to show a recent visit.

The vegetation, which appeared a massively thick wall beyond the edge of the open land, differed in shade from that he knew. It was a lighter green, broken here and there with splotches of a pallid yellow.

Not Inyanga! Then the tape—why had the tape been listed wrongly? Andas had the same disoriented feeling he had had when he first came to his senses in that unknown prison.

"I can guess that this is not what you expected." Yolyos's voice broke through his bemusement.

"Yes. I—I never saw this before."

"Instructive," was the Salariki's comment.

Instructive of what, wondered Andas. He could not have been mistaken—it had been the tape marked with the symbol of his home world that had landed them here. Perhaps—perhaps those had been purposely mislabeled to prevent the possibility of just such an escape as the storm had made possible for them! Perhaps it had landed them in an unknown port where they could be easily recaptured.

"Bait in a trap—" Either Yolyos had read his thoughts

from some change in his expression, or the Salariki's suspicions matched his. "If so, the one for Naul might also have delivered us here. But it would be of some value to know where 'here' is."

He worked an arm out of the protective belting of his pilot's seat and thumbed a button on the control board. Moments later the unaccented reply of the vocalizer reported atmosphere and gravity near to normal for at least two of them.

"We can survive. And we aren't going to take off again until we know more about where our choices will land us."

"They could all be for here—those tapes." Andas voiced his suspicion.

"Ingenious." Yolyos unlatched the protect-straps. "Worthy of a master of trade." There was honest admiration in his voice. "If that is true, we can look forward to being collected—by someone—sometime. I would suggest we make that collection as difficult as possible. Have you noticed one thing—"

"That there are no recent ship-burns? No one has been here—for years maybe."

"But at one time this field had been steadily visited. Yet"—Yolyos's extended claw indicated the visa-screen— "if this was a regular port, where are the buildings? Beyond the burns, that looks like deep vegetation which has never been penetrated."

"Fast growing, maybe." But even fast-growing vegetation would have taken some years to swallow up all port buildings. In the first place, even at a small way station, the buildings were generally made of resistant-to-vegetation materials. Such a precaution was standard when they had to have buildings that could be erected with a minimum of effort on worlds differing greatly. Either the time since this port had been in use was so far in the past that the vegetation had finally conquered or there had never been any standard equipment here to begin with.

A semi-secret landing place—only one type of ship would use that. Jacks!

He said that and heard an answering rumble from Yolyos.

"And"—the Salariki put the finishing touch on danger —"the Guild has been known to make common cause with the Jacks."

Normally the Jacks were the "peasants" of the crime confederation. They raided frontier worlds, selling the best of their loot to Guild fences. Now and then they were used by some Veep of the Guild for a project in which he needed easily discarded help.

"A Veep of the Guild!" Again Yolyos's thoughts matched his. "Turpyn" growled the Salariki.

"Then he knew—about the tapes!"

They could handle Turpyn among them. Why, Andas could take him alone probably. Somehow they must choke some information out of him. Andas got to his feet, ready to seek out the Veep and begin the job at once. His furious disappointment was chilling to that cold rage notorious in the House of Kastor.

"The tapes—" As if unconsciously, the Salariki moved between Andas and the ladder that would lead to his prey. "I am wondering about those tapes, Prince. A Veep of the Guild is a master at his craft. And I have seen Guild men who could lift a jeweled ring from a man's thumb without his knowing it. It could be that your In-yanga tape landed somewhere else than in the autopilot —that Turpyn was able to substitute another."

"He couldn't have! I was watching while he did it."

"As was I," Yolyos agreed, "but I do not say that I can better any master in his own trade. And how many encounters with Guild experts have you had in the past, Prince?"

"None. But if he could do that—" Andas drew a deep breath. If Turpyn could so cheat while they watched him!

All those tales about the legendary exploits of the Guild! It was said that they bought up, or took by darker means, new inventions that even the Patrol could not counter. But Turpyn had been a prisoner, possessing nothing but his garments. He could not have worked any hallucinatory tricks on them—or could he? At that moment Andas's belief in his own sense of sight, his own ability to outthink an opponent, was badly shaken.

"So we have two answers," Yolyos continued. "Either those tapes were left as bait, perhaps all of them, in spite of their markings, set to deliver us here. Or else Turpyn, for reasons of his own, made the switch. He took no part in our debate over Naul and Inyanga. Perhaps he did not need to, seeing that he could have his own choice after all."

There was a sharp ping of warning. Above the visa-screen flashed a signal.

"The ramp!" Andas jumped for the ladder. Someone was leaving the ship, had been ready to depart almost as soon as they completed fin-down. And he had no trouble in guessing who that was. They must prevent Turpyn from reaching whomever he had come to meet, get him first and learn what danger lay ahead.

Andas swung down at top speed, Yolyos so close behind that once or twice the Salariki's heels almost bruised his fingers.

"What is it—where are we?" Elys asked. Behind her stood Tsiwon.

Andas, unwilling to lose a minute, did not take time to

answer, pushing past the girl, heading for the ramp hatch.

They had made good time. As their sandals flapped upon that bridge over the ground, still hot from their rockets, they saw Turpyn out in the middle of the landing area. Andas had expected to see him running, heading for the protection of the growth. Once in there, the prince feared, they would have little chance of finding him.

But the Veep had slowed to a halt and was looking about him like a completely bewildered man. If he had left the ship with a goal in mind, it would seem he had lost his guides. He turned first this way and then that, shading his eyes against the strong sunlight, searching the vegetation wall for some break not there.

Andas pounded down the ramp, Yolyos still behind him. He expected Turpyn to hear, to turn and see them, to run. But the Veep continued to look about as if nothing mattered save to find what he sought.

He did not turn to look at them, even when they came pounding up. Andas caught at his shoulder and jerked him half around, ready to demand answers. But he never asked them, for he had not seen such an expression on the Veep's face before. Blank astonishment was as easy to read as if Turpyn had spent a life time cultivating the mobile features of a tri-dee actor.

"It's—it's gone!" He spoke as if to himself, trying to impress the fact of a loss on his own mind.

"What did you expect to find?" Andas kept his hold and now gave the other a quick shake to break through the maze of bewilderment that held him.

"But it can't be gone!" Apparently Turpyn was shattered. It was as if, up to this point, he had been armored by some certainty that he need fear nothing. Now that certainty had been reft from him.

"What is gone?" Andas began to wonder if the man had been shocked out of his full senses. He spoke slowly, spacing his words, in an effort to get through.

"The—the port. Wenditkover—the port!" Turpyn sounded impatient, as if he expected Andas to know already.

The name meant nothing to the prince. He glanced at the Salariki who made a gesture signifying like puzzlement.

"What is Wenditkover?" Andas asked again.

But then came a call from the ramp. Grasty was plunging down it at a pace that might be fatal for his footing unless he slowed.

The councilor's voice shrilled higher and higher as he ran, but Andas could not understand the words he sputtered. He had apparently in his excitement abandoned Basic for the tongue of Thrisk. His face was red under the muddy, greasy surface skin, and he pounded one fat fist against another as he spat forth what could only be abuse—aimed at Turpyn.

The Veep stood very still. That cloud of shocked amazement lifted from his face. He was once more the disciplined, enigmatic man of the prison. Andas could have cursed Grasty. If the councilor had not arrived at just that moment, they might have been able to learn something from Turpyn. Seeing the man now, he was sure it would take more than any art he possessed to force the Veep to talk.

Still half screaming, Grasty reached them. He paid no attention to Andas, but aimed a wild blow at the Veep, who avoided it easily. Then, not quite sure what or how it had happened, Andas found himself spinning away. He would have hit the ground had not Yolyos's arm, sturdy as a city wall, steadied him.

Grasty, though, had hit the ground with force enough

to expel the air from his lungs in an explosive grunt. Turpyn stood over him, rubbing the knuckles of one hand. He was as impassive as one who had watched Grasty take a tumble from a clumsy stumble.

The councilor wheezed, clutching his protuberant belly with both hands, his mouth working, but soundlessly as if he had run out of words as well as breath in that short encounter. Turpyn stepped away. He looked at Andas, at Yolyos, and then at that wall of green. Then he turned toward the ship.

It was then that the Salariki took a hand. Though the Veep had handled both Andas (who had prided himself on his skill in unarmed combat) and the clumsy Grasty with contemptuous ease, he learned that the warrior from Sargol was different. Yolyos's move was made so swiftly that his body, big as it was, seemed to be a blur. There followed an instant of struggle, and Turpyn again stood still as Yolyos loomed over him, his extended claws digging into the Veep's shoulder muscles.

So holding him, Yolyos shook him gently, or what seemed gently. Yet Turpyn's mouth twitched, and Andas did not miss the two telltale red spots beneath a couple of claws.

"So this place is Wenditkover. You must excuse our ignorance, Turpyn. Not having had your advantages, we do not know the name. I think that you will explain a few matters. First, where is Wenditkover—not in relation to us at the moment, of course, but rather in relation to where we thought we were going? Second, *what* is—or was—Wenditkover? At present you must admit it is very little. Third, who—or what—did you expect to find here? We have a great deal of time, since there is no use trying to lift ship until we know why we came here in the first place."

"And in that time, Turpyn"—the Salariki's voice was a

rasping purr of promise that made Andas glad he did not
stand in the Veep's place—"there can be more than one
way of asking questions. Politely in this fashion, or more
roughly. That you have tried to betray us in some manner is very evident. So there is no reason why we should
treat you gently."

Andas believed that Yolyos would do exactly as he
hinted. The Salariki's voice carried complete conviction.
And it must have impressed the Veep, because talk he
did, in short, toneless sentences. Nothing he said had any
reason to make them happier.

"Wenditkover is a Jack port—or it was. I don't know
what has happened. Or"—emotion touched his voice
fleetingly—"how everything could have gone *this* way—"
He shook his head. "It doesn't make sense. You'd think
no one had finned down here for years. And it is a regular refit and unload station."

"With a Guild fence in residence?" suggested the
Salariki. "Like that pirate's hold of Waystar?"

"Smaller, but like, yes.

"I tell you," the Veep continued then, "I don't understand this at all! There should be buildings here—maybe
a ship refitting. It couldn't all just disappear!"

"Suppose"—Yolyos did not loose his hold on the Veep,
rather propelled the man ahead of him toward the green
walls—"we just go over and see what is behind this
growth."

Andas matched them stride for stride. But Grasty remained where he was on the ground, breathing easier
now, but watching the Veep with a murderous glare, a
glare that perhaps included the rest of them, too. Had the
councilor been armed, Andas would never have turned
his back on him. But the prince did not believe the fellow was dangerous now, not at least for a while.

It was when they approached the green wall more

closely that they saw buildings were still there, at least in part. But they had been taken over by a jungle of growth so that only small vestiges were visible.

"It might be fast-growing vegetation," Andas suggested. But that shadow in the back of his mind was darker. No matter how fast growing that vegetation was, it could not have taken such a stranglehold in less than years. Yet Turpyn had been confident that this was a well-known Jack port, important enough for Guild connections.

"Not that fast." It was Turpyn who answered. "And this isn't that kind of growth either."

"You have been here before then?" Yolyos asked.

"I was taken from here—at least my last memory—"

That struck home like a blow. Andas had only one question: "What year—galactic?"

For a long moment Turpyn did not reply. Was he trying to reckon the time or change some planet accounting into galactic? Or had the question of time startled him into that silence? But at last he spoke.

"The year 2265."

Thirty-five years after Andas's reckoning, forty-five after Yolyos's—and differing widely again from that of Elys and Tsiwon! Time—Andas's shadow fear was gathering substance—how much time lay behind him in that prison?

"You say 2265," Yolyos commented. "And how long would you say that this port of yours has been abandoned?"

"I do not guess." But Andas thought that sounded rather as if the Veep did not choose to. Also he knew that once implanted in Turpyn's mind, that fear would be as hard a companion for him as it was for the rest of them.

"Since we know now what Wenditkover once was and what you expected to find here, may we also believe that

63

you fed its tape into the ship's pilot?" If the date bothered the Salariki, he did not show it, but had returned to
the business of getting straight answers from Turpyn.

"I recognized the symbol on one of the other tapes. It
was easy to palm and exchange." He was impatient, as if
they should have guessed the truth at once.

"But you still have the Inyanga tape?"

"Yes."

"And I think that we can believe that Inyanga will not
have disappeared into some waste of time as thoroughly
as this has," Yolyos continued. "So—"

He staggered back, the coverall on Turpyn's shoulders
ripped, there were red furrows on the skin beneath, but
the Veep had broken that hold. He burst from them,
heading into the mass of growth where the ruins of the
buildings offered so small a defense against the jungle.

Andas started after him when Yolyos's voice, having
the snap of an order, brought him up short.

"Let him go. You cannot find him in that tangle. And
once he sees that there is nothing there for him, he will
come back."

"Liar—cheat!" The rasping cry came from behind.
Grasty, bent over, his hands clasping his belly, his face
gray, tottered toward them, this time crying his abuse in
Basic. Then he sputtered again in his own tongue. But he
did not follow the Veep. Perhaps the folly of such a
chase struck him as quickly as it had the Salariki.

"Liar—cheat?" repeated Yolyos. "You seem even more
heated over this matter than the prince here, yet he had
good reason to believe he was on the way home. Or,
Councilor, did *you* have reason to think that *you* were
headed in some other direction? I remember you were
talking confidentially once to our late guide. Had you
made a separate deal with him? Did you think we were
coming to Thrisk?"

"But there were no tapes marked Thrisk." However, Andas thought Yolyos had hit upon something. When the Salariki growled that question, Grasty had actually flinched. The attack on him must have shaken him as badly as the first sight of this deserted port had Turpyn. And while he was in this state, they had better get to the bottom of any private deal he had thought he had made.

"I am Chief Councilor of Thrisk." Grasty might have been trying for dignity, but he could not stand straight. And he groaned and clutched at the belly so cruelly outlined by his clothing. "I have resources—"

"And you made an offer to Turpyn," Yolyos supplied when the man seemed unable to continue. "Where did you think we were going?"

"He said Kuan-Ti. They have a strong tie with Thrisk."

"And you believed him?" Yolyos was plainly amused.

"He was to get a million credits." Grasty choked out the words as if each hurt.

A million—what kind of personal fortune did Grasty have to draw on? Or did he intend for that to come from the safekeeping of Thrisk? Or had he intended not to pay at all, having once achieved his purpose? Andas suspected the last as the truth. Two of them making a bargain neither intended to keep—well might Grasty curse.

"It would seem that your trust was not mutual," commented Yolyos. "I do not think you are going to see Kuan-Ti, nor Thrisk for a while—"

"Help!"

The cry came from the ship, not the woods into which Turpyn had plunged. Tsiwon stood at the foot of the ramp beckoning wildly. And crumpled at his feet lay Elys. Andas reached them first and went down on his knees beside her.

She lay with her eyes closed, and those odd growths

on her neck had an unhealthy look, shriveled, puckering up in scaled patches.

"She said," Tsiwon cried out breathily in his thin voice, "that she must have water, that she smelled it and must reach it or she would die. She started to run—in that direction—" He pointed.

"Aquatic race." Yolyos had gone down on one knee, too. "I wonder how she has managed so long. But she will have to have her water or die. There is undoubtedly a limit on the time she can remain dry."

"But her prison cell seemed no different from mine—"

"We don't know what type of mind-lock we were in back there. The point is—she needs it now and in a hurry." The Salariki scrambled to his feet. "Can you carry her? If so, I'll break trail."

Andas got to his feet, glad she was so light of frame—unusually so. He had not been aware on the ship that she was so thin. Her bones seemed almost starting through her pale skin. Maybe that was caused by dehydration.

They headed to the spot Tsiwon had pointed out. There Yolyos went into action, beating down, breaking off branches and vines, clearing a rough path through which Andas could steer a way with Elys resting across his shoulder. He had not moved or made a sound since he had picked her up.

"She's right—water—" Yolyos was sniffing, as though water might have a scent—though at that it might, for the Salariki. For a race whose sense of smell was so acute that they habitually wore scent bags about their persons, the smelling of water might not be too great a feat.

What had Yolyos endured without his scents? It was customary that off-worlders coming to Sargol had to steep themselves in aromatic odors before having any dealings with the natives. What had Yolyos endured without his scents—pent in the ship? It must have been very hard on him, yet never once had he complained.

They broke through a last screen of brush and came out at the side of a pool.

"What do we do?" Andas was at a loss.

"No telling how deep this is. Do you swim?"

"Yes." Andas laid the girl down and unsealed his coverall. The air was humid, warm enough so that he felt no chill. He lowered himself cautiously and found that the waters curled only slightly above his waist. Good enough—he could manage.

"Let me have her."

Yolyos lowered the limp body into his grasp. The coverall dragged as he dipped her below the surface, save for her face. Her hair floated out, hardly differing in shade from the water weeds. Andas steadied her as best he could and hoped that the pool had no dwellers interested in meat meals. There were always unpleasant surprises on new worlds, and only a great emergency would drive a man to take such a chance as this.

Elys sighed and her eyes opened. Already those scaled patches on her throat were less shrunken, more the normal color of her skin. She wriggled in his hold.

"Let me go!" There was such force in her order that he did that. She pushed away, disappearing under the surface of the water before he could prevent it. He started to splash after her when she bobbed to the surface some distance away.

"This is my world. Let me be!"

Already she seemed to have regained her vigor. If that was the way she wanted it—but she had already gone under the water again. Andas climbed out of the pool and found the Salariki waiting with handfuls of dried grass. The prince toweled himself as dry as he could with those and dressed again, wishing he had fresh clothing to wear.

Yolyos had gone a little way along the pool side. From a bush there hung festoons of creamy flowers, and the Salariki buried his face deep among them, his wide chest rising and falling in deep breaths as he drew in all of their scent his lungs would hold.

5

It was a new Elys who finally emerged from the pool in answer to Andas's calls, though it was apparent that she came reluctantly. As a starving man might have reacted to some weeks of careful feeding, her too-thin body was normally rounded once again.

"I feel"—she flung her arms wide as she still stood with her feet awash—"like a priestess of Lo-Ange who has flung her name tablet into the sea and so is reborn again!"

Andas was impatiently pacing up and down. A thought pricked at him. What if Turpyn had made his way back to the ship? Neither Grasty nor Tsiwon would be prepared, or perhaps wish, to prevent the Veep's taking off to locate some other Guild lair. By lingering here they were offering him a chance to do just that. And to be marooned here—no!

He looked to the Salariki, but Yolyos had wandered on, like a man drunk with Formian wine, or else bemused with happy smoke, to sniff at some purple veined leaves, which, after smelling, he crushed between his hands, rubbing the resultant mass up and down his wide chest. Their aromatic scent was strong enough to reach even Andas's nostrils.

"We have to get back to the ship!" The prince said to Elys. "If Turpyn tries to take off—"

But she was too fascinated by her own form of refreshment, stooping to catch up palmfuls of water, splashing about like a child. He was thoroughly exasperated by both of them.

"Ahhhhhh—" A rumble of sound from Yolyos, who

had now wandered out of sight, was startling enough to bring Andas on the run.

The screen of flowering and scented growth that had been planted about the pool was a thin one. And the prince pushed through it to see the alien facing a small glade.

For a moment of surprise and awe, Andas was misled enough to think he might indeed be fronting the owners of this overgrown garden. Then he saw the truth. Tree trunks had been rough-hewn into those figures, gathered in a half circle about a spring bubbling from a stand of rocks. Bleached, perhaps by some rotting process of the jungle from which they had been hacked, they had an aura of life. Their bodies were humanoid, if gross and clumsy, but their faces were pitiless and alien. Some jungle vines had rooted on their bulbous heads, perhaps by accident, perhaps by long ago design, presenting them with tendrils of hair. And these vines produced purple blooms around which buzzed a multitude of insects. But there was also a sickly scent that made Andas give an exclamation of disgust and retreat a step or two.

Perhaps the aromatic leaves with which he had rubbed himself prevented Yolyos from catching that odor strongly, for he had drawn near to one of those figures and was peering into its blind-eyed face. Then he shook his head and came back to Andas.

"I have not seen their like before."

"And I have seen enough! The sooner we get back to the ship, the better. If Turpyn gets there first, he could try to take off."

"A possibility," Yolyos agreed.

"Come on then!" Andas did not move until he was sure that the Salariki was coming.

But as they went, the other still dallied, snatching a handful of leaves there, one or two blooms here, until he

72

carried in the crook of his arm a mass of highly scented growth.

Elys still lingered ankle-deep in the pool. Her thoroughly soaked overall clung to her. But she seemed to relish that instead of finding damp clothing a discomfort.

"The ship! If we ever want to get away from here, we must make sure of the ship!" Andas tried to make his fear plain.

The other two acted as if they were drugged, each by his own form of pleasure. Finally Andas urged them on before him as a Yakkan herd hound might round up a flighty flock to keep it moving.

They retraced the route Yolyos had opened and so came to the field. The ship's ramp was still firmly planted out. Seeing that, Andas gave a sigh of relief. At least the ship was not sealed against them. Of any of the others there was no sign at all. Still that passage across the open made them targets either for an enemy in the ship or one in hiding, and it was one of the longest walks Andas felt he had ever taken. Neither of his companions was in the least hurry. Short of pushing or dragging, Andas could not make them alter their pace. Elys was singing, a low, contented hum, drawing strands of her wet hair through her webbed fingers, while Yolyos did nothing but bend his head to take long sniffs of the mingled scents of his huge bouquet. A less alert company, Andas fumed, he had yet to see. Show Elys water, Yolyos some flowers, and they would be out of a fight from the start.

There was no sign of Grasty or Tsiwon near the ramp either. They climbed that, Andas crabwise so he could keep watch on the edge of the jungle, expecting trouble and Turpyn to erupt from there. He did not accept the fact that the Veep would give up so easily.

They found Grasty standing over the bunk on which lay the Arch Chief of Naul, his eyes closed, his age-pinched face more sunken and skull-like than ever. The councilor looked up as they came in.

"About time," he wheezed as if he had not yet recovered from the blow Turpyn had dealt. "He"—he nodded to Tsiwon—"has it bad—some kind of seizure. Went down as if he were blasted."

The Arch Chief looked dead, but when Andas examined him, he found a faint slow beat of pulse. Again panic touched him. A trained medic might be able to bring the old man back to consciousness, even save that spark of life. But they had no medic. To his surprise, it was Elys, steaming with damp, who moved up to push him impatiently away.

Her hands were sure, as if she knew exactly what she was doing, the fingers of the right just touching Tsiwon's forehead, those of the left his breast above the faltering heart. Her eyes were closed as if she concentrated or listened to what the others could not hear.

Andas was impressed by her air of assurance, enough not to disturb her. After a long moment of silence she opened her eyes.

"His heart is weak. He must go into san-sleep until we can get him to a healer."

San-sleep meant nothing to Andas, but a man with a weak heart could certainly not survive a takeoff. He said as much. Elys shook her head.

"In san-sleep he can. And here what chance has he? I do not believe you will find a healer out there." She pointed with her chin. In that she was right.

"But how do we get him in this san-sleep?" Andas wanted to know.

"I shall sing him," she answered. And having nothing better to offer, Andas agreed.

Elys shifted her position to the head of the bunk. Then using both of her hands to cup Tsiwon's head, the fingers spread to the widest extent, Elys began a low and monotonous humming note. Three times she gave that. Then looked to them.

"Go hence now. You might be caught also—if to a lesser degree."

They urged Grasty, in spite of his protests and groans, up to the control cabin, leaving Elys with her patient. As Andas went, he could hear a continuous wailing note, which made him uncomfortable.

"Do you think she can do it?" he asked as he joined the others.

Yolyos answered. "Who knows? Without a medic we shall do the best we can. It is a pity that survival techniques were not included in the past training we received. In fact, it becomes very plain that much education can be considered uesless when one is faced with a situation such as this."

He had laid his untidy harvest down on the astrogator's seat and gone to the tape file, flicking it open. There were three inside, and he hooked them out with a claw. Andas saw again the symbols, save that the one for Inyanga was missing.

"Do we choose Naul now?" the Salariki wanted to know.

"No!" Grasty heaved himself up and tried to grab at the tape case. "Not Naul!"

"Now I wonder why? What do you know about Naul?" Yolyos's cat eyes were dangerously narrowed. "You made a deal with Turpyn—what do you know about Naul that you do not want to go there?"

The man picked at the waistline bulge of his coverall. His natural reddish flush was overlaid with a gray look.

"Naul—Naul is overrun by the Jauavum Empire."

"The what?" Andas stared. "But Tsiwon—he wouldn't want to head into that—"

"He—he was the one who started it all!" Grasty replied. Then in a burst of words as if he must tell it, he said, "Iylas Tsiwon gave the orders that brought the Jauavum fleet first to Naul. Everyone in the Eighth Sector knows it. He need only to say his traitor name on any world there and he'd be torn to pieces!"

"And when did this treason of his happen?" asked Yolyos.

"In 2250."

"But Tsiwon said he could not remember past 2246."

"He said!" Grasty gave a nasty laugh. "Any man who has made his name stink over half the galaxy would say anything."

"No!" Andas cut in again. "Don't you see, if Turpyn is right and we have all been put in storage so doubles could take our places, that was what must have happened. Tsiwon's double—the android—was the traitor. You," he demanded now of Grasty, "if you knew what happened in 2250, what was the *last* date you remember?"

"The year 2273. But you mean we could have been in that place for *years?*" His voice shrilled higher and higher. "But Thrisk—what has happened on Thrisk?"

"You might well ask," Yolyos said dryly, "seeing what apparently happened on Naul after Tsiwon was substituted. If that is what did happen. So we have 2273 now—"

Andas was busy with subtraction. Forty-three years galactic time! But how could a man—it must have been stass-sleep. Yes, in the earlier days before hyper space travel, men had managed to sleep for centuries in stass while the early First Ships made their blind galactic voyages. Forty-three years—and how many more? How long had Grasty been one of their company?

"Turpyn can remember 2265," Yolyos continued. "And

he expected this to be a going port. Instead, there is every indication that it has not been used for a good many years. According to your dating, I myself have been in storage somewhere for seventy-three years, Elys for the longest period of all—seventy-eight. We shall, I am afraid, have to face up to the fact that whatever our absences were supposed to accomplish has long since come to pass, like Tsiwon's apparent treachery in Naul. I—I wonder what my double did for the trade mission. And you, Prince, perhaps your double now rules your empire in another's plan. We cannot be sure of anything until we learn more. But suppose you tell me, Grasty, what do you know of Sargol or Inyanga or—"

The Chief Councilor shook his head. "Nothing—I never heard of this Sargol nor Inyanga. The galaxy is too wide. A man could spend a lifetime voyaging and yet not visit a fraction of the inhabited worlds—you know that. I know about Naul because it was Eighth Sector and Thrisk is Ninth. We have had refugee ships from the Jauavum invasion."

"Well, we need not have thought that repatriation under the circumstances was going to be easy," Yolyos commented. "But we had all better be prepared to face some disaster upon our return. Do you still want to go to Inyanga, Prince?"

"Yes!" Andas supposed that the Salariki's speculations and his own fears were the truth. But still he had to know. Only what if he returned to find he was a traitor, or worse, as was old Tsiwon? More than ever he must make sure that his visit to the Triple Towers was in secret until he knew the truth.

"You'll have to find the tape first," Grasty pointed out. "It might be better to take a chance on one of those other two."

Yolyos had already clicked up the fastening of one. He

77

brought out the coil of tape and turned it over to inspect it before returning it to its case. Then he did the same with the second. Holding that out to Andas, he pointed with claw tip to a very small symbol on its spool.

"Inyanga?"

"Yes! How did you—"

"Guess that Turpyn might have switched cases for hiding? In the tight quarters we have here, it would be the most obvious way of keeping it safe. Remember he thought he was going to set us down in territory where he had friends—he might want to use the other tape later. If our kidnaping had something originally to do with payoffs to the Guild for our disappearances, he could believe that he might hold us here and try for a second sum to dispose or deliver us—whichever paid the best."

"Then we can take off for Inyanga! But Turpyn, what about him?"

They were back now to one of the oldest and most fundamental laws of space flight. You did not abandon a fellow spacer, no matter if he was your worst enemy, on an alien world. But if Turpyn did not want to be caught, to lift off in their ship, how in the world were they going to find him? It would take days, maybe weeks, and a much larger and better-equipped search force than they could muster to find him against his will.

"Yes, Turpyn—"

"Let him rot here!" Grasty snarled.

"A fate he may well deserve," Yolyos returned. "But one we shall not grant unless he asks for it. Yet I do not think we can stay here very long waiting for him to change his mind. And we cannot hunt him tonight."

Andas looked to the visa-screen. The Salariki was right. Shadows were creeping from the jungle like dark fingers reaching for the ship. To venture into that wilder-

ness in the dark was folly. They had no trails, no knowledge of what hostile native life might now lair in the
ruins.

Elys came up to them carrying E-ration tubes from
their supplies.

"Tsiwon?" Andas asked.

"He sleeps, but the life spark is very low. I do not
know whether he can survive the voyage. Yet he must if
he is to have any hope of a future."

Andas watched her hand around the tubes. Seventy-
eight years according to their reckoning! Yet she seemed
a girl his own age, maybe younger, though one could
never be sure of the true age of another species. It could
be a short life span or one as long as the Zacathans who
had outlived empires. Should he tell her of their new discoveries or what Grasty said had happened to Naul of
how long she might have been separated from her own
people? He decided against that for the present.

It was an uncomfortable night, and Andas got little
sleep. They had turned on the nose light of the ship,
thinking perhaps Turpyn might be honestly lost and
could use that for a beacon, though they drew in the
ramp as a logical protection. The visa-screen remained
on, and twice Andas started up at a spark of light ap-
pearing on that, thinking maybe Turpyn had found some
planet dwellers and was returning. But each time he
watched the erratic actions of that spark he was forced
to conclude it must mark the flight of some luminous
night creature.

By morning he was even more tired than he had been
when he had dropped into that astrogator's chair. But it
would seem that his unrest had not been shared by his
companions, for Grasty's snores and the Salariki's even
breathing were those of sleepers. Andas lay for a while
watching the change of view on the screen.

A dark hump moved out into the field. Andas darted a finger to a button to freeze and enlarge the scene. A man crawling? Turpyn injured? No, it was a beast coming slowly because it grazed at some small plants that had sprung up among the old burn scars. From a long, pointed muzzle a blue tongue snapped out, curled about a tuft of the growth, jerked it loose from the soil with a sharp tug, and brought it back to the waiting mouth, all with methodical regularity like a servo robot.

The humped body was shiny and dark, and the legs were very short, but its tail did not taper to the end. In fact, that reversed the usual pattern by uniting with the body in a narrow portion that then thickened and widened into a club. And the club seemed to have a coating of quills, which the creature either consciously or unconsciously flexed at intervals, so that they bristled out in an ominous display.

But it was what was caught on those quills that riveted Andas's full attention. Something fluttered, a small flag, bedraggled and stained. And that appeared also to annoy the creature, for it turned now and then (with difficulty because of its short neck and heavy shoulders) to snap out its tongue, as if it would so pull loose the rag from its quills.

Some freak of the wind finally brought it within reach of the creature's tongue, and the animal tore it loose and mouthed it. And then, with a very readable disgust, stamped upon it and turned aside, to eat its way through another patch of vegetation.

Andas was already on the ship's ladder. He descended as fast as he could, triggered the ramp controls, and then was out in the morning, heading for that rag. It was a wet mass, but he used stems of plants to straighten it out on the ground, only to have his suspicion proved correct. Chewed, torn, muddied, it was also otherwise stained.

And it was part of a coverall—Turpyn's.

The tracks of the animal were easy to read. These could be back-trailed. They must be. Andas started for the ship.

Grasty refused to go, and they overruled Elys when she volunteered. So it was Yolyos and Andas, with all the caution they could summon, who went down that trail. It led them to the buildings engulfed in the jungle. In the center of what had once been a courtyard they found what they sought.

It was not good to see, and they scooped a hurried grave, both working as swiftly as they could to get it out of sight; "it"—because what lay there had no resemblance now to a man. The Salariki kept sniffing, and when they had finished, he indicated one of the doorways that gaped about them like toothless dead mouths.

"In there—a lair—the smell is strong. He must have disturbed it. Perhaps it has young hidden. We had better move out before it returns. If I only had a blaster—"

His hands worked as if he wanted to draw that desired weapon out of thin air. They had searched the ship, hoping to find some cache of arms, without any success. To be bare-handed in such a situation made a man feel singularly naked. Andas agreed, ready to return to the ship as quickly as possible.

"What was he hunting, do you suppose?" Had Turpyn hoped to discover something in those dark interiors—a weapon, a message?

"Does it matter? Death found him. And we had better make sure it does not come sniffing after us," returned Yolyos.

They trotted back to the ship, watching both sides of the trail, alert to any sound that would herald the return of Turpyn's killer. The strength of the creature in relation to its size must be immense. Of the efficiency of its armament, they had had ghastly evidence.

But their problem was now solved. There was nothing to keep them here on this forgotten world—they could lift for Inyanga. In spite of what he had just been doing and the horror of their find, Andas was lighter of heart as they climbed the ramp. He was going home! Though what he would find there—well, there was no use hunting trouble. It had a way of presenting itself unbidden. At least once he was on Inyanga, he knew the kinds of danger he would have to face. One always had the idea one could cope with the known. It was the unknown—like that Turpyn had met in the dark—against which one had no defense.

"You found him?" Elys met them at the life level.

"Dead," Andas told her, but never would he let her know how.

"Tsiwon also," she said then. "I found him so when I went to him a little while ago."

Two of their number gone, and perhaps in the end those might be the lucky ones. But Andas was too young to accept such a view as that for more than a fleeting moment. He climbed purposefully to the control cabin. The sooner they lifted, the better. He found the Salariki there before him, the tape in his hands. But he looked to Andas searchingly before he fed it into the autopilot.

"You are sure, Prince? What if you find such a world as Tsiwon might have faced had his First Ancestress not been kind to him, as Turpyn found here?"

"At least it will be a world I know." Andas spoke his thought aloud. "And with a world I know, I have a chance. Be sure"—he faced the Salariki soberly—"that all I can do to aid you, the rest of you, to your own homes, that I shall do. As an Imperial prince—"

"If you still are an Imperial prince," Yolyos reminded him. "Count no heads until you take them and set them

82

above your doorway. Which is a bloodstained saying of my own people, relating to barbarous customs now followed only by the wild men of the outer plains. But still perhaps it fits too well the present situation. Heads may still roll—be sure that one of them is not yours!"

Andas tried to match the slight smile of the other, but he was afraid that what he produced was closer to a wry grimace. "I shall take every precaution."

Already he was planning ahead. The trip tape would set them down without any choice of port on their part. And the public ports on Inyanga were policed. He must find some way to escape official notice until he could learn what awaited in the Triple Towers. If he had knowledge, if any of them did, of how to bring the ship in on manned controls, they could land secretly. But there was no chance of that. The one man who might have had such knowledge (though he concealed it if he did) they were leaving behind them as part of the earth of this world.

The tape was snapped into the board. But before they activated the autopilot, they had one more task. Tsiwon, wrapped in a covering from the bunk on which he had died, was carried out, to be laid in a second grave scooped out of the earth. Elys lingered as they built a cairn of such small rocks as they could find.

"I do not know in what gods or spirits or powers he may have believed," she said in a low voice. "But that one such welcomes him now, let it be so—for no man should go alone into the shadows without some belief to make smooth his road." It was as if she recited some farewell, and they stopped hunting rocks for a moment to stand, one on either side of her, and give silent farewell to the Arch Chief of Naul, of whom they knew little, but who had their good wishing on his long journey into the mystery no living creature had yet solved.

6

Where on Inyanga would they land? The question bit at him during all his waking moments and brought him one nightmare after another. In his dreams Andas saw the Triple Towers in ruins, even as Wenditkover had been, or else a detachment of the guard waiting to take him prisoner for some crime his double had committed in his name. Such speculations could provide almost endless possibilities, and he could make no concrete plans without knowing more. He might have worked himself into a state of unsupportable tension if Yolyos had not challenged his preoccupation with the future.

"Would you step into danger without weapons to hand?" the Salariki asked.

Andas wanted to pace, to wear off in physical exertion the tension in him. But with weightlessness he clung instead to the astrogator's seat.

"Weapons?" he repeated. "What weapons do we have? Or"—he was suddenly more alert—"have you found an arms cache?"

"Your own weapons," Yolyos returned. "Your mind, your two hands. Accept that you cannot foresee the situation awaiting you, and do not try to be prepared in half a hundred ways when you need all your attention for one alone."

"I don't understand." Andas thought that argument had little meaning—except it was true. He could not defend himself without knowing the enemy.

"Just this—this ship has been used for illegal purposes. Of that we have simple proof. And where did Turpyn's chosen tape take us? To a base that was secret. Therefore—"

But Andas had already fastened eagerly on the suggestion and wondered why he had been so thick-witted as not to deduce it for himself. "You mean that a tape which would bring us to Inyanga might not do so to a port where the authorities would mark its arrival!" Why, that might solve so much. Then once more cold logic froze his first feeling of relief.

"That would be little better. A Guild port—with the Guild waiting—"

"Yes, but they would not be expecting our arrival. They might not even be occupying such a field at the time. Where on Inyanga might such be situated? Can you foresee a little helpfully in that direction?"

Andas closed his eyes on the control cabin and tried to mind-picture the continents of his home world. One needed certain physical attributes for a secret landing field. And Inyanga had few stretches of wilderness left to conceal such. At last he decided it was between the Kalli Desert and some hidden pocket in the Umbangai Mountains. And he said so.

"Desert or mountains," mused Yolyos. "And how well patrolled are either?"

"Not very well. There are two roads across the Kalli, but both follow old caravan routes from oasis to oasis. In fact, though there are aerial survey maps, most of the northern part has never been explored. As for the Umbangai—they lie to the north. A large section of those was once a royal hunting preserve. Now they are government conservation experimental lands. They are patrolled by rangers, but not often—they can't nose down every canyon. There is too much land, too few men."

"But of these two possibilities then, perhaps the desert is the best?"

"I trust not!" Andas could see some chance of getting transportation if they finned down in the Umbangais.

But suppose they hit the Kalli at some secret but non-manned Guild field—there would be no way of getting across that blazing waste to civilization. On the other hand, he did not want to land in the midst of a Guild crew either.

He decided that Yolyos's suggestion had really done little to relieve his state of tension. It seemed that if the authorities did not loom as possible opponents, the Guild did. Andas sighed.

"You see"—Yolyos's tone was mocking, or did the Salariki get some satisfaction from ramming home the darkness of the future?—"you can plan for little either way. So the more you exhaust your mind trying to fore-see, the more failure presents itself. You had better for-get the whole matter."

"Easy for you to say!" flared Andas. He sulked silently, trying to remember all he had learned about the Kalli. That must surely hold their port.

Once more ship time could not be planet time, and a voyage of unknown length added to their misery. Elys again took to her bunk, unable to adjust to non-grav. And this time Grasty declared himself as unfit, swearing that the blow he had suffered had left him in permanent pain. He might be right—at least he ate far less.

At last the warning of exit from hyper came, and then they swung into landing orbit. On the visa-screen Andas saw the mottled shape of what the tape declared to be Inyanga, though he could not recognize any feature. And he wondered, with a new chill, if once more they had been deceived.

Andas felt sick, closing his eyes against a new and shattering disappointment as they went into a breaking orbit. Soon the ship would set down. In the Kalli, the Umbangai, or a port? There was no way he could alter that—he would have to accept the gamble. But he did not want to feel anything more until they three-finned on solid soil. He willed himself to that state.

He roused when Yolyos asked, "Do you know where we are?"

The Salariki had triggered the visa-screen into action, and the slowly passing landscape was indeed desolate. They had planeted in an expanse of very barren waste between two cliffs.

Where the soil was not slicked over with the glassy surface left by old rocket burns, it was red, streaked by vivid green and wine-color, marking mineral deposits. The rock walls of the cliffs were layered with strata in red, white, and yellow. There was no sign of any building or of another ship. They were not at a regular port.

Then the turn of the screen showed a wide-mouthed opening in the face of the cliff and within that something—

"Stop!" Andas ordered, and Yolyos pressed the button.

The scene stilled, and they were able to study it. This was not altogether forsaken country. There were objects well within the hang of the cliff mouth, and they were covered with protecto sheets.

"I think nobody's home now," commented the Salariki. "Luck is with us to that extent. But do you recognize the country?"

Andas shook his head. "But if we are on Inyanga and there has not been another tape substitution, then this is the Kalli."

Sometime later he had no doubt that this was both Inyanga and the Kalli, for upon exploration the covered objects within the cave proved to be skimmers, made for air travel, well suited to the waste. And not ordinary skimmers either, but master craft. Behind them was a rack of energy units, each canister also in protective covering.

Blown sand had gathered in pockets chance had formed in the coverings of the skimmers. Andas thought that good evidence that they had not been used for some time. Any one of the craft provided with a unit would give him transportation.

"So it would seem that fortune runs at your shoulder, Prince," the Salariki commented. "Now, do you just take off—and in which direction?"

"If I wait until night, the stars will give me that," Andas said with assurance. As the good luck Yolyos commented on seemed to hold, he would trust it as long as he could. "I go north from here, and once I strike the Manhani Trail, then I will know where I am in reference to the Triple Towers. But—"

He rested one hand on the skimmer he had chosen, from which Yolyos had helped him strip the protecto covering, and glanced back at the ship. Now that they were down, Elys was no longer plagued with weight-lessness, but she needed water. Her body once more showed signs of that drastic dehydration. And where in all Kalli would she find any moisture?

"But—" prompted Yolyos.

"Elys, the rest of you, if you stay here—"

The Salariki did not reply, only watched Andas with those brilliant blue-green eyes as if Andas must come to some decision for himself.

Andas knew that he could invade the Triple Towers in his own fashion secretly. His training in the hidden ways was the core of that belief. But to take Grasty, Elys—though he did not feel the same way about Yolyos. Somehow the Salariki from the start had impressed him as being the one of their party well able to care for him-self. Andas could go on to the Triple Towers, send back for the rest as soon as he could—

But what if he never made it? Chance had put him

into this company. He owed no house loyalty to any of them. But now that the moment had come to cut loose, he hesitated. Elys on a waterless desert? He remembered how light she had been when he carried her to the pools that meant her life. And Grasty with his complaint of pain—what if he had been internally injured and his whining was more than a claim for what comforts they had?

To carry more than two would crowd the skimmer, and the future was uncertain—so uncertain he did not allow himself to think too much about it so his own fears might not weaken him.

"Do you go soon?" He had not realized how long that pause had been until the Salariki asked a second question.

"Choose!" Andas rounded on Yolyos. Let them make the choice, each one of them; then the future would be as much of their own bargaining as it was of his. "Stay with the ship, or come with me."

"And them?"

"Let them do likewise."

"Good enough," the Salariki agreed. "Though we may hang like deter weights about you in the future."

"In some cases I am not certain of that," Andas answered.

So he put it to the others. There was a way to civilization out of the waste. But he was careful to lay out the fact that he was far from sure their troubles would then be over.

Elys raised herself on one elbow. Even within the short time they had been finned down here, her dehydration had grown worse. She was close to skin over small sharp bones again. Grasty nursed his paunch between his hands,

"It is a small choice," he groaned. "Stay here and die of

the ache in my belly; go hence and perhaps fare as bad, if not worse. But I will go."

Elys still searched Andas's face, as if she would read there some more hopeful sign than his words. "This is desert and no water." Her voice was weak. "I will take the chance."

It was going to be a very tight fit into the skimmer, the more so because Andas saw to rations also. But, with the coming of night, the heat, which had fitted a tight lid over the valley all day, lifted, and his guides were the stars overhead.

They lifted in the dark, Andas, a little rusty at the control, raising them in a leap that brought a harsh protest from Grasty. Then he settled the small craft into straight flight, and they winged their way north over the waste.

By dawn they had reached the scrubland that fringed the waste and spiraled down over a sluggish river, which in this season had shrunk to what was little more than a series of scummed pools. Elys must have water. Andas had grown continually more uneasy about her, though, unlike the groaning and grunting Grasty, she had asked for no aid since they had lifted her into the flier.

He brought the skimmer down on a sandbar that divided two of the drying river pools and, with Yolyos's aid, carried the now inert girl to the nearest. Using a piece of driftwood, Andas cleared off the ugly scum along the edge, and then they laid Elys in the turgid water, Andas kneeling in the stinking liquid to support her.

The cracking clay about the edge was marked with a lacework of animal tracks, but nowhere were any footprints of men to be seen. He hated to hold her in this soupy stuff, but it was all he had. She began to stir, moaned, and her eyes opened.

"Lower!" Her head twisted on his arm. "Lower!"

He hesitated. The smell and the muck of the pool were so disgusting that he did not want to obey her order. But at last he let her down so even her face was submerged in it.

Once more her recovery was quick. She wriggled from his grasp. So submerged, with the water so thick, he could not see her, though the surface was roiled with movements.

"Let her be." Yolyos caught Andas by the upper arm and pulled him out of the pool. "She knows what is best."

Andas had to accept that as he squatted on the sandbank, using that grit to rub from his body the slimy deposit the water had left. But he kept watching the pool, wondering if he should plunge back in and try to bring her to the surface even against her will.

She arose at last without his aid, her hair in dark strings about her head and shoulders, with none of the exuberance she had shown at the jungle pool on the unknown world. She spat, raking her fingers through her hair, her face betrayed her disgust at her present state.

"You could do no better," she said. "That I know. But never, do I believe, could you do worse, not even by intention. Where are we, and where do we go?" She looked around as if only now was she aware the ship was not standing by. "Where is the ship?"

"Back in the desert," Andas answered. He was suddenly very tired, wanting nothing so much as to rest. "We are on our way to the Triple Towers."

"I have been thinking." Yolyos looked up the fast-drying river. "Are those mountains?"

Andas followed the pointing finger westward.

"A spur of the Kanghali." At least he knew that much.

"There might be more water closer to them. A better place to camp? Or do you intend to keep on by day?"

94

Andas shook his head. If they were lucky, very lucky, they might come in after dark. In the day the skimmer would be sighted by any patrol. But Yolyos's suggestion made sense. Elys needed water, certainly a better supply than she had just dragged herself out of. And closer to the mountains they would find that.

"Yes." He did not elaborate on his agreement. They climbed back into the skimmer, Elys sitting stiffly as if she hated the very liquid that had restored her to life, and then they took off along the river westward.

By the time the sun was mid-point in the east over the horizon, they had emerged into a green land where trees stood and there was more water in the river, running with some semblance of current before the heat of the waste attacked it. In the foothills they found what they wanted, a curve of open land where the river made an arc and they could set the skimmer down.

Elys was out of its confinement before either Andas or Yolyos could move. She ran straight for the water, plunging in with a cry of joy that reached them like the call of a bird. Then she was gone, and they left her to her own devices.

She returned much later to pick up the E-ration tube that was her share of their meal, the traces of her ducking in the desert pool washed away, her spirits once more high. Grasty, on the other hand, lay in the shade the skimmer offered and grunted when anyone spoke to him, refusing food but drinking avidly from the mug Andas filled at the stream edge and offered to him. Here the free running water was chill from the mountain heights and clear so that one could see the bed sand where small things scuttled around stones or hid in burrows excavated in the clay.

They slept in turns, Elys, Yolyos, and Andas sharing watches, knowing that they could not get Grasty to aid.

They waited until the twilight was well advanced before they took off again.

"You have in mind some landing place?" Yolyos asked. "I think you must want one as secluded as possible."

"The Triple Towers are built on the west bank of the Zambassi. They can be reached from Ictio only by triple bridges, one for each tower. By land, that is. On the west there is a ring of forts and outer walls. It is forbidden to fly over the royal grounds. However, if one comes in near to roof level at a point between the Koli and Kala forts, then one can set down in the section I told you of, the quarters that were once my father's. Unless there have been drastic changes in the palace, that is one of the long deserted portions with no regular inhabitants. I need only to set foot there—"

He did not continue. With Yolyos he could share the secrets of the Triple Towers. And—he might almost have also spoken of them before Elys. But Grasty he did not trust.

"What do we do?" Elys asked.

"Stay hidden. This portion of the Triple Towers is—or was—uninhabited. A man might live for a year without being found if he did not wish it."

"But you speak of a palace—is that not so?" she questioned.

"It has been added to, built on and about, for so long that all of it has not been in use for generations. The courts facing the three bridges, the traditional ones of the Emperor, the Empress, their suites, and those granted to members of the royal clan houses, are in use and have been since they were built, nearly a thousand years ago. Some of the rest were constructed for pleasure at certain seasons of the year, deserted in between. Others housed secondary wives when it was necessary for the

Emperor to keep the peace by choosing mates from each of the military clans. More arose merely because some emperor was fascinated by a new form of building and wished to have an example.

"When Asaph the Second went traveling through the Fourth Sector, he gathered artists and architects as one would pick luden berries in the river woods. He set them to work to duplicate in miniature buildings on their home worlds that had taken his fancy. And before he was assassinated, ten years after his return, at least five were finished. The others, still incomplete, were abandoned. Those are now largely shunned.

"So the Triple Towers is like a great city in itself, a city in which perhaps only three out of five wards are inhabited. If we can land where I hope, we shall have our choice of hiding places."

"Hiding places!" Grasty cut in. "What of your big promises, Prince, to return us to our own worlds? What lies here that you must hide from or keep us concealed from? I think that you have not been frank with us if we must skulk in ruins in your own palace."

"If an android has taken my place," Andas pointed out, "what would it profit me—or you—to go charging in without caution. I give you all the safety I can while I make sure of what has happened in my absence." He did not add that his main fear now was just how long that absence had been. If the term of years was what it seemed at their comparing of dates—well, it was long enough to bring about a whole change of government. Surely his grandfather would long since have died. But who wore the crown of Balkis-Candace, the cloak of Ugana fur, and carried the pointless sword of Imperial justice?

The skimmer had left the foothills. Beneath them showed the wink of lights, in clusters to mark towns, singly for farms and villas. He had the power up to full speed, knowing he must reach his goal before the first graying of the dawn sky. And in so close to the palace, there would be no safe hiding place to wait for another night.

Andas picked up several reference points and knew now he was on the right course. He began to lose altitude. There would come a moment he must choose correctly, shut off the propulsion unit of the skimmer, and swoop in all the silence possible over that one strip of wall, and he mistrusted his own judgment so that now he was tense and stiff, his hands on the controls. The light glare in the sky ahead marked both the palace and Ictio on the other side of the river. Andas could count the beading of forts along the wall.

Down, down—cut speed—slacken—slacken—

He nursed the controls inch by inch, then cut off the power entirely. They swept between the two forts, over the wall, probably with hardly a handbreadth between them and it. Were they lucky, or had their passing been sighted by a sentry? There was nothing Andas could do now about that. If they could get down before any search party was out, they still had an excellent chance of playing a successful game of hide and seek. He could, in a last extremity, take them all into the passages.

Now he still had the engine off, but he dared to snap on the hover ray. Without the buildup of engine power it would not last long, just enough to cushion their descent. A loom of pallid white—Andas cut the hover and brought the skimmer to earth.

Its tail caught with a crackle, which sounded like a roll of doom drums. The light craft overbalanced and skidded ahead on its nose. Andas slammed the protecto, and its frothy jell squirted out about their bodies, thickening instantly as it met the air. By the time they had stopped, they were encased well enough to spare them more than a few bruises.

It took Andas a moment or two to realize that they had made it. And then the memory of the crash noise set him at the hatch. Surely that must have been heard in the watch towers. They would have to get under cover and fast. He half tumbled into the open and then turned to help, pull, and urge the others after him.

The skimmer, like one of the water insects it resembled, though giant-sized, was tilted forward on its nose, its battered tail upflung, looking as if it had been met in midflight by a blow from some fan of ceremony. It had earthed just where he had planned—in the Court of Seven Draks, though whether that was its rightful name he never knew. As a small boy he had called it that because of the fearsome drak statues that crowned the pillars at one end. This was one of the unfinished building enterprises of Asaph's planning—consisting mainly now of only a smooth pavement of some treated stone that resisted the passage of time.

From here Andas knew well the way into the maze he defied any guardsmen to unravel. Of course, he had not meant to crack up the skimmer. But among all the various kinds of ill fortune that might have attended them this night, that was far less than most.

"Come on!" he urged them. "We must get away from here as quickly as we can."

7

"Where do you take us? This is dark and smells of old evils!" Elys stood, her feet firmly planted, a little away from the opening, which was a narrow slit that Andas had just opened, thankful his memory served him so well.

"Old evils," the girl repeated. "I do not go in there!"

Before any of them could move, she drew out of reach, flitting across the bare room into which Andas had guided them, her form alternately revealed in the moonlight through the windows and hidden in the shadows between.

"Elys!" He would have taken off after her. Yolyos caught his arm.

"Leave her to me." The Salariki's voice was the throat rumble of a hunting feline. "I will see to her. There are other hiding places here beside your hidden ways. And the sooner you learn what rights you may have, the better. I shall watch Elys and Grasty. Return here when you can."

Andas wanted nothing more than to do as Yolyos urged, yet he felt a responsibility for the others. And when he did not move, the Salariki gave him a push.

"Go! I swear by the Black Fangs of the Red Gorp of Spal, I shall see to them."

With an inward sigh of relief, Andas surrendered. But before he left, he made sure that the other understood how to open the door panel. Then if danger threatened, he could, with his charges, take to the hidden ways.

Andas went in, the panels slipped into place, and he was in the dark.

Always before he had carried a torch. But there had been times when, under his father's instructions, he had snapped it off and learned to advance a few steps at a time, trying to train other senses to serve him. One developed a guide sense through practice. And this part of the ruins held no unpleasant surprises.

Still he advanced with extreme caution, one hand running fingertips along the surface of the wall. Three side passages he passed, counting each in a whisper. At the fourth he turned into the new way. He should be passing now from the long deserted portion of the palace that had been erected at Asaph's orders, approaching the section in general use in his time.

In his time? How far back was that? But he must not think of that now. It could even be that while in prison their memories had been tampered with to confuse the issue should they, as they had, escape.

Far ahead he saw a very faint spot of light. Toward that Andas crept, fighting down his desire to rush heedlessly to that spy hole. He sniffed. There was a scent here now, one strong enough to battle the dank smell of the ways. Flowers?

He reached the spy hole and flattened himself to the wall to get the widest view possible of what lay beyond. It was easy to see where that scent came from. This was a bedchamber, and the floor had an overcarpeting of scented flowers and herbs fresh laid. Also the handles of several spice warmers protruded from under the bedcovers, which had been drawn up over them to contain their scented vapors.

By twisting and turning against the wall, Andas was able to get a partial view of the rest of the room's splendors. The ceiling, of which he could see only a palm's breadth, was studded with golden stars against the pale green that was Inyanga's sky tint on the fairest of days, while the floor under the herbs and flowers was a mosaic of bright color. The lower part of the wall was also a jeweled mosaic, and he focused on that. There was a line of figures in that company, all wearing dress of state. He could see four, and there was an empty space beyond the last of those as if the mural was not yet complete.

But there was no mistaking the robed and crowned man he faced the most directly. His grandfather's harshly carven features were set in the impersonal stare that was the formal "face" worn at audiences. And next to him was another—two others.

Standing on equality with the Emperor Akrama was another wearing the state diadem and robe, plainly his successor. Successor! But Akrama—dead! Andas's teeth closed painfully upon his lower lip.

If there was a new emperor—who? The face in the mosaic was familiar—he must know him—but it was not that of Anakue, Jassar, or Yuor. He could not set name to him.

A little beyond and lower than that unknown was the third portrait, this of a girl, plainly one of the Wearers of the Purple, undoubtedly a First Daughter. But her face was strange to Andas.

There was no one in the room, he could see, and he was fumbling for the release of the panel door on this side when he heard voices. The great empear shell and silver door opened, and two women, wearing the green and white of ladies of the inner chambers, backed into the room, bowing low before a third.

The newcomer was the woman whose face was pictured on the wall, save that it was not now set in the awesome, stiff pose demanded by Imperial art. She looked much younger and more human than her portrait.

Her hair, like that of her attendants, was completely hidden beneath a tall, bejeweled diadem from which fine chains depended to take some of the weight of massive earrings. Her robe was of the Imperial purple much overlaid with jeweled embroidery until it made such a stiff encasing for her body that she moved very slowly under its weight.

Involuntarily Andas's shoulders twitched. He remembered only too well the weight of such garments and the way they plagued one through the long hours of some ultra-boring court ceremony. She must be glad to be in her inner chamber, able to free herself of that regalia.

She stood statue-like, stiff as her portrait, as the two ladies struggled with clasps and ties until they could bear away that robe. In her soft undergarment she looked again younger. And she continued to wait patiently as they bestowed the robe somewhere beyond Andas's line of vision and returned to take her crown. Then she raised her hands to her head and stripped off with a quick pull the tight net that had bound down her hair, allowing its wiry, curling lengths to puff up from her skull.

With the overshadowing of the crown gone, Andas could better see her features. She was no real beauty, yet there was that about her that drew a man's eyes.

"The Presence wishes—?" One of the ladies fell upon her knees, holding out tray bearing a crystal goblet filled with a pale pink frothy drink.

The girl shook her head. "I have supped, I have drunk, past the point of feeling comfortable. One eats to forget the speeches of those who have nothing to say but recite it in a never-ending circling—" She stretched her arms wide. "Duse of the Golden Lips, how those trappings wear upon one! I think that some day when they are taken off, there will be nothing left of me but bare bone.

You may go, Jacamada. Wait a little before you send my night maids. I need a moment to rest—"

"As the Presence wishes, so shall it be," intoned the lady.

Andas moved impatiently. How it all came back—this smothering life of the Triple Towers! One might speak freely—a little—as this princess had just done. But the answers from all—save a tiny number of equal rank—would never be more than the formalities frozen into a set court speech by centuries of custom. Soon he would have no more freedom, perhaps even less than she whom he watched.

If this chamber was that of one of the Imperial princesses, he must now be on the outskirts of the Flower Courts. Yet his memories of the inner ways could not be that far wrong. This section of rooms had not been in use before. They were—he probed memory—yes, this was the court of Empress Alaha, who had been first wife to Emperor Amurak a hundred years ago.

Empress? No, the lady had addressed her as "Presence," which was not a ruler's title. It was safer to assume she was First Daughter. He was trying to imagine their relationship when he saw that she was staring at the panel behind which he stood.

"Creeper—spy!" Her voice was cutting with its cold anger. "Carry what tales you will, but remember two can play at this game. And remember this also—I have a way of knowing when you watch me. It is one beyond your discernment since it comes from the hands of the Voice of the Old Woman of Bones!"

Andas's astonishment for a moment was true awe. Then the last name made the chill of fear touch him like a hand of ice reaching into this stuffy confinement.

Old Woman of Bones—but how had a First Daughter in the heart of the guarded Triple Towers had recourse to the Old Woman? Unless—dark rumors of old, stories that had been many times told within these walls, flowed from his memory. The Flower Courts had their own intrigues, and sometimes death had stalked there more ruthlessly even than in the Emperor's dungeons.

She raised her hand, drawing from the forefolds of her robe a chain on which slid a ring. This she was about to put on her finger, while her lips curved in a small, secret smile.

"I do not think," she said, and the threat in her voice was open, "that you will return to your mistress with the same joy in life with which you left her—"

Because those old stories had a more potent influence on him than he would have believed, had it not been put to the test, Andas found the catch of the panel and watched the narrow slit open. He leaped out, his hands ready as if to meet an enemy.

He must prevent her using that ring, as the old tales said it could be used. She already had it halfway to her mouth. Let her breathe on it, activate it—

But she stared at him almost wildly, her gesture not completed. He was able to reach her, imprison her wrist, and twist it behind her back, using his other hand to cover her mouth lest she bring in guards with a scream.

She fought him, but he was able to pull her closer to the passage door. Now he released her hand long enough to grab at the ring. It was a tight fit on her finger, and he could not get it free as she battled him. Once more he tightened his hold until she could only get her breath in half-sobbing gasps.

For a moment he held her so; then she spoke.

"You have doomed yourself to the ultimate death, laying hands upon the person of the First Daughter." Her voice was calm, almost too calm after the violence of her fight seconds earlier.

"I think not." He spoke for the first time. "Look to your own safety, First Daughter, for you would have loosed the power of the Bones against the Chosen of the High Throne."

She laughed. "Your wits are gone, skulker in the dark. There is no Chosen prince. I can say that in truth. I am First Daughter, without a brother, to whom my father, the Emperor, has promised the throne to share with a husband of our mutual choosing."

"And what is the Emperor's name," Andas asked then.

She looked puzzled, but she had regained her composure. When she spoke, it was not to answer his question, but as if some other subject were far more vital.

"I do not think that Angcela sent you." She looked to the ring. "No, I have strengthened the warning with her blood and hair, she not knowing. She is not behind your coming. So, who are you—and why do you creep secretly so?"

"I asked you"—Andas shook her, hoping thus to establish some authority over her long enough to get straight answers—"Who is the Emperor?"

"Andas, son of Asalin, of the House of Kastor." She studied his face, frowning. Then she asked, "My father was in Pav in his youth, but for the rest of his years he has been ever in the Triple Towers. He took no full wife before my mother, nor was it ever known—and you cannot long keep such a secret in the Flower Courts—that he ever made a lesser choice. Yet, you might be my father in his youth. Are you some secretly gotten son of his?" And her eyes blazed with what he was sure was pure hate.

"I am myself, Andas, son of Asalin." He wondered if he could convince her, and beyond her the others, that another man ruled without right. But, she was the *daughter* of this false Andas! How long then— Once more he shook her.

"The year—in galactic reckoning—what is the year?"

"It is 2275."

"Forty-five years—" he said, and without his realizing it, he loosed his hold. She, ready for such a chance, tore out of his hands. But he caught her quickly again.

"I do not know what you mean. If you are some ill-got son, you have no claim on the Emperor or the throne," she spat at him.

"There is no true emperor on the throne," he got out, hardly believing it himself—though it must be true, for here he was, and he did not doubt that she was telling him the truth. In other words, she was the daughter of the android who had taken his place. But could an android father children? He had no idea—many secrets could be hidden by the Emperor's will. She might be a substitute brought in to bolster up the other's claim to humanity.

"You are mad—totally mad!" She had lost most of her assurance and began to struggle again.

"There is no Emperor Andas because I am Andas—kidnaped and hidden."

Her mouth twisted. "Have you looked into a mirror? You are a youth. My father is a man who has already had one renew-life injection. Do you think he could have deceived the medics then? You are the android—and mad in the bargain! Though the ring does not warn me, this must be some trick of Angcela's. She wants the crown so much that it has become food and drink, and she will die without it! But in you she has an imperfect tool."

Andas hardly heard her. The court intrigues she mouthed about meant nothing. What did was that long tale of years he could not account for—the fact that here on Inyanga an Andas sat in power—an emperor who was

—who *must* be—an android! Yet, had the stass at the prison kept him young? And if the Emperor had had an age-arrest injection, why the medics should know they were dealing with an android—

"I am not," he said dully.

He did not see the spark flare in her eyes. She watched him now with a small cruel smile, like that she had worn earlier when she had detected him in hiding.

"Do you still doubt it? Come then, prove it! Look into the mirror yonder and tell me truly that you are an aging man. Come!"

She pulled at him, and hardly knowing why, he came with her to stand before a tall mirror, which reflected all before it with pitiless clarity.

There he stood, not quite as he had seen himself in the past, for the torn and stained coverall was far different from the clothes he had last worn when he looked at himself so. But he was as he had always been, his brown face thin, with the high bridged nose of the royal clans, his hair springing on his head like a dusky halo, dark eyes, teeth that shone the whiter against his skin. On his forehead was the delicate tattoo of the Imperial house— the Serpent of Dambo, a crown he could never erase in his lifetime.

She stood close beside him, for he still had wit enough to hold her beringed hand. And in this mirror she was a slighter, more fragile copy of himself. She could have been his sister, the relationship closely marked—he had to admit that. Though with the royal clans so intermated in the past, such a resemblance could well exist. Only, she was the Emperor's daughter—that he was forced to accept. The daughter of an emperor *Andas* who was not he.

He could see her in the mirror as plainly as he saw himself. She had lost that teasing smile that promised ill.

In fact, she had changed somewhat.

"You—you are like my father in the tri-dees taken of his coronation. You are like—too like! What sorcery has Angcela brought into being?"

She tugged to free her hand and bent her head to raise that ominous ring to her lips. But he held it to him so he could see it the better. The setting was a round stone with a heart of coiling light. Then the light changed and made a shadow face, which grew stronger, sharper.

"Anakue!" He hailed that tiny portrait.

The girl stared at him as if she were frightened at last.

"Anakue the traitor! But—how comes he? I did not summon—and he was long dead before my birthing."

"When did he die?"

She still stared at the ring and did not answer.

"I said," Andas demanded sharply, "when did he die?"

"When—when my father was made Chosen. He tried to kill him. There was much trouble, and Anakue and several of the nobles were executed. My father, he uncovered the plot, and Anakue tried to claim that he wanted to kill the Emperor. But no one believed that, for my father could prove his loyalty."

The planted android—had Anakue been behind that? But if *he* were the android—Andas shook his head. It was like being caught in a fog.

"Why did he show in the ring?" the girl continued. "I did not summon him! Was it because you held my hand and looked within? But the ring was not sealed to you! I saw Rixissa draw it from the fire heart, and she sealed it to me only. And you are a man, so cannot serve the Old Woman more than as a slave."

"Which you would have made me, had I let you," he said grimly. "Now—what is your name?"

"Abena, as you must well know. Yes, I would have in-tied you with the ring. It warned me that I was spied upon. I could have made you my tool against Angcela."

"I do not know who this Angcela is, and I am no servant of hers. What I am—well, that I must prove. And, Abena, this is now necessary."

His free hand rose and pressed a spot in her throat. She had no time for protest, and he caught her before she slipped to the floor. He brought her to the bed, turned back the covers, and pulled out the spicers, laying her in their place. And he lingered long enough to work that ring from her finger. He could not take her with him through the runways, but he made sure of her strongest weapon against him.

There was one way of proving, at least to himself, that he was who he claimed to be. If he were not of the authentic blood, or if he had not undergone, before his grandfather's eyes, the first of the Three Ceremonies, he could not hope to lay hands upon what he now sought. But the very fact that he could find it, hold it, would be an argument to prove his tale.

But, now he needed light. Fearing any moment to hear the scratch of a maid's warn stick on the door, he toured the room, finding what he sought in one of the window seats. They were deep enough to provide a slender set of shelves against the frames, enough to hold tri-dee tapes. And there was a small porto light there also, clumsy for a hand torch but usable.

Andas had sealed the ring into a seam pocket of his coverall. Nobody was going to see it much longer. There were a couple of wells down which it could be sent to oblivion. He paused for a moment by the bed. As she lay there, the princess looked very young and innocent. Yet the fact that she knew how to use the ring meant she had ability to draw on deep and dark knowledge that most men loathed and few women had courage to claim for their own.

Andas got back into the hidden passage and snapped the panel shut behind him. He might have a very limited time to reach what he sought—so the sooner he was on his way, the better. So far he had come by a roundabout way. Now he must seize the chance on a passage that led into the heart of the Towers—the private quarters of the Emperor. And there was no telling about the ways there —maybe the Emperor knew them.

He switched the lamp on low. If the Emperor was the android, then he must have been provided with Andas's memories—which meant that he would know all about the exploration of these ways in the old days. So he would be prepared, once he had heard Abena's story, to hunt Andas through the very passages he had confidently trusted to hide him. He could even set up ambushes!

The only deterrent to the android against putting the guard in the passages as hunting hounds would be that too many secrets would be so revealed. But what that might mean in the future had no bearing on the present. Andas had to find the Emperor's chamber as soon as he could, and he only hoped that his memory was correct.

He began to count side passages, three, four—it was the sixth one that he wanted. Yes, it was here, five almost wall to wall with six. That gave onto a flight of stairs where dampness oozed. And there was a dank smell of— what had Elys called it—evil! Yes, if evil had a smell of its own, this was where one could well find it. There had been death walking these narrow ways through the centuries before him.

Andas counted twenty steps, and then the passage leveled off. But there were slime tracks on the walls here. They glistened in the lamplight. He never rememberd seeing any of the things that left such traces, nor did he want to. But he dared now to turn the lamp up full strength to shine ahead.

The pavement under foot was crossed and recrossed by thicker trails of slime. He slowed his pace a little as his sandals slipped and slid. If he remembered rightly, this was the worst section of the way, for it ran under the moat pond that surrounded the Emperor's pavilion.

Steps ahead, going up now. He turned the lamp back to low and climbed. It was like progressing out of the foul air of a swamp, for here the walls were drier, and now and then there was actually a whiff of incense or herbs wafting through the spy holes along this passage. But Andas did not pause at any of those holes. Time was important, and what he sought was at the very end of this way.

8

He must reach the bedroom of the Emperor, and if it were occupied— In his day (Andas found himself now separating past from present) there had always been guards in the outer chamber. But the Emperor was usually alone, even though on two sides of the pavilion wide vista windows opened on the Garden of Ankikas. And there were, according to custom also, small night lights made fast to the trees out there, illuminating moss and flowers. In addition, when the Emperor pleased, a transparent landscape could be thrown by concealed tri-dees on the walls, off-world scenes. Andas recalled more details as he sped along until at last he faced the wall where there was no spy hole but which should contain a small pattern of depressions.

Press—three together, then three more, then four. A band of light outlined a door panel. But opened no more than thumb's width. He worked his fingers into that and exerted his strength against an ancient and apparently long-unused latch.

There was a sound, a dismal grating that froze him for an instant. But it heralded the giving way of the obstruction. The panel slid open, and he looked into the room. He more than half expected to front a blaster or else the ceremonial dagger worn by all of noble rank. There were too many times in the past when emperors had been trapped, even in their own quarters. He was a little surprised the panel opened at all. If this false Andas had his memories, he would have known about this entrance.

Luck favored him again. The room, under the soft radiance of lamps set on shoulder-high pedestals around the wall, was empty. Andas wasted no time in crossing to where there was on the wall a great mask, impressive in its solemn beauty. Three times life size, it was supposed to be the representation of Akmedu, the first emperor, he of the House of Burdo, who legend said was more than human, having great knowledge, daring even to go against the Old Woman—thus making Inyanga a world free of her bloodstained shrines.

Andas paused, looking up into those wide-set eyes, so fashioned that they lived and held his gaze with theirs, as if there were indeed a spirit yet imprisoned behind the great bronzed metal face. The full lips were curved in a very faint smile, as if what those eyes looked upon provided lazy amusement.

He brought up both hands in the salute for one facing his overlord.

"Rider of the Storm Winds, Bearer of the Whip of Ten Lightnings, Judge of Men." His head turned from right to left and back again. "He who is sought but comes only at his own will, who is desired but does not desire, who stands tall in the shadows watching those who follow in his footsteps, though their feet fill not the prints left by his mighty boots.

"He who is one with the sun, with the rain, with the cold, with the dark, with all that comes to Inyanga—look upon me, who am of royal blood, who has come here to undo a wrong, who needs that which lies in secret waiting—"

Once more Andas raised his hands as if to shield his face and his eyes from some awesome glare. And so he stood for as long as a man might count ten. Then he moved closer to the wall. There was directly below the mask a table of polished black-heart, and set into its top were various symbols in the red ivory of nurwall teeth. At mid-point there was a censer of gold from which now curled a wisp of scented smoke.

Facing him, as if to threaten, there lay on either side of that censer a weapon. Both were very old, treasures no man might touch, save after certain rites and ceremonies had been performed, for they were, according to tradition, those that Akmedu himself had carried. One was a dagger of ceremony, its blade concealed in a gemmed sheath. The other, to Andas's right, was a blaster, of a type so old that he thought its like might not now be found anywhere else in the galaxy.

But the weapons were not what he sought. It was what they and the mask symbolically guarded—that which was death for a lesser man than the Emperor or his rightful heir to lay finger on.

Raising both hands to the mask, leaning at an angle across the table, Andas pressed his thumbs as forcibly as he could to the corners of that faintly smiling mouth. And though the mask appeared to be cast in a single unmovable piece, the mouth slowly opened. Between the lips protruded what he wanted. But again it was a case of using force on a long-untried spring. He pushed with all his strength, stretched as he was in that awkward position.

The mouth opened farther. What it held safe through the years fell with a metallic tinkle to the surface of the table, just missing the lid of the censer. Andas, with a sigh of relief, reached for what the mouth had disgorged.

He saw a key as long as the palm of his hand. The wards were intricate, the shaft a plain bar ending in curiously wrought combinations of symbols, so curled and embedded together that it would take much time and the searching eye of an expert in cyrmic script to translate, though Andas himself knew their message.

This was the heart of the empire. What it unlocked— that was not here but in the great temple of Akmedu's Shadow. Only two men had the right to hold and use the key—one was the Emperor, the other his heir.

It lay before him. Andas wiped his hands nervously back and forth across the front of his dingy coverall. He believed he had the right—he must! But to take it up would in reality prove whether he did or not. Otherwise, there would be vengeance, dealt by something above and beyond any justice of humankind. So it had happened in the historic past—there was even a visual record of such punishment.

But, he *knew!* If his grandfather was dead, then there was no rightful emperor but Andas Kastor, and he was Andas. He picked up the key. It was cold and hard in his hand, feeling no different from any other piece of metal. No lightnings flashed; the mask did not denounce him with a wail of sacrilege. So, he was Andas!

He was alive with triumph, perhaps too much so, for he did not hear the sound until too late to retreat. The man who had entered the room was now between him and the panel exit. For the second time Andas reached to the table top. He held the key in his right hand, but his left closed about the ancient blaster.

It was like facing a queer, half-blurred reflection in the mirror. He should have been prepared for this after what he had learned from Abena. But it is given to very few men, if any, to see themselves as they would be after a long toll of years has passed. Rejuvenation had worked in that the man facing him was apparently in the prime of life. But his eyes were weary and older than the face framing them. Now Andas saw those eyes widen a little, though otherwise the other showed no surprise.

"So"—his voice was low, almost toneless—"after all these years Anakue is proven right. And we thought he raved."

Andas had aimed the blaster. Its charge might be long since exhausted. That it would even fire he had no reassurance, but it was the only weapon to hand. He moved along the table cautiously, always watching the man by the bed. He hoped to get the other to move with him and so force him away from that line of escape. But the false emperor remained where he was.

"Clever—" When Andas did not answer, the Emperor stood with his head a little to one side, studying the intruder with growing curiosity. "Very clever indeed. They were artists, those Mengians. Lucky indeed that Anakue cracked and betrayed it all so we could clean them out. Or did we?" His eyes narrowed a little. "You are here, and you must have been decanted somewhere. But why a replacement years out of date? I am no boy. They could not even enthrone you by claiming some miracle of rejuvenation—my basic pattern is in too many files. Now, what did you come for—or were sent for?"

"To take my throne." Andas refused to believe in that flood of words. Of course, this usurper would claim to be the rightful Andas Kastor. And apparently he had had years to build that claim into almost certainty. He had everything but what Andas held now in his right hand!

"*Your* throne?" The false emperor laughed. "Android doubles have no thrones—in fact, they are outlawed since the Mengian plot was uncovered during Anakue's abortive rebellion. Whoever started you on this wild venture must be mad."

"No one started me." Andas had reached the side of the bed now, but he must win around its wide expanse to reach the panel, and the other had not moved. "I am Andas Kastor. This is rightfully mine as you know—*android!*"

"Android? Did they program you to believe you were real then, half-man? Where did you come from?"

"Where? In the prison where you had us all kept in stass."

123

"Keep him talking," Andas thought. Perhaps, just perhaps, he could hold the other's interest long enough to make a rush. He did not trust the weapon in his hand to fire, but there was a trick in which it could be used.

"*Us* all? By the teeth of Gat, do you mean there are *more?* How many Andases did they have with which to inundate our poor empire?"

"I was not the only one of importance kidnaped. There were others—from other worlds."

"Keep him talking!" Andas could not see that the other had relaxed any of his air of vigilance, but there was always a chance.

"We always thought that could be true"—the Emperor nodded—"though the Mengians followed their usual method of destroying their records when threatened. But perhaps we did not get their headquarters after all since they must have had you and these 'others' filed somewhere. But I don't see what moved them to loose you all so late and uselessly."

"They did not release us—we escaped." That he was telling their story did not matter as long as he could keep the false emperor from summoning the guards.

"That explains it." Again the other nodded. "Well, it is a pity that—"

"That what?" Andas held up his right hand, the thumb across the shaft of the key against his palm, so the other could see what he held. "That you should be unmasked at last, android? Do you think that anyone save him who I truly am could hold this—and live? You know the precautions—"

The other stood very still. It was as if the sight of the key had turned him into a statue after the nature of sorcery in the old legends. Then his lips shaped a word Andas read rather than heard.

"That!"

"Yes, that! I have it as my right."

"You are—it is impossible!" The surface of the other's calm cracked. "It is totally impossible! I am human, as has been proven many times over. Why, I have children —three daughters. Can an android breed?"

Andas smiled bleakly. "We have been told not—but by an emperor's orders children could be substituted or otherwise arranged for. We both know that in the Triple Towers there is only one law—the will of him who has the right to this!" Once more he held up the key.

"Now, call your gaurds if you wish. Let them see me— with the key!"

"I have guards the sight of that will not affect. Times have changed since the days of my youth. If you have been in stass, you have not been lately briefed."

His hand raised, and Andas did not try to aim the weapon he held. Instead, he threw it in a way he had learned at Pav from a mountaineer of the Umbangai. It struck the other between the eyes, and he staggered back and went down. However, he had not been rendered unconscious, but was struggling up again when Andas was on him. This time he applied nerve pressure that kept the other limp until he had him bound into a chair.

"Now"—Andas went to the open panel—"tell your guards when they come to hunt if they will. But what I hold is the heart of the empire, and I take it with me. If I fail, I shall make sure that it does not reach you again. And I shall assert my claim where it can be seen by all, in the temple of Akmedu." Then he thought of something else. With his left hand he felt for a seam pocket and brought out the ring he had taken from Abena.

"You boast of daughters, Emperor who has no right to be. You have a First one—Abena—is that not so?"

He had not gagged the other, yet he did not answer, only watched him, his eyes filled with an emotion Andas could not read. It was not hate as he first thought, but something darker still.

"Look you at what she threatened me with, Lord of Five Suns and Ten Moons." Mockingly he used the archaic address of the court. "A ring of the Old Woman. So it would seem that filth has once more bespattered the court. A like daughter for a false lord!"

"Not so—"

"Would you see it closer to make sure? Look then!" Andas felt so much the master of the field that he took three swift strides so that he could hold out the ring at the height of the Emperor's eyes, close enough for him to make sure it was as Andas reported.

"No male can wear this, but it was against her breast when she brought it forth against me. What now of your First Daughter? Though I shall see this does not serve her again. But once one deals with the Old Woman, there is no retreat before death—or after. So, I leave you to think on that also, android, during the short time left you—"

He never finished the sentence. The wide door of the chamber opened without warning, and only his reflexes saved him, for the thing that came scuttling in was a robot, and it aimed a cloud of vapor at him.

Andas jerked back, coughing, his eyes smarting as the edge of the mist touched him. His head whirled dizzily, but he made it to the panel. And, thank the five powers of Akmedu, it snapped shut under his frantic shove. He was still coughing, reeling, not sure how long he could keep his feet, but he forced himself along back down the passage. The false emperor, if he carried all Andas's memories, could comb him out. He would have to fog his trail as well as the robot had almost fogged him! And right now he was sure of nothing, save that he had made it into the ways, that in one hand he held the key and in the other the ring. The latter he fumbled quickly back into his seam pocket. The less he had to do with it, the better.

How had he avoided the robot's attack? It would—it did—seem impossible now that he considered it, unless it was true, that other old legend, that he who rightfully carried the key had for the space that it was in his possession the strength of Akmedu!

But powers of the unseen, while they might be potent enough in the right time and place, were not to be depended upon. By all accounts they acted erratically and sometives even turned against believers who strove to use them. He put no faith in the key except that it would do for him exactly what he planned, prove that he alone had the right to bear it into the temple and use it to unlock the secret there. And if he lived through the next few hours, when he was sure that the false emperor would exert every effort to take him, that was just what he was going to do.

The lamp—what had he done with the lamp? He could not remember now, and there was no time to return and hunt for it. But that meant he must slow his pace, not take a headlong tumble down those stairs at the under-moat section. And it was very hard to slow when every bit of him drove ahead. He must keep alive and out of captivity until he could reach the temple and prove his identity.

Beyond that he did not think. Steps—yes, he had reached the underwater way. He shrank from allowing his fingers to slide along the wall, for they crossed those trails of slime, and he had to center his will on keeping touch in spite of such defilement. He wished he had paced off this dank section and knew by counting where he was and how far he had to go. The smell, dark, and slime seemed to last forever.

Then, steps again, and with them a lift of spirit. He had the key pressed tight against him. Though its cold metal never seemed to warm any in his grasp, yet it was to his spirit now what a lamp could have been for his body. The last step—he was in a corridor comparatively free of the moat section's taint.

He had time now to think coherently, if that whiff of vapor had not left him dull-witted. To return the same way he had come would be the rankest folly. The princess might already have started the hunt. So there remained a long detour, and of all its windings he was not sure.

If only he had not the responsibility for the others, was free to pick his own route, retire into one of the more hidden ways! But if the false emperor had been schooled with all his memories— How had they accomplished this recall for their android anyway? They must have kidnaped him first, put him in two-com—thought that was risky. But it did not matter how they had done it, only that it had been done. And he could not hope to have a secret that grinning non-man back there did not share.

So, his own choice was to weave a wild pattern that would eventually bring him to the Court of the Seven Draks and those he had left. How had they fared? The hunt must have started after the crash of the skimmer. But somehow he believed that if any being could escape the guard, it would be Yolyos, though burdened with Grasty and the girl. Well, they would have to take their chances, just as he was doing.

He had had an amazing run of luck. Not that he dared build on that. Only a fool believed that fortune always turned a bright face in his direction. Count now—

He tried to make better time, but still he had to count passage openings. And he slipped into one that took him at an abrupt angle from the corridor of the princess's room. Andas cursed the loss of the lamp until he was aware of that queer little gleam from the front of his coverall. His fingers probed and found the ring.

What—? He pulled it out of hiding and was answered by a heightened glow—perhaps no greater than that of the songul's lower wing at mating time. It was nothing he could really see by, yet it heartened him. He dared not slip it on his finger—it was too charged with all he had been taught to fear from earliest childhood. Yet neither did he put it back into hiding, but held it before him between thumb and forefinger as if it were a lamp and could give him the sight he needed.

There was a forking of the ways at sharp angles. Andas hesitated and then chose left. It was hard to think of what lay above the surface and translate that into what portion of the assemblage of buildings he might be heading for. His only guide was memory. This might almost be the maze in the Garden of Scented Fronds. If one continued to choose always the left path, it would eventually bring him out close to the Court of the Seven Draks.

Andas had made his fourth such turn when he stopped short and forced his breath to the lightest possible in and out flow as he listened. No, he had not been mistaken—sounds! Andas knew of old that such carried through these passages in an odd fashion, sometimes sounding farther off than they were, sometimes reversing that process. So he could not be sure how close the trailer was.

He thought, or rather he hoped, that there were not robots after him. Those he feared more than any guardsman. Men could be, with luck, fooled by someone who knew these passages. But a robot, perhaps set to hunt for only the faint emanations of human body heat, would track relentlessly.

If he were at all sure of his present position, and he clung to belief that he was, there was a chance ahead he might have an opportunity to see his hunter from a position that would be safe for a short time.

Andas felt along the wall carefully as he went. But it was that so-faint gleam of the ring that served him better than he thought could happen, for with it he caught a glint of metal and so located the first of those loops set deeply into the stone, intended as a skeleton ladder. He tested the first by swinging his full weight on it, though that did not mean they were all as stable.

Stowing both ring and key safely within his coverall, Andas began to climb. He was well above the second floor of the palace apartment in which this was hidden as a shaft when he thought himself safe enough to brace inside that opening and wait. No robot he knew of could climb in such a narrow way as this. And long before it could broadcast his position, he could reach the roof above and strike out in the open for a while if the need arose. Now the dark below showed a glimmer of light. A robot would not carry a lamp, nor would it trail with one —too easy to alert its quarry. Guards then, so Andas felt above him for the next hoop. Still he lingered. Guards could follow him up if they saw the rungs on the wall; guards could even aim a stunner up this vent and bring him down helplessly without exerting any trouble. Guards could—

The light of the torch was very dim, yet to one who had moved through the utter dark of the ways it was bright enough. If the one who bore it was alone, Andas could leap down behind him, knock him out, and take that torch and the weapons he must be carrying. The plan built in his mind as a mason would set stone to stone for a wall, though anyone coming on this hunt alone would be a fool—unless he was playing bait—

Only one half-seen figure passed below. And the more he thought, the more desperately Andas wanted the torch and the weapons the other had. He rested his forehead against the gritty stone of the vent side and tried to picture more clearly what lay ahead.

Yes, there were two side passages not too far beyond. And if the hunter had come too far ahead of his fellows, Andas could be on him and away, giving any who followed a choice of three different routes down which to trail him. He had not been in their hands, so they had no personna reading they could feed into a trailer to follow him exactly.

He made his decision and slid down as fast as he could. The light was still ahead. He caught glimpses of it, though it was shut off from time to time by the bulk of the man who carried it. Andas listened—and then he ran lightly forward.

His hand was already aimed for a knock-out blow when he caught better sight of the man he hunted. That was enough to blunt his blow so that he did not kill, or even stun, though he carried the other before him to the floor where they lay, the attacked struggling feebly under him.

"Yolyos!" Andas pulled back. Luckily the light, a very small hand torch, had not smashed during their fall. Andas grabbed it up and turned it full on his own face.

"Yolyos!" he repeated, hardly able to believe that the Salariki was really here.

9

Andas switched the light from his own face to that of the Salariki, who was holding his head, giving low growls of pain. There was a dark smear of blood just above that aggressive bristle of coarse mustache, and Yolyos's ears were flattened to his skull, his eyes narrowed to warning slits.

Then Andas noticed something else. The fur-hair on one of the alien's broad shoulders was crisped and singed, a red mark rising under the blackened stubs of hair. He had had a very narrow escape from the blaster.

"Ssss—" the sound was close to a hiss. "Sssooo I have found you, or you me, Prince. And by your welcome, you expected others." The Salariki's voice had begun with that angry hiss but became more articulate.

"The others—where are they?" Andas listened intently but could pick up no other sound.

"You might well ask. But for the fact I proved faster than he expected, I might well be cooked now."

"Who expected? How did you come here?"

"It is something of a tale. But do we sit here while I tell it? I think by your manner of greeting you have reason to fear other life in these wall roads."

Andas was recalled to the peril at hand. "Yes!"

He arose, the Salariki with him. But Andas had to know what had happened. If it was unwise to continue back to where he had left the others, then he must revise plans.

"You were discovered? I must be sure, for if we cannot go back to the Court of the Seven Draks—"

"The idea when I left seemed to be that you would. They have a reception party waiting. No, I should advise

135

hastening in the other direction, any other direction!"

"Elys—Grasty?"

He heard a snarling sound from Yolyos.

"Yes, our delicate little Elys, she deliberately brought this about. I think we misjudged her as badly as if we were cubs to be netted by the first pair of eyes turned in our direction. Elys who would die without water, who was to be protected, who—"

"You might tell me what happened, or do I play a guessing game?" interrupted Andas.

"I am not quite sure myself—that is the trouble. One moment I was trying out the secret fastening that controlled the door through which you had gone. I thought it well to know how to do that quickly. The next, something struck me on the side of the head, and I was on the floor. I saw more stars for a second or two then than can be sighted in the heavens of any planet I know.

"While I was still seeing double and triple, Grasty landed his big belly on my back, and he had a force knife to my throat before I could get my wits to working—"

"A force knife! But where did he—"

"You can well ask. Perhaps Turpyn supplied it. How can we be sure how deeply that one was concerned with our kidnaping? Or maybe that she-wyvern conjured it out of midair. Grasty was only her claw man in the matter. She made that clear.

"And what she was going to do—well, she was prepared to bargain with the guard. Had it all worked out, she was sure she could appear before them, an unarmed woman, and they would not flame first and ask questions afterward. When they gave her a chance to talk, she would tell them all about you—buy their favor so. She was very sure that you were not going to achieve anything with your own actions here, and she would gain credit with the powers in control by her play of being more or less your prisoner, ready to tell all about your invasion of their palace. If you remember, she had plenty of time on board ship alone with Grasty to work out a plan to be put into action at the first chance. And Grasty's playing injured was a part of that.

"They were both sure that whoever had put up the fortune it must have cost to get you out of circulation would be most grateful to anyone who would push you back under his claws once more. Practical and logical, that is Elys. You really have to admire her straight thinking, always accepting that her ultimate goal is the preservation and aid of her own plans."

"But you got away—"

"Yes. We heard the arrival of a guard unit. I think they were wearing anti-grav belts and had come across the roofs. So Elys ran out into the middle of the court to meet them. She raised some very pitiful screams for help. I would have believed her—you would have too, Prince.

"Grasty is no fighting man—was, I should say. He was distracted by the action in the court. Elys was doing some splendid acting, running to throw herself at the first man to set foot down. She took a chance there. He might have turned her into a cinder, but she gauged his reaction correctly.

"By that time I had my wits back in my skull, and I took action, too. Grasty, I am sure, never tangled with a Salariki before. We have our own little tricks. At any rate, I got to my feet, his wrist in my teeth, and there was no using the force blade then. He squealed, and I was trying to knock him out when a blaster flamed us. One could see the entire beauty of Elys's plan then. She wanted to get us both burned to a crisp. Then it would be her word against yours—if you lived long enough to say anything. And who would be believed?

"However, the First Ancestress was with me. Grasty took that blast. I continued to hold him as a shield and backed into your doorway, pushed him out and slammed it, hoping they did not know the trick of its opening. I went along, I can't tell you now in which direction. But I found a box with some things in it, a large torch, which was burned out, this one, a container or two, supplies, I think. They were dusty—must have been there a long time."

"One of my father's caches. He left them so when exploring sections new to him," Andas answered. He was still bewildered by Yolyos's story. That Elys would so turn on them—he could hardly believe it. Yet, as the Salariki had pointed out, her actions had a cruel logic. And, after all, what had he known of the alien girl? Also no one could judge an alien, or even a man of another world, by one's own standards of conduct. What was accepted, a matter of established custom and moral right, on one world might be high crime on another. Elys was undoubtedly acting according to her own ethics. Not that that made it any more acceptable— But what of the ring in his own possession?

What that represented was evil according to his beliefs. Yet it had been worn and used by a woman of his own blood. So how could he sit in judgment on Elys? It only remained that their party had been cut to two. And inwardly he was glad that it was the Salariki out of their number who was left to accompany him now.

"What about you?" Yolyos asked. "I would judge you have not been too successful if you are expecting hunters to sniff along your trail here."

Andas hesitated. The accusation made by both Abena and the false emperor (though there was good reason to discount them both) gnawed at him. But he could *not* be the substitute! He was alive, he felt pain, he had to eat, sleep—he was *real!*

"You have learned something that has clouded your mind."

Andas was startled at those words. How had the other guessed? Esper? But never before had the other given hint of esper powers. And if he had concealed such a talent, could he otherwise be trusted? Again Andas halted and turned to flash the lamp directly at the bloodstained face.

"You—you are esper!" He made the accusation boldly, bluntly, hoping to shock the other into the truth. But how could you surprise an esper, his common sense demanded a second later. It was impossible.

"No. We do not read minds," Yolyos told him. "We read scents—"

"Scents?" What could the alien mean?

"You know how we are addicted to our scent bags? Well, those are worn not only for the purpose of enjoyment, but they are also protective. We can scent fear, danger, anger, unease of spirit—emotions. And think you what that would mean to have always in your nostrils! You would find it hard to concentrate. So we set up our own scent screens."

"But you did not scent Elys's coming betrayal."

"No, because she was alien, more so than she looked physically. To me she was always—fish!" He brought out that last word as if he were in some way at fault for not being able to penetrate the natural defenses of the girl. "Now Grasty was so filled with fear that that overlaid everything, so with him I had no warning either.

"But you I can read, for in ways your species is not too far removed from mine. We are both mammals, though our distant ancestors were dissimilar. I have seen a creature called 'cat' on one of your trading ships and have been told that such is a more primitive example of my own line. We had a creature on Sargol—now extinct—which might have been your far-off ancestor. Your emotions are not too far different from ours, save that at times they can be overwhelmingly strong. Any of us leaving Sargol for other worlds, even on short visits, must undergo conditioning—just as a mind-reading esper must build up his defenses against crowds, when the burden of their mingled thoughts could well drive them mad.

"So, yes, I can scent that you are highly disturbed, that it is more than just the fact you are hunted by those who have no reason to wish you well. But if you will not share your fear"—the Salariki made a gesture akin to a human shrug—"that is entirely your choice."

What if they were right—but they could not be! But should he warn Yolyos? In his own world the Salariki might face the same accusation. If he were prepared, he could perhaps be able to prove he was not android as Andas would use the key as proof.

So he told the alien just what happened, that a false emperor was Andas in this place and that his only chance of proving the truth was to reach the temple.

"Android." Yolyos repeated the word thoughtfully.

"But it is false! I am human! I eat, I feel pain, I need sleep—"

"What do you know of androids?" The Salariki cut in. "It is not a science that has ever been used on Sargol, but I am under the impression that they were not like robots—which we also have no liking for. Is that not true?"

"Yes. That's why they were prohibited on most worlds long ago. It is even against all laws to make a robot the least bit human in construction. The first androids were destroyed by mobs whenever they were found. Men fear anything that can resemble them and yet be unhuman—deathless—"

"Deathless? Yet this emperor has seemed to age in the normal fashion, has had your life-prolonging injections."

"So he says. With absolute power a man can claim many things, and there are none who can prove it is not so."

"But such a deception would have to have partners, your medics—and surely at least one woman of his inner courts, perhaps more, if he has been thought to have had children. A secret is only a secret when no one shares it. I do not think that your human households are so far removed from ours. And I know that in my clan house what is known to one woman in that respect is, less than a day later, known to most others, and within two days by their mates. Do you think that a score of people could, or would, keep such secrets here?"

Andas found himself shaking his head. No, rumor and gossip had always spread, sometimes as a dark, almost destroying wave, throughout the Triple Towers. There were wild tales told of his father (he had heard some of them whispered) merely because he lived apart. And if they could so embroider invention and get it accepted as truth, what could they do in turn with explosive facts?

There could be a cold-blooded answer—that those who did know might have sudden accidents or fatal illnesses. But only a certain number of those might ensue without raising the very rumors the Emperor was trying to avoid. Andas had to accept, whether he could believe it or not, that this Andas could not cover up a medical report.

"If"—Yolyos proceeded relentlessly—"he could not cover these matters with a lie or by his will, then they must be true. Again I ask you, what do you know of androids? You have said that among your kind they have been regarded with aversion, that they are forbidden. So, we have a form of scientific research that is under restraint. But in the past has that ever worked successfully? Can men be kept from research, their minds turned off by orders? The Mengians Turpyn spoke of—the records that we found in that prison—would that not be the very type of forsaken, hidden place where such researches could be furthered—to higher points unknown before? Suppose that the end result of such experimentation was an android that could not be told from a normal human being?

Logic—devastating logic that he could, had to, agree to at every word! The Mengians were the heirs of the Psychocrats, and the Psychocrats were men (or emotionless superendowed likenesses of men) who admittedly knew more about the human mind and body than any scientists before or since. The remains of their autocratic experiments were so widely scattered that now, two generations after men had rebelled against their yoke in the Ninth and Tenth sectors, discoveries were constantly being made of some new facet of their planning. Yes, given the Psychocrats' resources and knowledge, and unlimited chances for research, there could have been androids that were beyond the boundaries known to history.

"If we are such—" he blurted out.

"Will we ever know?" countered Yolyos. "After hearing your tale, I do not doubt my counterpart is in action somewhere, either on Sargol or engaged on some mission off-planet even as I was at the time I can still remember. You say that you have that which will prove your case if you can reach the place to put it to the test. This I want to see, for it may also affect my future plans. But are you sure you can reach the temple? Have you any idea where we now are?"

Andas was not surprised to have Yolyos make that challenge. They had been plodding on, the dim light of the torch picking out side passages at intervals. And how long he had been in the maze he could not have told.

He was hungry, and more than that he was thirsty. Even to think of water made him draw a dry tongue tip over drier lips. They would have to find sanctuary and both food and drink soon. And all he knew was the general direction in which he had been heading since they left the vent. Not, of course, back toward the Court of Seven Draks, but into a series of ways that, if followed to the end, would bring him to the only place he recognized as home, the pavilion that had been his father's.

"I know enough to get us—" He was beginning and then paused, for the danger in his plan was suddenly clear. They knew who he was, and knowing that—if indeed the false emperor did share all his memories—what better place to lay their trap than there? No, he could not go that way. But where then?

"To get us where?" demanded the Salariki.

Andas sighed. "I am afraid not where we have been heading. They could well be waiting for us there. There is just one place—"

He had tried to push that out of mind, but he could not. Only a very desperate and reckless man would choose that path. But certainly he was desperate enough. And when all roads but one are closed, one either fought like a hopelessly cornered beast, or one took that open road. He knew what would happen if he tried to fight. They could cook him in blaster fire, pick the key from his charred body, and no one would know who he really was. But that other way—

"You are afraid, greatly afraid now."

Andas grimaced. So he smelled of fear, did he? Well, perhaps this furred alien would also if he knew as much as Andas did. But it was the only way, and unless Inyanga had changed radically since he had last walked these ways, the false emperor was going to have a very

143

difficult time sending anyone in *there* after them.

"There is a place we can go," Andas said slowly, and then decided to tell the whole of it, whether the other would believe him or not. To one who did not know history, it might sound like the most primitive superstition.

"It is the Place of No Return."

"A cheerful name, that."

"Not always does it work that way. But from the earliest records of the building of the Triple Towers, there have been notations of disappearances at that place. Sometimes—in the early years—there would be four or five in a year, or less, and then a longer time when one could go and come there without harm. It was a matter of concern, for the guards' second barracks was at one side, and there were many men there on duty. The old north gate was situated near that point.

"It made no difference who the man was—sometimes a common soldier, twice officers of high rank, and then the Prince Akos. And he was *seen* to go! Five men, one his bodyguard and two generals, watched him dismount and start to walk across the inner court. They saw him—then he was gone!"

"There was a search, I presume?"

Again Andas ran his tongue tip across his lips. "One that turned the Triple Towers inside out. They explored more than had been done for years. On the third night they heard the calling—"

"Calling?"

"Yes, near the place where Prince Akos had vanished. Very faint and far away, as if it came from a great distance. They brought the Emperor to hear, and the Princess Amika, Akos's wife. Both swore before the altar of Akmedu later, when the final record was made, that it was truly the prince's voice they heard. For the space of two hours he called, his voice growing fainter. And he called names that all heard—first those of the men who had been with him when he had disappeared, and then, later, that of his wife. And at last his voice faded, and they never heard him again, though the Emperor stationed a constant sentry post there for two years thereafter."

"When did this happen?"

"About two hundred years ago. The Emperor had the old records searched then and counted all such disappearances. There were almost fifty—which surprised everyone as no one had completely reckoned them all before. And when, after two years, they heard nothing, found nothing more, he had that section put under ban. They closed that north gate and erected a new one. You cannot even reach that part of the palace now except by ways such as these. And I do not think guards will follow us in."

"But you have been there?"

"Once, with my father. There is a passage that reaches the inner corner of the old barracks—running to the commander's quarters. We stood in a window there and looked down on the courtyard where the prince vanished. A storm must have struck part of the enclosing wall, for stones were scattered inward, and we could see little of the pavement."

"And what explanation did they have, these people who watched your prince disappear and heard him call?"

"The ignorant spoke of night demons and sorcery. The Emperor had all the scientists called in. There was only one explanation my father thought made sense—that perhaps there was another world, one on another plane of existence, and that at intervals there was a break between that world and this, so a man might be caught. Since then I have listened to off-world travelers, and I have heard of such. Alternate time streams are spoken of,

145

layers of worlds in which history has taken some different turn. These, they say, may exist in bands side by side, so a man knowing how to go from one to another may travel, not backward in time, nor forward, but across it."

"A most intriguing suggestion. But since that emperor closed it off, no one has gone exploring there?"

"No. That is why we will be safe there. If we do not reappear for a while, they may even think we are caught in that invisible trap."

"Always supposing we are not! But it is within the court itself that this tricky piece of ground exists. And if we stay away from that we are safe?"

"Yes." Good common sense. Andas's spirits began to rise. It was true that they might shelter on the edge of danger and yet avoid it. He remembered how the empty rooms of the barracks had spread before him on that other visit. And there was even a small garden beyond, which had been attached to the commander's quarters. There was a spring-fed pool there. Water—they would have water—and there could even be fruit growing wild—

He quickened pace, but there was still a difficult journey ahead. In the first place, they must pass a dangerous portion of the ways running near to his old living quarters, for only from there could he take direction to the Place of No Return. Time dragged as they made that careful circuit. When he reached a stone-walled cell into which fed four passages, Yolyos suddenly tapped him on the shoulder. The Salariki's lips were very close to Andas's ear as he whispered in a hiss.

"Someone is here. There is a stink—" His broad head swung back and forth, his nostrils wide, sucking in the dank air. "There!" With a foreclaw he indicated the passage to his left.

"Can you tell how far away?" Andas murmured. That passage soon became a flight of steps leading to a garden house where his father had enjoyed the night blooms of the qixita.

"It is not too strong."

They could hope then, Andas believed, that the ambush had not been set within the passage, but rather where an unsuspecting fugitive might emerge into the room above. But he did not have to brave such a meeting. He was oriented enough now to find his way. He pointed to the opening directly ahead.

Not that this way was easy. The passage dropped deeper, at such a sharp angle that they soon had to clutch at small stones set in the walls to provide steadying handholds. When they reached the foot of that incline, they were walking again underwater, as the thick trickles on the walls told them. The passage narrowed, running now beside a conduit from which the lake above drained in rainy season. And there was a slime deposit where things that had never seen the light of day crawled and bred, while from it arose a vile odor.

Andas heard a coughing grunt from his companion and thought how much worse must be the torment for the sensitive nose of the alien. But at least their way led them along above that ooze and did not run beside it for long.

Three steps up and they were in another corridor surprisingly dry. This had one wall that was a series of bars chiseled out of the stone, with narrow slits between.

"What is that place beyond?"

"A wine cellar, or used to be—when the Crystal Pavilion was the home of the Empress dowagers. We are lucky, for all this section lies close to the old north gate."

"A wine cellar. A pity that we cannot sample some of what is stored there. I am carrying a dry throat."

"There is a garden with a spring at the old barracks," Andas promised, though he spoke with more assurance than he felt. There could be many changes with the years, and he still flinched from thinking how many years had passed since he last walked this way, though, by his own reckoning, it was not more than ten. Yet Abena had told him it was forty-five. Could she have spoken the truth?

They climbed again, Andas counting steps. Once more they were in runways with peepholes, so there might once have been reason to spy on the inhabitants here.

"Where are we going?" demanded Yolyos as they began a second climb.

"To the roof. We must reach the upper ways now. The tunnel underground is closed."

That was the one danger spot if they had guards with anti-grav belts on duty aloft. But there was no other way the fugitives would go.

10

They emerged on a very narrow walk of stone much be-
spattered by generations of bird droppings, where some
spindly plants had taken root in small crevices. Their
doorway had been set in the wall of a chimney, and they
must walk this ledge to the end, then scramble down to
the eaves, from which they could swing across to the
next roof, Andas hoped.

He had lost all reckoning of day and night since he
had been in the wall ways. It was now early evening.
There were still sun banners in the sky at his back, giving enough light for this difficult maneuver.

Something crunched under his sandals, and he glanced
down at a pile of splintered bird bones. There was no
marking in the green wash of moss and plants to suggest
that anything save winged creatures had come this way,
but he hurried along at the best speed possible, the
Salariki following effortlessly.

They slid down to the eaves, Andas expecting at any
moment to be sighted by some guardsman on patrol duty
aloft. That they had escaped this long seemed to him un-
believable, though it could be that the false emperor,
knowing what Andas carried, was wary enough to lay
nets closer to their goal. Should the key be lost, the result
would be black for the empire.

It was when they reached the eaves that Andas knew
desperation. When he had made this crossing before, his
father had carried devices he had worked out for safety
during his strange explorations. They had shot a magnet-
ic dart across and rigged a line to which they had
snapped safety belts before they took the leap. He had
nothing and must depend upon his own muscles.

"We go there?" Yolyos pointed to the slightly lower roof.

"If we can make it." Andas admitted his fear. "I only went this way once, and then we used tackle."

The Salariki crouched, drawing his legs under him in a position that looked almost awkward. Then he took off with speed and precision, leaving Andas gasping, to land gracefully on the roof ahead.

Yolyos turned to look back, his mouth a little open so that his pointed side fangs were visible in the fading light. Fading light—Andas knew he must go now, that he could not take that leap in the dark.

"Come on!" There was impatience in Yolyos's hissed call, as if he believed that leap of no importance and could not see why his companion hesitated.

Trying to summon all his self-confidence, Andas went as far back on the cramped take-off point as he could. Before he dared have any second thoughts, he jumped.

Hands shot out, claws ripped into his coveralls, and he had only an instant or two to realize that, but for the alertness of Yolyos, he could have missed his goal. Then the other drew him to safety. He crouched beside the Salariki, shaking so that he could not immediately move on.

"Where now?" Yolyos gave him no respite. Andas realized later that the Salariki had been wise in that.

He steadied himself with a hand against the parapet of the roof and tried to forget the swimming sickness in his head, to concentrate on half-remembered landmarks. They were standing on the roof of the Tower of Alikias. Here were no inner ways; they must use the regular stairway and seek the ground floor before they could return to the dark warren.

They found the trap door. It took some anxious moments to force it up. Time had settled dust about it like a corking. And by the time they were on the narrow stair within, the evening had closed into night. Andas had stopped shaking, fastening his mind on what lay before and not behind. He was sure that they had, for the moment perhaps, baffled or outrun the hunters.

Even if he and the Emperor shared a common knowledge of the hidden ways, the other was still no thought reader and could not be sure in which direction Andas would head. In fact, their present path was so far away from the ultimate goal of the temple that it might not be suspected. He hoped that the false Andas and those obeying his orders would believe that their quarry would head at the fastest possible speed for the temple. It was there that they would be setting up the most intricate of their traps.

But the longer they had to do that, the less favorable Andas's chances became. Yet his tired brain saw no other plan possible.

He *was* tired, fatigue weighting him down with a thick smothering—just at a time when he needed to be thinking sharply, his reflexes acute. If they could reach the walled-off place, then he could rest. He said so, and Yolyos answered, his voice a purring murmur through the dark.

"True, we are not made of metal like robots. And if we are androids, it would seem that we are also heir to the ills of our prototypes."

The air in the tower smelled of dust and faintly of animals—as if some of the long-empty rooms had been used as lairs. But they did not explore any of the chambers on the levels they passed, using the limited beams of the torch to bring them into the section just below the surface of the ground outside, where once more Andas's memory found the door to the other ways.

He set the fastest pace he could maintain, needing to

find refuge where he could rest, drink, perhaps find something to ease his aching stomach. This passage ran straight, with no branching ways, until they came again to one of those very narrow stairs and started to climb. It was short, taking them up past perhaps two floors. Then Andas inserted his fingers in certain slots, having first blown the dust from them, and pulled. They stepped at last into what had been the private chambers of the guard commander in the days of the old north gate.

The windows still had protective panes, so grimed by years of neglect that one could see them only as a very vague light against the velvet dark. There were sliding inner shutters, and though the runs of these were badly rusted, they beat and hammered until they got the windows covered. Only then did Andas switch the torch on the high beam and look around.

Against one wall stood the frame of a bed, so massive that it had probably been deemed too much to be moved. Their own footprints patterned the floor, together with the tracks of small creatures that had roamed the deserted barracks at will. There was nothing else.

"You mentioned water—" Yolyos said.

"There was a garden." Andas turned his head to the west wall as if he could see through it. "When we were here last, there was a spring there. There might even be a loquat vine in fruit. They live for years without tending."

"I would suggest we test the existence of both—now."

But Andas felt a reluctance to leave this shuttered room now that he had gained it. It was as if outside the walls of this one place waited all the menaces he had fled. Only the needs of his body drove him to battle that vague sensation of brooding danger.

Below the quarters of the commander stretched halls and rooms stripped now of everything that might suggest they had once harbored companies of guards. Passing these, they came out into a space between the barracks and the inner gate—to be assaulted, not by the stale, dusty air of the deserted building, but by a wave of almost overpowering fragrance, where a vine, grown wild and assertive beyond all resistance from its fellows, had run thick cables across the ground, bushes, and intervening trees, throttling them into dead skeletons fit only to support its vicious luxuriance.

Great white flowers burst in clusters along its stems, almost as if their growth was as explosive as blaster fire. And the ground was deep with rotting layers from past bloomings. Loquat indeed. Andas stared. He had never seen such a wild stand of the vine.

Beneath the clusters of flowers now in bloom hung the fruit of earlier blooming, smaller than the globes he had known, as if the strength here had gone more to flower than fruit. But it was ripe and ready for eating. They could eat, but however could they batter their way through that netting of leaf and stem to find water? He had no idea in which direction to search, and he doubted if they could get well in without jungle knives to clear a path.

"Water? I will find it!" Yolyos had been drawing deep lungfuls of the scent, as if the odor, well nigh too powerful for Andas, was as much a restorative for him as the food and drink they sought.

"That way—" He was so confident as he went that Andas followed him without question.

The Salariki did not rip and tear at the vines as Andas would have done. Rather he spread and pushed with gentleness, as if he handled something he would not harm, turning many times to hold open a space for his companion to squeeze through. It might be that he disliked the thought of breaking a path more brutally.

They had lost sight of the barracks, so deep was that growing curtain, when they at last found the spring. Once it had been piped in to feed a pond, but that bowl had long ago been broken by the roots of the vine, so that now the water gathered in a few shallow cups, trickled from one to another, and formed a stream beyond.

The water was good—how good Andas did not realize until he plunged his hands into one of the depressions again and again, bringing them cupped and dripping to his parched mouth. He had tasted wine from the Emperor's finest stock in the old days that could not compare with this.

There was a constant murmur of sound in the garden, the rubbing of vine stem against stem, blown by the night wind, the cries of insects, the gurgle of the water. But he heard also the appreciative slurping of his companion as he shared that boon of a long cool drink.

Andas had mouthed two of the tart-sweet (more tart than sweet in this wilder stage) loquat globes before he thought of what might be a serious problem for the Salariki. Though his species was omnivorous, their tastes were still strongly carnivorous. But that was not the greatest difficulty—could the alien safely ingest what was Andas's native food? Anyone traveling from world to world had immunity shots. But that did not mean that they were safe from the effects of another's food—which to them might be deadly poison.

He held the bunch of fruit he had snapped free and looked to Yolyos, who in this gloom was only a shadowy bulk still dribbling his fingers in the water.

"Maybe you cannot eat these."

"There is only one way to be sure. And one does not welcome starvation if there is any form of food available," returned the other calmly. "I am duly warned, Prince."

There was a rustling, and Andas guessed the other was culling his own bunch of fruit.

"It is not bad to taste," Yolyos announced a moment later, "though that can be no warning of future trouble. Many traps are overlaid with pleasant bait. I would rather have a well-covered xar leg bone in my hand, but one does not miscall what the First Ancestress desires to set before one. So—I eat."

But Andas continued, as he fed himself, to listen for any sounds from the other to suggest that this *was* a deadly trap covered with pleasant bait as far as the Salariki was concerned.

"It is food, but not too filling," the alien remarked at last. "However, for the smallest favors a man in need must be thankful. That we have this private food and water is another piece of good fortune to be paid for when one is free to concern oneself again with debts to the First Ancestress."

As he tried to get up, Andas found himself dizzy. Perhaps it was the lack of rest, but it seemed to him that some of that vertigo came from the cloying scent of the flowers. Suddenly he wanted to be away from the garden. He said so sharply that he must have surprised Yolyos, for the other asked, "What danger do you feel here, Prince?"

"The flowers—that smell—I must have fresher air!" He lurched and would have fallen had the other not steadied him. In the end Yolyos had almost to carry him out of that lush growth into the sterile dustiness of the barracks. There Andas drew as deep breaths of relief as those the Salariki had taken when he had fronted the banks of perfumed bloom.

"You are all right now?" Andas heard the Salariki rather than saw him. Out in the garden, though no moon had yet risen, the masses of white flowers seemed to give light.

He jerked free from the other's hold, feeling shame that such a thing as a flower, even in bulk, would weaken him so. "Yes. We can rest above—in the commander's room." He wanted to be near the exit he knew while in a place of such ill repute.

"You go on." Yolyos was back at the door. "To me that scent is all meat and drink. I shall come when I have had my fill."

Andas was too tired, too uneasy to argue. After all, he had warned the other. If Yolyos, knowing the danger, wanted to go and smell flowers in an overgrown garden, then let him.

Andas climbed to the upper chamber. The bed was but an empty frame. He could have brought some of the vines and grass from the garden to soften the floor. But he wanted no more of the loquats. With a sigh he stretched out on the hard surface and closed his eyes.

Dark—but with a kernel of red light that drew him, so that without knowing why, save that he must, he went toward that. Then that kernel enlarged suddenly, as if he had covered some length of distance in a single step or by willing it. There was a fire, and the weaving flames were the only illumination of a grim scene.

That fire burned not on any hearth but in the middle of a room, and not a room of four stout walls and an intact roof either, for the flames, now revealing, now dying so that they hid again, showed a ragged hole larger than any window in the wall facing him across the source of heat and light. When the fire burned higher, he could see that the roof was only partly overhead. There was little protection against a thick, creeping mist, such as Inyanga knew just before the winter came.

There was one who fed the fire, coming now and then

on her hands and knees, pulling pieces of roughly broken wood to push into the flames with caution, as if she drew upon a scant supply. Andas, from his days at Pav, recognized the technique practiced in survival course, though by the looks of her she played no training game but lived life on the thin edge of survival in truth.

That she was a woman he could tell only from the hair braided tightly to her skull in the many small braids of a desert nomad, for her body was a huddle of coarse garments from which protruded arms near as thin and curveless as the sticks she handled. Her face was as close to a skull as that of any living human being could be. And, save for her eyes, she might well have been one of the dead-alive of the old, old tales.

As she fed the fire, the light it cast grew so that Andas could see the other occupant of that ruined room. He had been propped up so that he sat facing Andas across the flames. But there was something about the way his limbs were stretched before him under a tattered rug that made the prince think they were useless.

On the stranger's lap lay—was it a voice-harp? Andas could not see it clearly in this bad light, and the woman with her fire-feeding kept blocking the view. It did have some resemblance to that elegant and courtly, if very old-fashioned, musical instrument, save that from one end of it projected and then rose a fan of slender rods. Woven back and forth, uniting the rods into a transparent fan, were wires or threads that gleamed and glistened as the light touched them.

But the man did not seem to be in the act of playing. Rather he held, gripped tightly in one hand, a splinter with a wad of candle fluff on its tip, which burned with such restricted light that the holder had to bring it very close to what was in his other hand in order to see, if he could see at all.

And what he was trying under such difficulty to see was a book—not a reading tape such as had been in use over untold centuries now, but an ancient *book* with pages to be manually turned, words printed on them. Andas knew books. They were curiosities and brought high prices from dealers of antiquities. There were at least a dozen in the Triple Towers, among the treasures collected by dilettante emperors in the past. But those were treated as treasures, kept in gem-set boxes.

The volume that the frowning would-be reader held in this place of dark and ruin had a cover of what appeared to be thin slabs of wood, the pages as thick as plasta sheets, but yellow and tattered on the edges. The prince looked beyond the wonder of that ancient book to the face of the man who held it and—

Did he cry out, or was that sound only uttered in his mind? At least neither the reader nor the wraith woman who fed the fire were startled or looked up to see him. But that other's face, thin, with a half-healed scar upon the temple—that face was his own!

This must be a dream, yet there was a feeling of reality in it such as Andas had never known in any dream he had walked or drifted through before. Could it be true then that men lived many lives, as the priests of the half-forgotten cult of Kaissee taught? And that some men were allowed to see these past lives? That the deeds of one life, good or bad, influenced the next? If so, was he looking now upon a self that had been his in the dim past?

He could see the lips of that other Andas move, but he heard no sound. And now the reader must have said something to the woman, for she came away from the fire, hunkered down by him, and took that dreary taper into her hand, holding it close to the page of the book, while the man's right hand, now free, moved to lie on the keyboard of the harp.

The fingers pressed, one, two, three— Again Andas heard no sound. Rather there was a vibration in the air. Once more he cried out as that vibration closed about him like a net, drawing him toward the fire in spite of his struggles.

Again the fingers moved, and the vibration tightened. Now he heard sound, too, very faint and far off. But it echoed and rang in his head, a torment that could not be shaken off. The reader looked up from the book, straight at Andas. The prince saw the eyes in the thin, starved face widen. It was plain he himself was seen.

The woman started, letting fall the candle. And Andas heard another sound, a thin cry of distress.

But he was free of the net the harp had woven. And he pulled away with all the strength he had, seeking the dark that lay beyond the fire, away from the man wearing his face.

Andas opened his eyes, afraid for a moment to look about him lest he see the fire and know that he was a prisoner in that place where a man wove a spell with a harp. But the acrid smell of dust and the silence told Andas that he lay safe (if one could term his present situation safe) once again in the commander's quarters.

Had it been a dream? He tried to compare it with dreams he had known. But most of those had been very fleeting and lacking in detail after one awoke. This was a different matter, for against all reason, his instinct and his emotions told him that somewhere, or sometime, the scene he had just witnessed had been real. Perhaps his fatigue, his exposure to thirst, hunger, and the strong scent of the flowers had unlocked some unknown portion of memory and he had spied upon his own far past. But then—

Andas sat up, drawing a deep breath of wonder and then of relief. If he could believe that, if he had, as the priests of Kaisee taught, remembered another life—that was proof he was no android!

By some experiment he could have been imprinted with all the memories of a man he had been made to resemble. But he could see no possible way he could also have been made aware in deep unconscious parts of the mind of events from the other man's past life. If he could only believe in the creed of Kaissee, then his own fears were stilled. Now he could only hope.

The presence of the book—that certainly meant the scene had been in a very ancient past. Books were treasures never to be used as that stranger had done. And the harp, while in part it was akin to one he himself had been taught to play as one of the graces of his rank, was different. The past—he had seen into the past—

Was it because he had the key? He had heard many legends concerning that, though privately those of royal blood discounted most of the old stories. Yet there must be an aura of power that clung to a talisman that had been venerated by generations upon generations, so that such objects took on a patina from that worship until in themselves they kept shadows of the very forces they represented.

His hand slid across the breast of his coverall, seeking the shape of the key. But first he touched that other thing he carried—the ring. And he jerked his fingers away as if the fire he had looked upon in his dream had licked them. That—that *was* a thing of power and one which he had forgotten or he would not have carried it so long. It should be destroyed, though he had no means for doing so. If he hid it somewhere here among the ruins, it would still have a way to draw to it the one to whom it had been sealed. Men might question the power

162

of the key, except when it was put to the use for which it was fashioned. But there was altogether too much proof of the influence of such a ring. He had a duty to see to its destruction. Luckily he could accomplish that also when he took the key to its proper place.

Andas lay back on the stones, but he was too wide awake to sleep again. Instead, he began to recall detail by detail the dream, and instead of fading as such normally would, it all became more sharply fixed, until he could remember things he had not noted at first—such as the bandage that had shown on the breast of the man when a movement of the stranger's hand on the harp had pulled aside the clumsily patched tunic he wore. There had been a crusted black-red stain on that bandage.

So it had been more perhaps than hunger and cold that had set those dark shadows under the stranger's eyes. He had the look, now that Andas had time to consider it, of a man sore hurt.

Of the ruined building in which those two had sheltered so poorly, he was not sure. It was certainly not of the Triple Towers he knew. He had seen tapes of warfare, and this dream scene reminded him strongly of such a picture taken in a refugee camp. War could reduce men to such a plight.

There had been wars in plenty on Inyanga—he could not deny that—though for the most part those had occupied only the claimants to the throne and their liegemen and had very seldom spread to the country at large. In fact, one of the pacts made by Akmedu had been that when disputes were to be settled in blood, the fighters must withdraw to the Red Waste. It had worked out very well. But the last "war" to be fought there in any force was now generations back. He himself had gone into the Red Waste from Pav—there had been nothing there like the scene he had witnessed.

"Prince!"

Roused out of his thoughts, Andas got up. He was stiff from the hardness of his bed and gave a little catch of breath at the complaint of a leg muscle.

"Yes—?" he did not need to ask who came. There was so strong an odor of loquat blossom accompanying the new arrival that the Salariki must have been rolling in a blanket of the moon-white flowers.

11

"There are doom dealings here!"

To Andas the words made no sense, but he could read the emotion in the other's voice, that growl he had come to identify with anger as far as the Salariki was concerned.

In spite of the shutters they had forced into place across the windows, Andas could see the dark form, and he turned on the torch to catch the other in its rays. Yolyos had his back turned. He was facing the one window that overlooked the fatal Place of No Return.

As the light centered on the alien, the prince could see the fur ridge along the other's upper arms and backbone. The hair did not lie sleek and smooth but was erect, while Yolyos's ears appeared flattened, folded in against his skull. Now the Salariki turned his head and looked at Andas over his hunched shoulder.

"It stinks of the doom here!" he growled again.

"Doom?"

"Doom—that which those who dabble in drum talk and fang work bring upon them in the Hidden Moon time." He still made no sense. "Give it what name you will then—but this is what the Death Drummer raises—death from no weapon but by stealing men's lives, sucking their breath unseen." Now he swung around to face Andas squarely, his lips flat, drawn back from his fangs, his eyes glowing as no human eyes could. "What do you here, Prince?"

In spite of himself, as if the very force of the other's suspicion drew it from him, Andas answered with the truth.

"Nothing but dream."

"Dream? But do not say that is nothing! There are true dreams and false ones. Some are sent as warnings or enticements. You have said this is a place of ill omen avoided by your kind. Now you dream. And this room has the stink of doom dealings—and you call it nothing!"

The longer the Salariki spoke, the more Andas realized that the alien was genuinely aroused, that the easy relationship between them was threatened. In turn, his own unease grew. He had not chosen Yolyos as a comrade in this wild venture. That had been thrust upon him by chance. Yet now he discovered he did not want to lose what he had in common with this warrior of another species and world.

"None of my doing," he said with, he hoped, enough force to impress. "I went to sleep and I dreamed—"

"And what manner of dream?" Yolyos relaxed none of his defensive stance. It was plain Andas had to prove himself.

Andas told him, though whether he made clear to the other what had happened, he did not know. He waited for a long moment until the Salariki spoke.

"This man wore your face?"

"With the addition of a scar," Andas amended.

"And the place, that you did not know?"

"It was too dark to see much, but I am certain I never saw it before."

"And the woman?"

"I swear to my knowledge I have never seen her, though she was of my race—a desert nomad perhaps."

There was a subtle change in Yolyos, and inwardly Andas relaxed, sure he was no longer a figure of suspicion. Now he ventured to ask a question in return.

"What is this doom of which you spoke?"

"Each race or species has its own beliefs in intangible powers—in 'magic.' We have our adepts, too. I have seen a Death Drummer—" Yolyos broke off as if that touched upon some memory he would not resummon. "As do all emotions, this dealing has a smell. My people scent things others feel. And this is a foul smell. When I came in, it was rank. I think your dream was no dream but a sending. As you tell me—this net of sound drew you toward him who made it. Whatever touched you then—" He frowned. "No, I will not set name to it here and now. Such naming can draw influences when one least wants them." Andas saw his wide nostrils expand and his head swing from side to side, as if testing the stale, dust-laden air of the room.

"Now it is gone. Whatever spear it launched at you failed. But I would not slumber here long."

"The only door to our escape is in the wall here. As far as I know, there is no other entrance to the runs." Andas was half persuaded, yet to leave the way to such safety—poor as it was—that the wall passages promised, he could not bring himself to do.

"Then let me set such safeguards as my people know—I *shall* set them!" What had begun as a request was now a definite decision.

Before Andas could protest, Yolyos turned and used his unsheathed claws on the shutter they had pounded into place, levering it loose. The prince tried to stop him.

"No—we could be sighted!"

"By whom? You said this is a shunned place. We have no lights—if you will turn off the torch—even if your guards decided to fly over. I tell you this room must have protection or we do not stay in it!"

So strong was his conviction, Andas stood aside. But he did not help any as all the windows in the wall facing that ill-omened court were not only freed of the shutters but also were opened to the night. Then in the moonlight the Salariki padded back to the doorway where lay a vast mass of stuff, a mixture of vine, flower, and leaf, as if he had plundered the garden.

He picked that over, bringing forth a number of flowers, still waxy-white, though darkening bruises showed here and there on their wide petals. The best of these he proceeded to lay out on the windowsills in a pattern. When he had finished each, he held his hands in the full moonlight, cupping and flexing his fingers, as if he were actually gathering some of that wan radiance.

Then he turned palms down, opened his fingers, and murmured in the purring speech of his own people, as if he recited some charm or ritual. On each windowsill he did so. Then he stepped back, his face hidden in the dark. When he spoke, his voice had lost that threatening roughness.

"This is a potent charm of my people. If you have any you can add to it—"

Andas shook his head and then realized that the other probably could not see that gesture. "We do not believe in charms." But he made that denial conciliatory. To each species its own safeguards. And what had Yolyos said of the talisman? He had the key—though that was only a symbol.

Thinking of the key brought the ring to mind. Suppose that could be a focus for evil? Should he try to rid himself of it, if only temporarily? Yet he was determined to destroy it, and if he hid it, how did he know that he could recover it?

Yolyos spread the mass of foliage on the floor. Making a bed, Andas judged. Once more the heavy perfume of the now wilting flowers was thick, far too heavy in this room, making him dizzy. He was sleepy, too—very sleep again, with the same eye-burning fatigue that had sent him to dreaming on the hard floor earlier. He must not sleep! In sleep, dreams could return, could reach for him, but—

It was as if he were two people. One was a prisoner watching the other surrender, ready to curl up beside the Salariki on the fragrant nest of leaves and flowers. He struggled to withstand and failed.

The moonlight through the windows made white bars of light on the floor. Half revealed in one was the huddled form of Yolyos curled about, his head pillowed on his crooked arm, his breath coming evenly. The moon was so bright that it had a glitter like ice. It was cold—

Andas stood up in the moonlight. He walked to the window, looked out and down. There was no longer any fear in him, rather a growing excitement, a tension such as filled men on the eve of a fight or some contest of skill or trial by force.

On the sill lay the pattern of blossoms Yolyos had set with such ceremony. Andas laughed silently. Did this furred barbarian think that such a stupid trick would defeat what waited out there? He swept the flowers away with his hand. Then putting both palms on the sill, he leaned out to look down.

The broken wall had spilled its upper layers well over the court. But the rubble did not cover the whole; it did not even touch upon the important section. Still, the time had not yet come, only its warning to awaken him.

He watched and waited, without any fear or surprise, save that his excitement was hard to contain. He found it very difficult to stand still and mute, not to run down there shouting aloud—very hard, but the time was not yet.

It was beginning (not visibly before his eyes, but somewhere deep within him), a beat like the beat of his heart, save that it began slow and sluggish, and then grew faster, stronger. He could hear the rasp of his own breathing as that, too, grew heavier and faster, like the gasping of a man who runs a race. But the time was not yet.

Andas stood, waiting. Then came the moment with a signal his spirit recognized, but his ears did not hear, nor his eyes see. He left the window, passed the bed of vines, went into the hall, and threaded corridors and stairs as if they were not dark but brilliantly lighted and this was a well-known way.

Thus he came to a door that was not only closed but also fused shut. And by then the force that drew him was so strong that he hammered at the barrier, unable to think clearly. After he had battered the door for a space, the compulsion lessened. He leaned against the firmly sealed door, his bruised fists hanging by his sides.

No way through—his mind moved sluggishly. It was hard to think. No way through here, but there must be a way! Like a programed robot he turned back and retraced his path until he stood once more at the window looking down into the court, to that spot where he *must* be and soon.

Quickly he turned and made a dart at the vegetation that had formed their bed, on which Yolyos still slept. Andas's hands closed upon a length of vine, and he jerked it free with no thought for the sleeper. He had blanked the Salariki out. All that mattered was a way to get below. But this vine was too short! From this window, yes, but a floor below—

He heard a cry from the Salariki whom his action must have aroused, but he paid no attention. With the loop of vine about his shoulder, he ran, once more surefooted and fearless, through the dark to another room where there was another window.

That was closed, and the moonlight through it was dim and dulled by the dust. Andas looked about him wildly. There was a jumble on the floor here, as if the debris of the barracks had been pushed together to molder into dust. He scrabbled in that and came up with a bar of rust-flaking metal. But its core seemed stout enough, and with that he broke out the panes.

The bar was longer than the window was wide. It must serve as his anchor. He had no time to hunt a better one. He looped the vine about it, jammed the bar across the base of the window, and climbed out, the vine ends in his hands. At the same time there was a shout from the door of the room. He did not wait.

It was more a fall than a descent, but the vine kept him from crashing to the pavement. He no longer cared really. He must reach that spot—*now!*

Andas ran, vaguely hearing the thud of someone landing on the pavement behind him. Two steps more—a hand clawed at his shoulder raking his flesh painfully. Andas did not try to strike it away. There was no time. Reach the spot—that was all that was meaningful in the world now!

But there was no pavement, no bright moon, no crumbling walls. There was a time of transition through a place he could never afterwards describe, from which his memory flinched. Then he was falling, coming up against a solid object with force enough to painfully drive all the breath from his lungs in a single gasp. And propelling him forward in that dive was another struggling body.

Andas was occupied at first merely fighting to get a full breath again. But once that happened, he looked around. No moon showed. Rather a thick mist hung like a cloak, leaving cold beads of moisture on his skin.

"Fool!"

Beside him another body moved. He felt the softness of fur against his arm, wiping away some of that moisture. But the voice was a warning growl of anger.

"Yolyos?"

"What is left of him, yes. And into which of the Drummer's hells have you now plunged us?"

Ándas had no time to answer. The compulsion that had drawn him to the courtyard closed about him again. It was as if his transition to this place had jarred loose some tie, now once more firmly noosed about him. He scrambled to his feet, not looking for the Salariki. But as he started off, he said, "This way."

Whether Yolyos followed or not did not matter. All that did was that he, Andas Kastor, must reach that place toward which he was going. And there was a need for haste, great haste. His path led in and out among tumbled blocks of stone, many taller than his head. The mist continued—became a soaking rain. He could not tell how far he had traveled or how long. His sense of time had been disrupted by that passage through the other place. But at last he saw ahead a wink of light.

Memory stirred. Once before he had seen just that same small wink of red and yellow through the dark. Surely he had done this all before.

Fire—among ruins. The blocks around which he made his painful way were not stones, but the remains of buildings, or of a building. And those he sought were the people of his dream—the skeleton woman who fed the fire, the man who played the strange harp. He was caught again in the dream! Yet this time it carried even more the stamp of reality.

But the woman did not feed the fire now. She crouched a little behind the half-seated, half-lying man, her too-thin arm an additional prop for his shoulders, as if he needed all the support she could give him. And he held no ancient book, but instead both his hands rested on the harp and were in motion there, though Andas heard no sound, only felt that vibration, which shook and churned him and would not let him go.

He did not drift effortlessly to the fire this time—he walked on his own feet. And as he came to a halt on the other side of the now dying flames, the harper's face was filled with exultation. He spoke, and Andas heard and understood.

"The records were right. It is done well—"

The woman interrupted him. "Done, yes, but done well? Ah, dear lord, only time can answer that!"

"And I have so little time—is that what you think?" he asked half impatiently, raising his hands from the harp to press them against his chest over that encrusted bandage, as if he held there something precious and threatened. "There will be time, Shara. I have not accomplished all I have so far, not to have time to finish!"

The compulsion faded as he talked. Andas was free. Yet when he turned his head to look for some manner of escape, he was still sluggish, wrapped in the effects of that bondage.

"Yes, you are here! And you are Andas—a young Andas. Shara, show him to me clearly!"

The woman left her place at his back, moved out, took up a piece of wood, and thrust it deep into the fire's heart. When it blazed, she lifted it again and held it near enough to Andas so that he jerked his head back, the heat too strong for comfort.

"Strong, young—the rightful Andas, just as the records foretold." The stranger with Andas's face almost crooned the words, as if he sang a victory song. "An Andas for an Andas! I die—you live to fulfill all the promises—"

"Who are you? This place—where is it?"

"Andas!" But the woman did not look to him as she cried that name aloud, rather to the man on the ground. She whirled the branch around, stirring it to greater

175

burning, and held it before her as she might a spear or sword.

There was a clatter of stone against stone.

"Prince! Give me a lead to find you!" Yolyos's voice came out of the rain and the dark.

He answered, "Here—there is a fire for a guide—"

"There is a fire to kill!" The woman menaced him with her brand so he leaped back and away. But the harper made what was plainly a painful effort, seized the edge of her shapeless outer garment, and put his waning strength into a swift backward jerk, so she staggered, almost losing her balance.

"He is not alone!" she cried. "It is a trick!"

"Not so," the harper told her. He spoke in a quiet voice, almost as one would soothe a child. "We drew him. There was another who followed, who was with him at that moment when the gate opened. He knows this one, speaks to him as to a friend. Be not so swift to judge, Shara."

The brand had burned close to her hold. She tossed it into the fire and stood empty-handed. There was an empty look on her face, too. She said nothing more, but dropped in her old place, her hands on the man's shoulders, as if she needed that contact as much as he might need her support.

She no longer even looked at Andas, but kept her head bowed, her eyes ever upon the face of the man whom she now sat beside. Nor did she even glance around as Yolyos came out of the shadows.

But there was surprise on the harper's scarred face as he saw the Salariki. He surveyed the alien with a searching stare, as if he sought to read Yolyos's thoughts and weigh them to see if he were friend or enemy.

"You are not one of us." He did not speak Basic, and Andas was sure the Salariki did not understand.

"He does not speak our tongue," he cut in swiftly. "Yes, he is an off-worlder, a Salariki—the Lord Yolyos."

"Salariki." The harper rolled the word about in his mouth as if he tasted something strange, beyond his experience. "Off-world—oh!" Once more triumph flamed fitfully in his gaze. "In your world, brother, men still seek the stars?"

"*My* world? What world is this—if it is not a dream?"

The man sighed, his hands slipping from his breast and the bandage there as if he could no longer find the strength to hold it so.

"This is Inyanga, part of the Empire of Dingane that was—was—was—" He repeated the verb three times, as if in doing so he tolled some bell signifying the end of a living thing. "But it is not your world, save that in some parts it is a double of perhaps that much happier life. I do not know the rights of this, brother. It would take a man much more learned than I am to explain. I only know that our twin worlds must lie very close, so that in places, or at least one place, there is a touching. Have you no tales of men—yes, and women, too"—as he said that the woman beside him stirred and raised one hand to her lips—"who have vanished suddenly and never returned?"

"Yes."

"They came here, some of them. That is how Kioga Atabi first thought of this." His hand lifted and fell upon, rather than pointed to, the harp. "I—I was his student for a short time, before the rebellion. So I knew, or thought I knew, enough to open by intention a gate which before opened only by chance, to open that and draw through the man I needed—my people needed—"

"Me?" Andas was fast losing all belief in the reality of this. Was it another vivid dream? He could not be standing here in the rain and the ruins, listening to the man-wearing-his-face saying such things.

"You because you are who you are—Andas Kastor. Just as in the world I am Andas Kastor. But I am dying, and you are alive and unhurt. You can take up the battle I must leave—carried upon my shield after the right of the royal blood, though there be none now to bear me to the Tomb of the Thousand Spears, nor any to beat the Talking Drums of Atticar at my going. Still there is a war being most bitterly fought, and my people need a leader. Thus, I summoned one they will give allegiance to with-out—without—" His words slowed, he swallowed visibly once, twice, then coughed, and a dark tricle crept from the corner of his mouth.

The woman exclaimed and would have moved to his aid. But with one hand he waved her back, fighting to speak again.

"I leave you now the cloak of Ugana fur, the sword of the Lion, the crown of the great queen Balkis-Candace—"

Long ago those words had lost their meaning save as a ritual so sacred and old that Andas, without thinking, responded to them. That no one knew what a "lion" was or remembered a great queen Balkis-Candace did not matter. What did was that this man, wounded to his death, invoked something so sacred, so much a part of Andas's breeding, that he went to his knees and stretched forth both his empty hands. It was a gesture he had thought to make one day, but kneeling before the altar of Akmedu, and the man saying that to him would have been a tall and glorious figure in brilliant robes, the Emperor, an old man of his own house accepting him as heir.

The harper raised both hands, though they wavered and shook. And they fell rather than were placed on Andas's hands. They tried to grip Andas's fingers, but had no strength left. It was his hold that kept them linked.

"By the rite of the crown, the spear, the shield, the Lion, the—the—"

"The thorn." Andas supplied for the faltering voice. "By the water which freshens the desert, the clouds which veil the mountains, the will of Him who is not named by lesser beings, by all these, and the blood of my heart, the strength of my arms, the will of my spirit, the thoughts of my brain, so do I accept this burden and rise under it."

He spoke steadily, the harper watching him with feverish and demanding eyes, his lips shaping the words he did not say aloud as he followed the great oath with such intensity that it was plain the whole of his being was now centered on hearing Andas intone it to the end.

"Rise under it, to serve those who look to me for bread, for water, for life itself. So rest on me this burden until the end of that time written in the stars for me, when I shall go forth on the road that no man seeth. And this do I promise by the key, which I lay hand upon." He had dropped those lax hands and fumbled at the breast of the coverall. He drew out the talisman, and the fire seemed to leap higher at that moment, giving fiery life to what lay in his grasp.

The harper looked at it, and his face contorted into a painful smile.

"Well, oh well, have we wrought, Andas Kastor that was, Andas Kastor that will be! Emperor and lord, hold well the key—the key—"

Once more he fought for words, but this time he could no longer hold fast to the last wisp of strength. His eyes closed, and he fell forward, hunching over the harp. His hands tore at it in a last struggle, and in his frenzied grasp the strings broke with a horrible discord.

12

Shara put both fists to her mouth as if to stifle some cry. The Salariki spoke first.

"He is dead. But what did he ask of you?"

Andas still knelt, looking at the huddled body. He answered absently in Basic.

"He put upon me the Emperor's oath, passing to me rule and reign. Though if he had the right to do so—" He glanced about at the ruins. This was no housing for one with the right to pass the oath—which was done only in an atmosphere of great richness and ceremony.

Shara tugged at the body, drawing it back so that the harper's face could be seen. Since his driving will and spirit had departed from it, that face was now a mask of endurance and despair.

"Who was he?" Andas demanded.

"Emperor and lord." She did not look at him, but continued to pull at the flaccid body, straightening it.

"Of what? By the look of him he—"

"He fought when lesser men lay down and willed the coming of death. He believed and worked for that belief!" She came alive, on fire, facing him across the body, as if she had taken into her own wasted form the energy that had held a dying man to a fearsome task. "He was the only hope of the empire. And when he knew he had taken his death blow, he held off death that he might bring one to stand for him—"

"Stand for him? But how can I do that, woman, unless I know the whole of the tale?"

Though she appeared the poorest of desert nomads, yet this Shara spoke the pure court tongue. Also he was beginning to think she was much younger than she first appeared. What was she to the dead man? Wife, Second Lady? But at least she ought to make some sense now of what had happened to Andas.

She had taken off the piece of rough material she had wound about her shoulders as a shawl, straightening it out gently over the body, covering the face that was a mask of Andas's own.

"You are right. There is a time for mourning and the beat of drums, and a time when such must be forgotten. He knew he had but hours when he came hither, so upon me he laid the burden of remaining alive, of playing guide to the one who would come.

"This is a world twin to your own. I do not know why this is so. But it is true that those from your place have come among us from time to time. It seemed they could do this by chance but could not go back. The Magi Atabi worked to discover the secret. He made many experiments. The last was this—" She pointed to the harp with the now broken strings. "It was his belief that certain sounds could open the gate between. When he was an old man, a very old man, he came to court, to beg of the Emperor a chance to put his invention to the test.

"That was when Andas saw him. His tutor was a pupil of the Magi's and took Andas to meet him. And the old man, fearful of getting no notice from the authorities (which he did not), took much time and trouble to explain to Andas what he wished to do.

"But already the shadow reached over us. He had no listeners—save a prince who was a young boy."

She paused, and she no longer surveyed the shrouded body or Andas, but rather raised her eyes to the broken wall, rapt in some vision of her own. Andas spoke to her gently and as he might to an equal in rank.

"You speak of a shadow, lady?"

"Yes. And that shadow has a name—a foul name—one

to be spat upon! Kidaya—Kidaya of the Silver Tongue!" Her wan face flushed darker. "Kidaya of the House of the Nahrads."

Andas started, and she must have noticed it.

"Do you know of her then? Is your world also so cursed?"

"Of Kidaya I have not heard. But the House of Nahrad, the Nameless people of the Old Woman—yes, I have heard of them. How came one of the cursed line to your court?"

"You might well ask. Ask it of those who sing the Bones. It was decreed after the rebellion of Ashanti that none of the Nameless were to 'come within one day's journey of the Emperor. Yet Kidaya came to lie in his bed, to eat from his marriage plate, though she did not wear the crown. Even a man bewitched can be kept from some crimes! He took her into the Flower Courts, but he dared give her no First Honors. And for that Kidaya made him pay, and this whole empire crumbled into what you see about you—ruin and decay.

"Faction was set against faction by her cunning, and one rebel after another arose. She laid memory spells on the Emperor, so he felt hatred toward those who served him most loyally. Houses fell, their heads and all their families slain. Even Andas's life was saved only by a trick—" She laid her hand on the covered body.

"When he was of an age to take shield, he was the only true-line heir. She had seen to that by her web-spinning. The Emperor was too old, too sunk in her dreams, to be reached by those who would still save him and the empire. But she—she did not grow old! The witchcraft of the Old Woman held, so that she grew in outward beauty and in evil power as the years passed.

"But she bore no son—openly. There was a story that in secret she mothered a daughter, dedicated to the Old

Woman from the first drawing of her breath, and that daughter Kidaya determined would hold the key—"

At her words Andas's hold tightened upon the talisman. There was nothing to say that a woman could not rule in her own right. Twice over in the past had there been an empress who touched what he now carried. But that anyone tainted with the forbidden knowledge would so aspire—!

"When she thought she was strong enough to move, she wrought upon the Emperor until he turned his face from Andas. There was a silly plot uncovered, so botched a matter that all knew it was but a sham to give the Emperor reason for decreeing the Second Punishment—"

Again she paused, and Andas drew a whistling breath. In his own world the Second Punishment existed only in the dark annals of long past history, though it could still be used by law against any of the royal clans who rebelled. Yet it had not been so for more than a hundred years. To what barbaric state had this twin world sunk that this punishment could be once more invoked against a man?

"But his eyes—" he protested. The dead man's face was hidden, but Andas was sure he had not been mistaken. Those eyes had been normal—he had not been blinded.

"He had friends still, ready to risk their lives and more than the true line not come to an end and that witch sit on the Triple Throne," Shara said. "But he played a game thereafter such as few men would have the strength to do, for he wore the mask of the Second Punishment, and no man knew that he had not lost his eyes. As a blinded prince he had no chance for the throne. She could contemptuously let him crawl into any hole he chose to hide shame and disgrace. But he lived and so won a small victory, since she would not send against him, blinded, such evil arts as the Old Woman's blood-sworn knew, such as had been turned against others. He was a nothing, a grain of dust she had swept aside and need not remember."

"But he was not blind," Andas said slowly. A blind prince, a cripple, one slack or injured of wits, could not stand as emperor—an easy way in the dark old days to sweep away a rival. But for a man to play blind so cunningly to save his life, that required such patience that he marveled at the thought of it.

"He was not blind. And he was young, very young, but his wits were old and his understanding great. He played his part very well. At first she kept him about the court, a warning and a threat to others. Also, I think, a symbol of her own triumph to please herself. But at last she discovered that pity does not die under disfavor, and she sent him to the Fortress of Kham. There she made her mistake."

"The mountaineers have never welcomed those of the Old Woman," Andas commented. Though that knowledge was of his world and not this, he saw Shara nod.

"Is that so with you as well as us? It is true. They had a spirit caller of unusual power, one sworn to peace and well versed in the inner life. He had made several miraculous cures—publicly. The commander of the fortress then was of the House of Hungang—"

"So he would be shield-up against all the Nameless." Again Andas interrupted. This was like viewing a half-remembered history tape.

"That is so. And the spirit caller wrought another cure —but on that day also the news of the Emperor's farewell flashed from the Triple Towers."

"So civil war followed? Did your Kidaya have enough of the lords to back her?"

"She had built well. Three-quarters or more of those making up the inner circle of the court were her men. She need only close her fist to crush them, as they well knew. Yes, she had backing, and there was war. But it would have been an even judgment between us had she not brought mercenaries from the stars. And they had such weapons as beat the loyal houses out into the hills like beasts. Since then all has gone wrong." Shara raised her hand and let it fall. "The mercenaries hold the center of the land. But they have had no further help from off-world since our raiding parties destroyed the call tower at Three Ports two years ago. They have already had to abandon many of their weapons for lack of ammunition or repairs.

"Also there was the choking death, and they died from it, more of them than us. It is even said that the choking death was one of their weapons that was misused, since it spread out of Zohair after they occupied it. There are other ills, though, that Kidaya has loosed—the night crawlers—"

Andas shivered. "But those are only legends—to frighten children. Sensible men—"

"Sensible men believed not—and died! What we prate of as superstition in the days of pride and safety may seem different in the dark when men hide from death. The night crawlers here are real. Then—then there was betrayal in our own small ranks!" Her voice, which had held so even and colorless, suddenly quavered. "My dear lord was so struck down. He knew that he had his death wound, though he held to life with both hands as long as he could that he might bring aid to those who had put their trust in him. For months he has sought the cache left by the Magi Atabi, hoping that in it might be some weapon strong enough to turn against the invaders now that they are weakened. But when he found it, then that secret enemy struck. I think that it was in the mind of that unknown one to take what my lord had found and use it to bargain with Kidaya.

"But my lord beat off the attack, losing in it all save me. And he would allow me only to bind his wounds and aid him here—with what he had found in the cache—for the Magi had left a writing, and my lord believed that with this strange harp he could summon from the other world one who was himself there. As he did! So he passed to your hands the power, the task—"

"But, my lady, this is not—I cannot—" For the first time Andas realized fully what he had done when, bemused by the ritual of the passing of rule, he had taken those oaths to a dying man. This quarrel was not his. He could not possibly take upon his shoulders the burden he understood so little. The first who met him would know him for an impostor.

"You are Andas, Emperor." She looked at him sternly. "I bear witness, as can this alien—whom you so foolishly brought with you—that you are. And with my swearing so, who would believe otherwise? You have his face."

"He has a scar. There is a difference," Andas was quick to point out.

"That scar was gained but a few days before the final attack in which he was wounded," she told him. "None living, save me now, knew he had it."

"And who are you that your voice will make or unmake an emperor?" Andas demanded.

He could see nothing about her that would give credence to the certainty with which she spoke—as if she held the power she allotted in her tale to Kidaya. She was a bone-thin woman with her hair in the tight, small braids of a nomad, wearing tattered sacks as a robe of honor.

"I am Shara, the Chosen of Emperor Andas." Her chin

lifted, and there was about her a pride which was as illuminating at that moment as if she did indeed stand with her feet in the slippers of gold, the pearl diadem on her dusty head. "I am of the House of Brawa-Balkis. What say you to that, son of the House of Kastor?"

Kastor was a royal house, yes. But there were older clans with the right to provide a ruler at the Triple Towers, and of them all Balkis was the fabled, the legendary one. The last daughter of Balkis had chosen to unite with Brawa. But long ago that house had dwindled and disappeared in his own world. Chance could have kept it alive here, and Andas recognized a speaking of the Blood. No one would claim such heritage unless it was the truth.

He raised his hands in the formal gesture of one veiling his eyes before a sun-bright superior. "Hail, Blood of the Blood."

"Far away and long ago that." Her voice had lost that chill pride. "But here and now I am the Chosen. Do you think that my word concerning you will not be believed? You are Andas, Emperor. And he who lies here—he must be laid secretly with only the honors we can do him in our hearts, not even knowing where he lies."

But she was moving too fast for him. Andas got to his feet and, for the first time in many moments, remembered the Salariki. He turned to look for Yolyos and could just barely make out the alien's form as the other hunkered down some distance away, facing out into the rain and the night as if he were on guard. Andas went to him.

"You now have some knowledge of what this means." Yolyos greeted him with a statement rather than a question.

Andas repeated all Shara had told him.

"So he gave you the rule. And she says that you are

now the Emperor and plans to hide his death and pass you off as him. You will do this?"

Andas had been dodging the need for a decision. Perhaps that was why he had listened to her story, tried to keep his mind on the past rather than the present or the future.

But one fact was ever before him. Though he had not taken that oath in the temple or before the glitter of a court, he had given it. And all the conditioning of his life had set in one mold, that the Emperor had a duty of service. Once he had taken the oath, he was no longer so much a man as a symbol. Though that was cold and bleak, yet it was the position to which he had been born and bred.

Could he explain it so that Yolyos would understand? Andas sought to put it into words—only death now could dissolve his responsibility. He could not tell why he had been moved to answer the appeal, the determined will of that other Andas. But having done so, he was bound.

"And if you are not in truth this Andas, but an android?" Yolyos asked then as Andas stumbled through his explanation, finding his logic dwindle when he had to present it to an alien who could not understand long conditioning.

"I am Andas, Emperor, now!" He refused that other thought.

"This female tells you there is no going back. Can you believe her?"

"As she knows it, she is telling the truth. And the harp that seems to have brought us here, it is now broken."

"Conveniently, as far as they are concerned," Yolyos growled.

Andas was jolted out of his own concerns. He might be bound here, but what of the Salariki? He certainly had no duty pressed upon him by death and a ritual of words, and he would be wholly in exile.

"Perhaps there is other information kept by this Magi, to be found in the cache of which she spoke. We can—"

"Always hope?" Yolyos finished for him. "Yes. Also there is this. As you have found yourself so superseded in your time, perhaps I also have been long so. There has never come any good of counting the horns on a Kuay buck before one has shot it, nor the teeth of a gorp that escapes one's net. It is better to look to the foretrail than behind one. So we hide this emperor's body—then what?"

"She must tell us." So much would depend upon Shara's help. That she would be willing and eager to give it, he knew. And she must be able to brief him so thoroughly that he could pass as the proper Andas, even with those who knew him well. What he would *do* as that Andas, however, he had not even speculated.

They buried the Emperor in the ruins of the building he had chosen for a campsite, piling rubble from the walls up, over, and around him and then, at last, uniting their strength to push over a standing portion to cascade upon the mound, covering it.

Shara brought a bundle into the open when they were done. She opened a roll of mat-cloth and shared out twists of dried meat and some fruit as hard as metal pellets and tart enough to pucker the mouth.

"It would seem that your commissary does not do well, Emperor," Yolyos commented when they had managed to choke it down, washed by drafts of water they handscooped from hollows where the rain had gathered.

Shara tugged at Andas's sleeve. "He speaks with the tongue of the mercenaries. It is better that he learn ours as swiftly as he can."

Andas passed this suggestion along. The Salariki growled.

"Well enough, if you can teach it. But these mercenaries—are any of them Salariki?"

When Andas translated, Shara shook her head. "They are all like us, save that they have very pale skins and their hair is yellow. They wear it even on their faces—so—" She drew her finger across her upper lip. "And they speak among themselves with a sharp click-click—like a pang beetle—though they use the speech you talk in to this one also. They wear garments something like yours" —she touched Andas's sleeve—"so we shall say that you killed one of a patrol and took his robe. With supplies so few for us, this often happens. Even the enemy go ragged at times since there are no more ships setting down to bring them what they wish.

"White-skinned, yellow-haired, wearing mustaches." Andas was trying to place the enemy. He translated for Yolyos. The other had a suggestion.

"Mercenaries are now hired from only two sectors. I have seen men of Njord among the bodyguards of the Svastian overlords who resemble your description. But how can we judge the *here* with our own world? Mercenaries among us are largely outlawed. It could be for a similar reason that ships have ceased coming here. Your empire may be under ban by the Patrol."

Andas had heard of such bans—of planets, even systems, so deeply embroiled in some chaotic war that they were declared off limits for any space contact. Or it might be that the plague Shara had spoken of had isolated this world. There was nothing so feared throughout the galaxy as plague, and nothing that sooner put a whole world into a quarantine that might last for generations.

But if such limited the inflow of mercenaries, perhaps

this isolation was to be welcomed rather than deplored. However, it was what lay immediately to hand that mattered. Andas did not know how long they had been about the business of burying his double, but the rain had stopped and the sky was now lightening into day. The ruin they had demolished as much as they could to cover the grave was only a part of a vast, devasted area where the signs of fire, explosion, and the use of weapons that could melt and curdle stone were only too evident. He stared about him, seeing no relation to anything he had known in his own world.

Finally he asked, "What is this place?"

Shara had tied together her bundle, taking care with the scant remnants of the unpleasant field rations she had supplied. She looked up with a strange half smile.

"This is the one-time heart of the empire, my lord. Know you not the Triple Towers?"

"The—the Triple Towers?"

He put his hand to his head as if dazed by a blow. Nor could he believe that this wilderness of riven desolation was the vast spread of palace, pavilion, hall, courtyard, and garden that he had known so well all his life.

Andas turned slowly, pivoting, to seek out some point of reference, at least one of the towers themselves, or the bulk of the temple against the sky. But the change was too great. He could not guess where they now stood as compared with that other world.

"What happened here?" he demanded.

"Ask of Kidaya," Shara replied. "We were hiding afar, back in the hills. All we saw was the flash of fire. What survivors we have met were not in the palace at all, but across the river in Ictio, and they were all suffering from radiation burns."

"But if the burn-off destroyed Kidaya—"

"I did not say that! She and those who could best serve

her purposes were away before it happened. We do not know whether it came from her will or some accident—but it ended our chance of holding the heart of Inyanga. We had those planted here ready to further our cause. And could Andas have reached the temple—" She shrugged. "What might have been and is are far removed one from the other."

"The temple!" Once more Andas's hand closed upon the key. If the other Andas had had its equivalent and could have reached the temple, and if the old records were true—

Shara turned around, much as Andas had when seeking a landmark. "That way, I think. But it is high in radiation, and no one can enter without a protecto suit, which is as difficult to obtain as Kidaya's death. What want you with the temple?"

He turned the key around. But what was the use of thinking now about what that might have led him to. If the temple lay in hard radiation, it was as far removed from his penetration as the third moon of Benin.

"Nothing that matters now. But I think we would be better away from any source of radiation. Where do we go?"

"This is wasteland now." She swung her bundle under one arm. "And the only path I know is the one by which we came. It is roundabout but will bring us to the Garden of Astarte, or what is left of it. And from there we go to the mountains. It is a weary walk and one not to be taken too openly. The enemy still send out scout skimmers. I know not how effective the Old Woman's seers may be, but Kidaya has put them to good use in the past. And such events as your coming through the gate of the Magi should have set up a troubling in that spirit world and made them suspicious."

She believed in cold facts, the colder the better, Andas

decided. He translated her warnings to Yolyos, and they
followed behind her. It was a weaving path, swinging
wide at times to avoid places Shara told them still regis-
tered high in radiation. She had a small wrist detect,
which he was not sure recorded correctly, but it was
their only guard against straying into deadly territory.

All through that march Andas was unable to recognize
any building or part of a building that he knew. He concentrated on Yolyos's learning the new language. Except
that he had a hissing accent, the Salariki fortunately
proved to be quick at picking up their speech. Of neces-
sity his answers were curtailed and very simple, but he
retained words at a single repeating much better, Andas
thought, than he would be able to do himself under the
circumstances.

They came out at last into a place where vegetation
had survived, though it was an odd color and misshapen.
Pillars had been tossed back and forth, crisscrossing each
other on the ground as one might toss twigs in a game.
But this was, Andas knew, the Garden of Astarte.

Here they halted, sheltering belly down under a trio of
fallen pillars. Shara motioned at the ground stretching
before them. There was not even a bush of a size to give
cover.

"By day to walk there is to be seen," she commented.
"They patrol outward from the Drak Mount, which is
their stronghold."

"How far do we have to go?" Andas wanted to know.

"A day's travel, plus a night more, on foot. After we
reach the cache there are elklands for riding, if they have
not broken free."

"Wait!" Yolyos's hand closed upon Andas's upper arm.
"Listen!"

He could hear now, too, the high, faint whine from the
sky. There was a skimmer aloft.

13

It was a scout. Andas watched it hungrily. If they could get their hands on that now— He did not relish the cross-country travel Shara had described—not in this desolate waste.

"Are you thinking with me, Prince?" Yolyos was so close beside him the slightly raised fur of the Salariki's arm brushed his sleeve. "I believe that you are."

"How do we get it to land? By wishing?" Andas scoffed at his own desire.

"They must have a scanner," speculated the other. "Therefore, they can pick up the ground on their screen. Suppose they saw something—someone they had no reason to believe could be here—"

"Such as an emperor?" questioned Andas. "Their reaction would be to trigger a flamer!"

"Not an emperor, an alien." Yolyos's claws showed. "According to this lady, there have been no off-world ships here for some time. Therefore, they would want to know what a Salariki was doing at the ruins of their once First City. They must have a prisoner, not a dead body, to learn that."

"If we had even a stunner—" breathed Andas. It was utterly mad, but sometimes a mad throw in the very face of fate paid off. Above them was not only transportation but also men who could answer *his* questions.

"You plan something with this furred one?" Shara's voice was hardly above a whisper, as if she expected those cruising overhead to be able to pick up their voices.

"Weapons—surely you came here armed?" Andas returned. He had seen no blaster, stunner, or even sword or dagger with the dead emperor. But they were supposed to have fought their way out of an ambush to reach the ruins, and they could not have done that empty-handed.

For a moment she hesitated. Then her hands fumbled at the neckline of her outer robe, and she drew out a slender tube, hardly thicker than a branch a man could effortlessly snap between his hands.

"This—but the charge left is very small, perhaps only enough for a single firing."

She did not hand it to Andas. And when he reached for it, for a moment he thought she would not release it. Finally she let him take it. It was an officer's sidearm—a flame-needler. But it was strictly a short-range weapon and, if the charge was nearly exhausted, not too potent.

"They could turn a stun beam on you," he said to Yolyos. "I would under the circumstances, just to be on the safe side. They might even blanket the whole area—"

"Beam, yes," the Salariki agreed. "But blanket, I think not. They would carry only hand stunners on patrol. A skimmer is too light a craft to arm. They are sent to scout, not to fight. It only remains to be seen if I can make tempting bait."

Before Andas could put out a hand to stop him, Yolyos rolled out from under their pillar cover. But he did not get to his feet. Instead, he struggled only to his one knee, the other leg stretched out as if useless. He propped on one hand to balance himself, while with the other he waved, shouting aloud in Basic for help.

"He betrays us!" Shara snatched for the weapon Andas held. He fended her off.

"Quiet!" he ordered. "Yolyos is bait in a trap." He thought their chance was very slim, however. The skimmer had only to keep on hover and report back to its base. It all depended upon the temperament of those who manned the craft and whether they were cautious or otherwise.

Andas divided his attention between the Salariki, who was giving an excellent performance of someone hailing long-hoped-for aid, and the hovering craft. The skimmer had made a swift downward swoop and hung over the place where Yolyos was flopping about. Then a rope dropped from the belly of the craft, weighted with harness.

Why had he not foreseen that? Of course, with rescue equipment the skimmer did not need to land.

Yolyos's movements slowed. He was acting as one so weakened by some injury that his efforts of the last few moments had totally exhausted him. As the harness swung down, he made a very convincing grab at it, falling back to lie still. There was a shout from the skimmer. Yolyos lifted a hand in a gesture of appeal and let it flop on his chest. His other, hidden in the shadow of his body, held the force knife he had taken from Grasty.

The line of the harness jerked and arose to dangle in the air. Would they draw off now? No, a figure appeared at the belly hatch of the skimmer and took off with the leap of an anti-grav equipped sky trooper, spiraling down almost lazily. He made an excellent landing beside the prone Salariki and knelt beside him.

Yolyos moved with the speed of a trained fighting man of his own species, reacting faster than any human. He had one arm about the trooper, pinning his hands away from his weapon, yet holding him across his own body as a shield.

Andas leaped out of hiding, the flame-needler gripped between his teeth, both hands outstretched to catch the dangling line. He caught the harness, and his weight pulled it earthward as he began to climb. There was another after him—Shara had copied his run. The skimmer went out of hover into rise, or tried to.

But the very safety precautions built into the rescue equipment defeated the pilot. Though both Andas and the woman were lifted well above the ground, the harness could not be reeled in while it supported a double load, nor might the skimmer rise higher with the harness outside, for it had been designed for the ultimate safety of the unfortunate in the lift.

Andas could take no thought for Shara now. He had only moments of which he must make the most. He climbed the swaying line above the harness, and when the hatch was directly above him, he took the needler with one hand, prepared to fight his way in. It all depended now on the number of crew the skimmer carried, though these craft were not intended for many.

He was in the hatch. Behind him the rope of the harness began to coil in on its own since Shara's weight alone could not halt it. But Andas was facing the man, who, having put the skimmer on autopilot, was just emerging from the control section. He had a blaster at ready, but Andas fired a fraction of a second earlier.

The blaster ray was close. Andas cried out at the sear of it on his neck just below his ear. But the pilot had crumpled forward. The blaster, still blazing, spun past Andas, out of the hatch. He threw himself at the downed man, but the body was inert, and he scrambled over it to reach the controls. The rope of the harness was still winding in, and until it was all within the cabin, he could not set down. So he waited, tense.

Shara's unkempt head appeared above the edge of the hatch. She clung grimly to the harness, her eyes closed, her teeth set as if she were in the midst of an ordeal she could only endure. Andas moved back, caught her robe, and heaved her in with little ceremony. He let her lie gasping as he went to the controls and thumbed the button to set them down.

Even as the skimmer settled, he could hardly believe that their wild and hopeless ruse had paid off. But he was in the skimmer, the pilot was dead, and they were in command of the situation. By the look of it, Yolyos had finished off the other crew member.

Sometime later they hunched in the shadow of the craft, ravenously eating the rations the crew had carried. Andas had always considered E-rations as totally lacking in anything but strict nutritional value. But what he mouthed now from tube and container was equal to an Imperial feast.

Before them on the ground lay their prizes of battle. There was one stunner, a blaster (the one that had pitched from the skimmer had been too badly jammed when it struck the ground to use again), and another needler, as well as fresh rounds for the one Shara had brought. The dead crew of the ship had been stowed under the overlapping pillars where they could not be sighted from the air.

"The First Ancestress," remarked Yolyos, "is always said to favor the brave, though 'reckless' and 'brave' are not always the same. When I have time, I shall offer five jars of fine essences for her delight. And what do we now? We have a ship, we have weapons—"

Andas turned to Shara. "Where do we go? The skimmer can take us fast and far."

She had not said much since she had been so unceremoniously pulled through the hatch of the skimmer after her ride aloft on the harness. It was as if she thought, reserving speech for later.

"We must return to the Place of Red Water—there lie the Imperial forces now in the field. But we cannot fly all the way in this. There are defenses about the head-

203

quarters, and we would be sky-burned before we could signal. It would be best to set down in the heights. There are places there possible. It has been long since we have had any fliers of our own."

"And this is not a cruiser," Andas commented. "She is a scout and can give us little more aid than speedy transportation."

"I wonder if there is a tracer on her. Suppose there is and they send something heavier now to look for her? Yolyos remarked. "We'd best be off quickly."

They buckled on the weapon belts they had taken, Yolyos setting the force knife in a convenient loop on his. The stunner Andas passed to Shara. He found himself a little ill at ease with her now. Such feminine women (or as he thought feminine to be) as Elys and Abena he understood—a little. But this ugly, thin bone of a woman, with her tightly knotted hair, a woman who had so quickly risked her life to insure the success of their attack, was new to him. It was as if she expected to be treated as a battle comrade. And he found himself doing just that, speaking straightly as to another man—which was contrary to all his court training.

By Shara's guidance they flew north, in order to avoid any other air patrols. North was, she told them, largely wild country now. Where once broad farmlands and grazing uplands had provided most of the food for this whole section of the continent, now there stretched a desolate waste. Some of the farmers and herders flew south, forming ragged new settlements along the very edge of the Kalli. Many more had died on their own holdings or joined the Emperor's ragged force.

Beasts gone wild in the uplands were hunted and salted for the winter. But famine was a spector at every fire. They did not know how those at Drak Mount fared now, save that there was a rumor that stores had been laid up there before the outbreak of the war.

"The enemy must be fewer now," Shara continued. But whether that was true or she only hoped it, they could not know. "The plague was hard upon them even before the Triple Towers were destroyed. And that was years since. But the defenses at Drak Mount are such that even were it manned by dead men, the devices set on auto, we could not fight our way in."

"Then how did Andas—your Andas—ever expect to bring the war to a finish?" Andas asked.

"We have cleaned the whole of the north of the enemy," she spoke proudly. "They have really only the Drak Mount now. If they did not have such craft as this, we would not fear them at all. We reckon that they have at least two cruisers left with mounted flamers—though those we have not seen lately. My dear lord hoped to discover in the cache of the Magi some aid. Instead, he found his death."

"You spoke of treachery—"

"With good reason!" she said swiftly. "Only his own guard, three of his most trusted leaders, and perhaps the Arch Priest, knew what he would do. Also the cache was so well hidden that they did not find us there by chance. No, one of those he trusted betrayed him—for there was a party waiting in ambush. And it was only because of one of the Magi's safeguards, which my lord knew of, that we two won free. The rest died, for the safeguard was no respecter of right or wrong when it struck."

"You do not suspect one above the others?" Andas had no mind to be a second target.

"No." She answered him promptly enough.

They had set the skimmer on top speed, fleeing the vicinity of Drak Mount. Andas gave his attentio now to the sweep of land below as it was recorded on the visa-screen. She was very right. One could trace the boundaries of once prosperous farms and holds, but the area was clearly under a blight, which had reduced it from wealth to scrubby half-wilderness. Nor did anything creep along the deserted roads.

Some of those roads headed to the port of Garbuka on the eastern sea, the main outlet for Ictio with the sea trade. Andas remembered those arteries in constant use.

Mountains arose—the Kumbi ranges.

Shara spoke. "Steer by the Crown of Stars."

Obediently Andas went on manuals and swung the skimmer west toward the landmark mountain. The country below was rough. Once this had been used for the systematic planting and harvesting of bluewoods, those trees esteemed by stellar trade not only for their beauty, but also for the extreme durability of the lightweight, highly polished furniture that could be fashioned from them. Andas could see now their peculiar wide-branched crowns pushing above the lower growth, very noticeable from above, where they looked like large, flat platters laid upon the uneven covering of the other woodland.

"To the north of that crag, there is a landing place." Shara pointed a grimed finger on which the nail was ragged and broken. Again he swung to her guidance.

She was right. There was a level space, enough to set down the skimmer, and they made a straight descent, though Andas wondered a little at the future difficulties with mountain winds.

"We need anchorage," he said as they climbed out.

"So, not too difficult—ropes around the rocks ought to do." Yolyos indicated large stones that had slipped down the upper slopes to make a ragged fringe along the side of the landing space.

The harness hoist supplied some anchor lines, and they found another length of tough rope in the cabin locker. With these they wove such a netting anchor as would keep the skimmer where it was in spite of a storm.

Evening clouds were gathering, and Andas eyed them dubiously. Out of the skimmer's supplies they had assembled two packs, far too small, but all they could find. He and Yolyos could carry those easily, but the ledge on which they had set down was still well above the level of the forest. And he did not fancy a descent in the dark. Nor was he sure Shara knew the road from here.

"The Place of Red Water—where?" he asked as they trudged along the rim of the plateau looking for a place to descend.

"To the west, crossing through the Pass of the Two Horns." She spoke confidently, as if she carried a map with a vocal director in her hand.

He tried to remember. The mountains, yes, he had been here—enough to recognize the Crown of Stars. But the Pass of the Two Horns—no memory supplied that, just as the Place of Red Water was a name new to him.

"We cannot travel by night," she continued. "But that does not matter. There is a foresters' post near here. That will shelter us, and if it is manned, there will be news also."

"This way!" Yolyos gestured from where he had loped along ahead of them.

He had discovered a broken series of smaller ledges, like irregular steps, down which they could go. Andas fought his old fear of heights, keeping his eyes at a point immediately before him. But he was sweating and a little sick when they reached the scrub beginning of the woodland. Shara pushed ahead, eying the growth. A moment later she turned, much of her assurance gone.

"I can see no trail landmark that I know," she admitted frankly.

Yolyos's head was up, his nostrils dilated. "You may not see, lady," he said in his halting growl of her speech, "but smell I can! There are men—that way!"

"How does he—?" She looked to Andas.

"His species have a far better sense of smell than we do. If he says there are men that way, he is right."

Shara dropped behind Andas, to the tail of their party, as if she were so dubious about their present course that she wanted to be able to retreat in a hurry if disaster loomed.

That Yolyos was right, in at least the fact men had been here, was proven when they pushed through a screen of brush into a trail. Once in that slot Yolyos turned left. But as he went, he asked Shara, "Are your friends, lady, such as will shoot first and hail strangers afterwards? If so, how can we make sure we shall not be their targets?"

She did not answer in words but raised her head a little, testing the breeze. She pursed her lips and uttered a small flutting whistle. Three times she signaled so and then waved them on. But within ten paces she whistled again, this time twice, and, at a third time, once.

They had come to the foot of a bluewood, and her answer reached them from overhead when a vine ladder whipped down out of the foliage. Shara pushed by the others and climbed, Andas and Yolyos following.

What they came into was a very well-concealed camp. Its like had been known, mainly as curiosity, in the gardens of the Triple Towers, but here it had been put to practical use. The bluewood had branches that were inclined to grow from the tree trunk at sharp right angles. They were also relatively straight beyond that point. Use had been made of this natural peculiarity on three levels, planks laid across and fastened to form an arbor house of three stories, vine ladders leading from one to the next.

Those who sheltered here, once their entrance ladder was up, could not be sighted, for the underside of the planks that formed their springy floors had been covered with growing things, while the flatly spreading top of the tree, well overhead, was a roof no skimmer could sight through.

The man who awaited their coming was as thin as Shara, and his clothing was as coarse as hers, though it had been dyed in patches of green and brown, so that it matched woodland coloring. He had clumsy thong-bound leggings and a tight-fitting cap to which were stuck bits of leaf and vine. Andas could believe that in the woodland he could walk hidden.

"Hearth claim, master," Shara said.

He looked at her searchingly and then beyond, to Andas. When his eyes met those of the prince, his face came alive, and he dropped on one knee, both hands outstretched, palms up. His weapon, a crossbow, lay on the floor beside him.

"Sun of Dingame! That *you* should be here!"

"And glad for it," Andas answered. He made the traditional gesture, finger right to left on the man's palms. "We need shelter this night."

"And for once the hunting has been good!" The man's face still mirrored amazement. "I have meat, Great Lord."

Still kneeling, he waved toward the ladder to the next level. "Please to climb. There shall be food speedily. And here you may rest safely. There is none, not even the tree kangor, who dares this fort-place."

"You are named?"

"Kai-Kaus of the House of Korb, Great Lord. Once we held—"

"From the Upper Lumbo to the sea." Andas nodded. "And you will again."

"That we doubt not, Great Lord," the forester replied proudly. He was quite young, Andas saw, but there was about him the air of a man who was doing what he had to do with competence. Though he was dressed as a forester, it was apparent that he was of noble blood.

The next platform, which was the middle one of the three, was apparently the living quarters of those manning this post. There was a bed place wide enough for two, fashioned of ferns and leaves. Some calabashes with their stoppers well pounded in sat in a line, and a box had its lid thrown back to display crossbow bolts. Also there was a square of stone-rimmed clay where blackened embers showed fires burned.

Their host speedily joined them with a bundle of wood and a packet of bloodstained hide, which he unrolled to display dukker meat cut into strips and impaled with chunks of tree melon on skewers of green wood. Andas's mouth watered. This was far better than the rations from the skimmer, or the musty, dried stuff Shara had shared with them.

The forester laid his fire and brought it to life. Andas reached for the nearest skewer.

"There is no ceremony among comrades at war. We eat as one tonight."

For a moment it seemed that both Shara and the forester would protest. But when Andas held his skewer to the flames, they picked up their own. Yolyos was already pushing his to the fire.

Andas saw Kai-Kaus glancing at the Salariki. After all, now any alien would be suspect. And he must make sure Yolyos was placed above suspicion.

"This is our comrade in battle—the Lord Yolyos from off-world. He has also been a prisoner of those we hunt and are hunted by, and by his aid only have we come through a great peril. He is thus named Lion Friend and Shield Upon the Left." From old tales Andas dragged those titles, the meaning of which might be forgotten, but would still be honored by those loyal to the Emperor. He remembered that his grandfather had once named a warrior so who had saved his son's life. And thereafter the court gave that man, though a commoner, the honor due a first house lord.

"To the Lord Yolyos, greeting—" The forester raised his hand in salute.

Yolyos looked up from the skewer he was tending so carefully. "To Kai-Kaus, greeting. It is a good hunter who can provide so well for unexpected guests."

The boy shifted. "It has been a lucky day. Some fear sent the herd on the move down trail. I was able to pick off five before they stampeded. They have grown so wary from our hunting that it is seldom we can find them so. It is perhaps by the will of Akmedu that this happened so I would have food for my lord—"

"Or something else. If a thing is not natural, it is suspect!" cut in Shara.

"That is so, lady. And the reason why I am alone here. Ikiui, who is a trained scout, has gone to see what set the herd moving. There are no hunters now except us, and I do not think the enemy would venture into the wilderness."

"Never underestimate an enemy." Yolyos had withdrawn his skewer, though to Andas's eye the meat on it was hardly cooked. He used thumb and forefinger to jerk the end lump from it, waved the bite for a moment in the air, and then popped it into his mouth, chewing with the noisy good manners of his people.

14

There were no lamps to be lit in this tree house, and even the coals of fire were covered at the coming of full dusk by an earthen bowl. The forester swung down to the lower platform and crouched there, listening, and now the dark was such they could hardly see him.

Yolyos, once his hunger was satisfied, sought the same vantage point. And now Andas dropped down the ladder also.

"What do you listen for?" He stood beside Kai-Kaus.

"Ikiui. He has not returned. Yet we do not walk the forest trails at night."

"So?" The Salariki moved closer. "And why not?"

"The tree cats hunt by night, as do the great serpents. And lately, there are other things—" His voice trailed away, and Andas suspected he did not want to discuss those "other things."

But that very suspicion led him to press for information.

"Those being?"

"Nothing any man has seen—and lived."

"But some have seen—and died?"

"Yes. Four men of the southern range, Great Lord. Their bodies, two of them, were found in the trail easy to see—left as a warning, we believe. They had met the night crawlers—"

Andas froze. But legends could not live! The horrific tales that gave children pleasurable shivers up the spine had no base in real life.

"They were," Kai-Kaus continued in a low voice, as if by telling the story at all he could be invoking the evil he described, "drained of blood. We have found forest animals treated so, also, twice plainly hung on bushes to be seen—but those were earlier. Ikiui, he feared that the stampede might have been caused by such an attack."

The forester was so certain of his facts that Andas's disbelief was shaken. After all, the events of his own immediate past were enough to prove that anything was possible.

"The night crawlers serve *her*," Kai-Kaus whispered. "And that she-rat of the Drak Mount is *her* voice, as she has sworn openly. Also that one has danced the Bones before the eyes of the living and promised that all beyond her cloak of safety will be the meat of the Old Woman."

Danced the Bones! That anyone had dared so drastic a ritual—this Inyanga was indeed a bedeviled land; Andas's hand went to the seam pocket wherein lay the ring. Did these women know wherein they dabbled? Or was their hunger for power so great that they did not care?

He recalled those tales he had considered fiction. Remembering one thing after another, he shivered. The ring—he must rid himself of that talisman if Kai-Kaus spoke the truth and that which should never be named now crawled this forest land.

Where to get rid of the ring? It must be lost in some place where no follower of the Old Woman could sniff it out, for by all accounts those who had taken such oaths were attuned to these things and they could be drawn. Perhaps even to carry it with him now would make them a focal point of attack.

"There is trouble—" Yolyos's growl was subdued to a rumble hardly louder than Kai-Kaus's whisper. "I can smell it on the wind."

"What kind of trouble? Someone coming?"

"Not so. This is the doom thing again." He made a spitting sound of disgust. "Evil. It stinks worse than the rotting hole of a gorp's nest. Also"—he was silent a moment and then added swiftly—"one flees before it. And his fear is as great a stench as that which follows him."

Andas listened. He could hear nothing. Only, out of the dark, came Kai-Kaus's hand to close about his arm.

"Lord, I am your man to defend you to the death. Get up into the fort level, taking the ladder with you. What comes may be only seeking hunters—"

"Before I was an emperor, liege man," Andas answered, "I was a warrior, taking blood oath. And among the words of that oath is a promise of shield rights in battle. I do not let others fight my wars for me."

"An emperor has no choice, Great Lord. That other men die for his life is the pattern of things, for with the head of state dead, the state itself crumbles into nothingness. When you became Emperor, you put aside the rights and duties of a warrior to take on a greater burden.

Andas had to recognize the truth by which he had been reared. An emperor was no longer a man—he was the embodiment of all that made the empire, and his life must be bought, if that need arose, by the blood of others. Yet he was not going to let this begin here and now.

"Not yet," he said. "Yolyos, what else can you tell us?"

"He who runs is close. That which follows is yet a space away. But the runner is near the end of his endurance."

Even as he spoke, there was a rustling that was not wind. It came from below—someone was trying to attract attention.

"The ladder—drop it!" Andas ordered.

"He will have to go hence so that you be not endangered."

"Emperor or no, I do not reign in the Triple Towers," Andas burst out. "Nor may I ever. Those rules about the

Lion in Glory do not stand now." He could not be responsible for this. Groping across the floor, he found the ladder and dropped it before Kai-Kaus could stop him. The vine lines were taut—the fugitive was already on his way up.

Andas could hear the heavy gasping breath of the climber. He did not need Yolyos to assure him that the man came with death breathing at his heels.

"Kai-Kaus! The man crawled over the edge. "Night crawlers—"

"Quiet! cried the other forester fiercely out of the dark.

Andas's hands closed on the man's heaving shoulders as he sprawled up onto the platform. He dragged him away from the hole and pulled up the ladder as fast as he could. Perhaps whatever hunted would be baffled at the disappearance of its prey aloft and go on. He did not regret his decision. Emperor or not, he was not and perhaps never would be able to accept such sacrifices. He must walk his own road. Perhaps that others Andas had chosen poorly when he had summoned him through the gate; perhaps he would have been a failure himself had he indeed been crowned in his own world. It might be that he was not the material of which emperors were made, unbending, infallible to those about them. Well, he must be himself or be utterly lost.

"Close—" Yolyos's warning was a thread of sound.

Andas dropped belly down on the platform, his head over the ladder opening, staring at the dark below. Here and there he saw the flitting of huge ghost moths, their almost transparent wings outlined and ribbed with fluorescence. And there were some small plants that had the same eerie radiance, using that lure to attract prey. But there was something else—

Yolyos spoke of smells, stenches. Now Andas put his

hand to his nose, trying to shut out the odor wafted to his post. This must be pure torment to the Salariki with its sensitivity. It was decay, old death. Though he had never smelled either, he thought of both now.

And there was a wan light also, like that of the ghostly moths, yet unclean. If such a stink could have light, this was it.

With his other hand Andas worked the needler free of his belt and drew it forward. He did not know what hunted below, but he had never seen anything yet that could survive a needler attack at full strength. And having reloaded it, he could set it on that.

The thing coming along the trail moved swiftly, but it did not seem to walk or run on normal feet. He aimed and fired at the fat bulk.

The burst of needler ray lit up the trail. He heard a wailing that screeched up the scale until human ears could no longer detect it. But his body, his head, was pierced through and through by the sonic vibrations the thing was now emitting. He fired again, though this time, tormented by that vibration, he could not be sure he aimed true.

It threshed about, beating at the growth, flattening and tearing at bushes in its agony. Then that terrible sound ended, and it lay still, though Andas had caution enough not to believe it was yet dead.

"You have a needler!" Kai-Kaus had crowded beside him. "We have not seen one for seasons now."

If crossbows were the best armament the loyal forces had in plenty, Andas did not wonder at the other's pessimistic attitude toward fighting the monster below.

"I'll lay another shot—" He was aiming when Yolyos spoke.

"The thing is dead. Have you a torch? We had better

look upon this enemy so that we know it again," he said to Kai-Kaus.

"Here is your light." They turned their heads. Halfway down the ladder from the sleeping platform was Shara, in one hand a brand glowing red. She twirled this a little, and the fire came alive, giving them a source of light in the dark.

"My thanks, lady!" Kai-Kaus caught the brand from her.

"Is there anything else waiting down there?" Andas asked Yolyos.

"The stink overlays much. But I pick up nothing save the life forms that are harmless. I think this thing hunted alone."

Kai-Kaus made no objection when Andas descended the ladder behind him. The realization that the newcomers had the superior weapons had done much to allay his sense of responsibility for his ruler.

On the ground the smell was so terrible that Yolyos held his nose, gasping. Almost, if with lesser reason, Andas could have duplicated that gesture. But he forced himself to prod the white thing now curled into a half ball in its final convulsion.

He stared down as Kai-Kaus swung the torch close, and then he backed away, his shoulders heaving in a rising nausea he could not control. Thus, he leaned against a sapling along the trail and lost all his earlier supper.

Yolyos reeled away in turn. Andas saw him run for the ladder and pull himself up, as if the thing had come alive. Nor were the two foresters long behind him, though they waited at the ladder foot, urging Andas up before them.

The sight of that—that *thing*—had been such as to almost paralyze his mind for moments. Anyone familiar with tapes made by star travelers (and his father had

had a fine collection of such, which he had known from childhood) was aware that there were many strange— even horrifying—life forms in the galaxy. But never had Andas seen anything to equal what lay in the forest of his own world.

Unclean? It was more than unclean. It was so heavy with evil and filth that it seemed impossible for it to have held life. Yet there was a teasing sense that he had viewed something like it before—not exactly like, but near enough that this tantalizing resemblance now made him uneasy.

From whence it had come, he had no clue. Was it even native to any of the planets of the empire? He hoped not. He trusted that such spawn had never developed under the sun he knew. Yet, there was that familiarity—

"In the name of the First Ancestress"—Yolyos's voice was a little muffled by the hands still clapped across his nose, as if he could so strain the stench from the night air —"what is that thing?"

"I do not know—" Andas was beginning when a memory far buried came to the surface of his mind. "An eloplan—but it can't be!"

"An eloplan from the garden of the Old Woman." Shara cut across his denial. "An eloplan and something else—worse. *She* has more than gardeners serving her. She has the Nessi Magi—"

After seeing that dead thing, he could believe anything. But that any Magi, no matter how far from the true light, could serve the Old Woman—that was a contradiction of terms. The Magi were male, and their training forced them to keep to their own sex all their knowledge. The Old Woman could and would receive only the worship of women, women who had such natures that they were known as hers almost from their birth hours. Magi and the Old Woman—no!

"The Nessi Magi"—Shara could have been reading his thoughts—"are apart. They entered into an alliance with the Old Woman just after Kidaya began her ensorcellment of the Emperor. They acted truly as if their minds were turned about in their skulls, so they thought entirely differently. It was one of those three who brought about the death of the Emperor. And twice have they tried to set a sending on you. Do you not remember that, my lord?" Her voice was a warning, and he was aware that this was one of the things he must appear to know.

"With Nessi knowledge, creatures such as the night crawlers could be bred. We have no information concerning what they were, are, able to do. It was always research that interested the Nessi."

Andas forced himself to consider what he had seen dead as rationally as he could in the light of her suggestion. An eloplan—mobile at certain times of the year, able to travel from one favorable rooting ground to another—was a vegetable curiosity. He had seen small captive ones in the exotic palace gardens.

But this had been no plant—it had had a *head.* Andas clamped his teeth together and willed fiercely not to be sick again. This had been partly—horribly—human! And if the Nessi Magi were responsible for such, they must be rooted out, exterminated, and all their unholy knowledge eradicated with them.

"You said night crawlers," he said to Kai-Kaus. "There are more of these things?"

It was Ikiui who answered. He had been eying Andas with awed recognition as the prince stood in the light of the torch, and he saluted as he spoke.

"Lord, there are at least four loosed in the forest this night. All the warm-blooded creatures flee before them. They are driving out the game."

"And you know from whence they come?"

"Only that they move from the east. Nor do they turn aside, save to feed. Also, they are, I think, directed."

"How so?"

"There was a water loffin they surprised, and it ran past them east. One of the crawlers started after it. I—" He put his hands to his head as if in memory of some hurt. "In my head there was a pain. The crawler reared and cried out as if it were angry, yet it came back from the loffin trail."

"And where were you to watch this?"

"In the vineways above. I would not have been trailed, but there was a place where the vines did not run. When I came to earth, that one hunted me."

"As if you might have been sighted and that creature sent to make sure of you? There was a skimmer overhead then?"

"No. And if so, no one aboard could have seen through the veil of trees. Whatever spy is used was closer than the air above the forest."

"Close indeed." Yolyos still held his nose with one hand so his speech sounded odd. "Prince, that is not a good thing to look upon, but I think you should examine it again. I caught a glimpse of something—though I may not have seen aright."

The last thing Andas wanted was to approach the kill again, but he did not disdain the importance of Yolyos's suggestion. Very reluctantly he descended, Kai-Kaus coming with the torch. The Salariki remained behind at Andas's order—this ordeal was doubly hard for him.

That fat worm body still lay in the coil it had assumed upon death, but not so tightly. Andas took the torch from Kai-Kaus and forced himself to view the thing with searching intensity, though he gulped and fought nausea.

The light held steady on the round of body just behind the head. Luckily the head itself had dropped forward, to lie face down, so he did not have to view that. He spoke to Kai-Kaus.

"Hold steady, and give me your skinning knife!"

It took every bit of resolution Andas could summon to work with the knife, hacking free what was embedded in the fetid flesh, until he could stand it no longer and ripped and pulled in a frenzy that brought loose a be-spattered device, trailing horribly befouled wiring from the body of the creature.

Andas set his trophy on the ground and grabbed at leaves and grass to wipe it off as best he could. But he would have to take it with him, and his flesh shrank from touching it. Still he would not ask Kai-Kaus to do it for him.

At length he managed to wrap leaves about it and carried it up to the tree fort. Laid out on the floor, it proved to be a complex machine, probably of the electronic order. And his knowledge of such was less than adequate. He looked inquiringly to Yolyos, but the Salariki made a gesture of denial.

"I am no tech, Prince. But I would venture to say this is no simple thing. And undoubtedly it was used to control the creature."

"Could it be something of the mercenaries?" Andas asked.

"More likely Nessi," Shara returned. "But I would not believe they could make such a device now with most of the empire in ruins. Such technology is the result of highly specialized manufacturing. We have no factories or labs left. And I do not believe that the Drak Mount has either—it is a place given wholly to war."

"What of the Valley of Bones?" Andas had been poking at the box with the point of the hunting knife, taking care not to touch it directly.

He heard a whistle of breath from the others. One did not mention that name directly. It was so great a taboo that for him to break it was almost as if he shouted a curse in a place of honor.

"Kidaya is of the Old Woman's kin," he said slowly, making that a statement rather than a question, but watching Shara to make sure he did not make a mistake. "Perhaps it was she who brought the Nessi and her mistress together. And what better place would they find in which to hide their misbegotten experiments than the valley? I begin to think that it is not to the Drak Mount we should face, but in another direction!"

"My lord"—Kai-Kaus spoke up then—"we cannot stand against the Old Woman."

"So have we always been taught," agreed Andas. "And there was method in that teaching. The Old Woman is a woman's thing, and they have mysteries no male can understand. But if such mysteries now shadow this land, we must do as Akmedu did in his time—carry war to that heart."

He was still staring at the box that might mean so much, yet he was aware that all save Yolyos had withdrawn from him a step or two. Pledged they might be to the Emperor's cause, still he might discover that there were none to back him in this. But in his mind it was proven as true, as if he had tapes to support the idea that he was right—the war spread from the fortress held by the off-worlders, but it fed upon the flaw in his own people, from their clinging to custom, their long conditioning.

There had always been a strong strain of mysticism in his race. In some this took the form of formal religion, or a delving into philosophy, or experimentation with esper. With others it followed a darker trend—to such things as the worship of the Old Woman, the researches of the

Nessi. It was in him, too—when he had reacted to the ring he had taken from Abena.

But he would have to set aside beliefs and fears if he was going into this battle. Men—and women—who had been ground down to the extremity of these foresters, of Shara, half starved as she was, perhaps did not have the inner will to break old bounds. They would be easy prey for such devils tricks as the crawlers.

Perhaps because he was not fully one with them—and he had Yolyos who was not of them at all—he would have a chance. But it might be that he would be forced to take that chance alone.

Andas dropped the knife. He reached within his coverall and brought out the key. It shown ruddily in the torch light. And he kept it in his right hand. But with the left he freed the ring and drew it from that pocket in his closed fist, holding it well away from the key—for they still stood in his mind as opposite poles of light and dark, good and evil.

Then he gave an exclamation, for the cool metal circlet in his fist was not cool any longer. He opened his hand. On his palm lay the ring. And it glowed—but from no reflected torchlight. It was the gleam of life. And at the same time the device he had dug out of the crawler gave a spark of flame and began a low humming.

15

"A seer ring!" Shara drew away farther yet.

At her cry the others, except for the Salariki, stared at him.

"A seer ring." Deliberately Andas confirmed her identification. "One I took from a handmaiden of the Old Woman when she sought to use it to my betrayal. But think you that I could also hold this"—he raised the key so that they could see it clearly—"if I had surrendered my will to such a ring?"

Perhaps the foresters did not know the key, but Shara would surely understand. She had witnessed the other Andas's reaction to it.

"He is right," she said after a moment. "This is the key to the heart. But to bear it together with the ring—"

"The ring must be destroyed. But how can that be done until I find a place in which it can be forever hid?" Andas countered. "Bury it in the ground, throw it into a chasm or lake, and can you say that there will not be those whose nature will draw them to it? Also, perhaps it can be made to aid us—"

"Look at it!" Shara had been watching the ring. Andas did indeed look.

The milky-white setting showed a thickening swirl of color—something was coming through! But he had done nothing to summon— Andas raised the key between him and the ring as a protection, the only one he could think of.

"Back," he ordered, "out of line with this!"

The others were only too ready to obey, pulling away as if he had a live flamer in his hand, one about to spew destruction.

"Throw it away!" Shara cried. "My lord, meddle not with the things of that she-devil!"

Every instinct in Andas agreed with her. Yet he held tight command over his desires and continued to hold the ring. At that moment it spelled contact with the core of the enemy force. And all he could learn would be to his advantage. But he did flip the glowing circlet about so that he was not looking into the setting, but rather down from above, while it was focused on the device from the crawler.

In addition to sputtering sparks from that device, the wires he had ripped loose came alive, writhing on the floor as if they still governed movements in the body from which they had been pulled. The ring was now yellow-green, and in it moved, not the picture he had expected, but a series of spark impulses that made tiny patterns. But those came and vanished so quickly that he could not be sure of any.

"The question is"—Yolyos had not withdrawn as the others and now squatted on his heels by Andas, watching those sparks—"is that broadcasting or receiving? Does the ring activate that device, or the unit the ring? And can such a broadcast be picked up elsewhere?"

He was interrupted by Ikiui. "Listen, my lord!"

He need not have warned them, for it was plain to hear—that wailing that could be heard in the night, yet rang in one's head.

"Crawlers—more than one!" Kai-Kaus had gone on hands and knees to the entrance for the ladder. "They are coming—"

"The ring! Perhaps it called them!" cried Shara.

Andas closed his fist again about it and almost cried out at the head radiating from the metal. He slipped it back in hiding.

"Perhaps this is for the best." Yolyos had drawn his

needler. "I would rather meet those things on a field of my choosing than loose in the woods. Summon them in and pick them off—as we do the goop in the great hunts!"

"You are right!" With only crossbows for defense, the crawling horrors might seem menaces to the foresters. But faced with superior weapons, they could be disposed of with what appeared now to Andas as ease. And to have them gathered in one place for slaughter—

He dropped a hand on Kai-Kaus's shoulder. "Is there a way we can set an ambush above that trail—pick them off as they come?"

"For us perhaps, my lord. But you are not trained so—"

"Just show me a stable perch."

"If we have time." There was a new eagerness in Kai-Kaus's face. Their triumph over one of the weird beasts had given him confidence.

Shara moved into Andas's path. "My lord, you bear the ring, and you would go to meet those things which answer to it. I beg of you, do not leave with what may be a break in your defenses! You do not know how that acts, only that it has been alerted by the device which directs the crawlers. What if it can compel you to meet them on their own ground?"

"It did not before."

"Then, my lord, you had not deliberately exposed it. It was not 'alive'—not until you held it before that device. But alive it has powers."

Was it the old superstition working in her, or was her warning a legitimate one? Before he could decide, Yolyos closed in on the other side.

"A suggestion, Prince. If that ring is bait, let it be bait indeed. Set it or suspened it so as to pull them to our best advantage."

Andas was reluctant to let the ring out of his control. From the first he had feared that if he loosed it, it might escape him altogether. But Shara's warning influenced him somewhat. After all, to battle enemy forces holding that which might prove traitor was folly. And Yolyos's suggestion had good logic.

"The stranger lord is right, my lord," Ikiui agreed. "Use it for bait."

Andas left it to the foresters to select the proper ambush, and they moved swiftly. The wailing, which had only been a faint cry at first, was growing louder. Also the forest itself had come alive about them, its inhabitants fleeing a common doom as they might have run before a fire. Bushes threshed, flying things cried with small hoots and flutings, and there was a scurrying on the ground beneath their trees.

The prince discovered that the foresters were indeed right in mistrusting his ability aloft. He had to be pushed and shoved along one of the tree branches that supported the platform to reach another lower limb, which was not so comfortable and swayed under him. Kai-Kaus passed him a length of vine rope made fast to the tree trunk, so that he had a lifeline.

He was slightly irritated to learn that the Salariki was far more surefooted in his limb travel, having little or no difficulty in scrambling aloft in another tree across the trail. Andas knotted the ring, testing the fastening over and over again, before he allowed the vine end to which it was tied to drop. The glow of the set increased in color as it swayed back and forth. And now that wailing was silenced.

Andas turned to Kai-Kaus, not too far away on the same leafy perch.

"They are—?" he began when a faint hiss warned him into silence.

He balanced as well as he could, waiting, though the interval was not long, for out of the brush pushed the white mass of a crawler. It came at a pace faster than he would have allowed for its bulk to squat below the ring. The forepart of its half-seen body, visible because of its paleness in the general gloom, reared as it tried apparently to reach the ring.

Its repeated failures did not seem to matter. It kept on rearing, even though at best it was well below the dangling treasure it sought. And it was still single-mindedly busy when a second of its kind appeared.

The monsters took no notice of each other. It was as if their world had narrowed to the ring. The smaller rocked against the larger as they both reared, sending it off balance. There was a sharp grunt, and the head of the larger swung around to butt its companion away from the bait.

Since the smaller accepted the challenge, they were striking at each other when a third and greater one arrived, plowing up and over the struggling bodies of the other two, aiming at the ring. Its questing forelimbs (if you could call them such) came close to achieving the goal. Andas, afraid that a second try might be successful, fired. He had given no warning to Yolyos. But at the same instant his needler rayed out, the other fired also, so that the twisting bodies below were caught in a cross fire that was fatal.

Were there any more? And would the lure of the ring suffice to draw them even though some signal of their companions' ending might have been broadcast? The men waited in the branches above for what seemed to Andas such a stretch of time as must comprise half the night. But no more crawlers appeared, nor did they hear any wailing.

At last, Andas, stiff from his unaccustomed position

and wondering if he could cope as well with a second attack, hooked in the vine and loosed the ring, to stow it away safely. Evil token it might be, but tonight it had served them well. And there was a chance that they might continue to use its calling powers for their own ends. He was more confident about the future since they had won this engagement. First they had taken the skimmer by wild chance and now defeated these monsters.

When they were back again in the tree fort, Andas was willing enough to stretch out on the bed place. His body ached from that cramping vigil in the treetop, and he could not remember sleeping since that abortive try in the commander's quarters.

Green light sifted down through the branches when he awoke. At least it was day, but what hour he could not tell. He rolled over to see that he had shared his bed. Shara's head was pillowed beside his. Her sunken eyes were closed, but he thought she looked a shade less gaunt now and younger—

How old was she? She had announced herself the Chosen of the Emperor. There had been cases in the past of marked disparity of ages for dynastic reasons, but he began to believe that she was no worn woman as she had first appeared—haggard with the hardships of her hunted life—but a girl instead. And he was still searching her face for some clue as to the truth of that when her eyes opened.

There was instant awareness in those eyes. She was like a trained warrior who wakes at once to any alarm. But she said nothing, only returned his study, surveying his face with the same intensity he turned upon her.

They were alone on the bed platform of the tree as he saw when, embarrassed, he sat up, a little ashamed he had been detected spying on her as she slept.

"You are the Emperor's Chosen." He was at some loss

as how to approach the matter of his own feelings.

"But not yours." Her voice was the faintest murmur of sound, meant to carry to his ears only. "My choosing was a matter of state—or began so—"

For once imagination told him what he guessed was the truth. "But later it became otherwise between you two?" Inwardly he was now doubly ashamed at his own blindness. The death of that other Andas might have ended part of her world for her, but it had meant nothing but a burden for him. In his self-centeredness he must have been cruel where he should have been kind. He had thought only what events meant to him and inwardly struggled against enmeshment, resentful of the man who had committed him to this life. That the other Andas had been devoted to duty and had taken the only way left to save his plans, he did not doubt. But he, too, had been selfish, or he would not have sentenced a stranger to this.

"It became otherwise." Again her light whisper wrenched him from his thoughts to consider her. But she did not enlarge upon that admission.

The Chosen of the Emperor—his wife, though not his empress, until he could crown her publicly. He had a wife in the sight of his loyal followers and one he could not possibly disown.

That thought bothered him. His father's solitary life, which he had shared, had been devoid of feminine company. They had not even had a woman servant. And when Andas had been drawn into the life of the court, he had shortly thereafter gone to Pav for warrior training, again a world without women. There had been ladies enough at court on his return ready to toss him their flower bracelets. But he had been too shy, too ill at ease in such company, to react to their invitations. And there had been no official marriage made for him before that night when he had gone to bed in the palace—to awaken in the prison on another planet.

Since then, there had been Elys for whom he had been sorry, judging her by his own fears and feelings, only to learn that she had been more alien than the furred Salariki. And he had seen the Princess Abena—he smiled wryly at the memory of that meeting. Abena was supposedly *his* daughter. Now here was this frail-looking yet tough wraith, with her drab barbaric dress, who claimed to have been the other Andas's Chosen. How closely would she expect him to carry out that previous relationship?

He had no feelings about her, save a kind of impatient pity—impatient because she was part of the new life he could not discard. Could it be that lack of emotion was the sign of an android? The old fear bubbled in him. If he only knew more about androids! They had been forbidden for so long that the references he had were mainly hearsay. But could they have made an android so physically human that he could deceive a medic, even father children? But if the false emperor was not false— then he, Andas, was android!

"Your thoughts are troubled." He had risen to his feet, but she only sat up on the bough bed. "I do not claim more from you than you can give, save that before others we must make a pretence, for the truth shall be kept. For his sake will I keep it!" And the concern in her voice became a warning.

"Before others I shall play my part as best I can. And I can play it better if you will tell me more."

She nodded. "This is a good time for such talk. We are alone. Even that furred one you speak of as friend has gone with the hunters. With the crawlers dead, there is a chance hunting will improve. And any chance to increase our food supply must be seized.

"The headquarters of your forces are at the Place of Red Water. You have four first captains now. There is Kwayn Makenagen. He is the oldest, once Governor of the North Marches, a tall man but a little stooped, and he has a habit of pulling on his lower lip so"—she demonstrated—"when he is thinking deeply or is at some disadvantage. He is none too fast at that thinking, but once he sets upon a matter, he does not drop it until the end.

"Next is Patopir Ishan. He is younger, a valiant fighter, but reckless, and needs the curb hand. He limps from an old wound, but is very soft-spoken and charms women as much as if he wore a love mirror about his throat. His face is handsome, and he laughs much, but he is also shrewd. Only his reckless impulses to action keep him from being truly great.

"The third captain is the Lady Bahyua Banokue."

"A woman!"

"Just so." Shara made a reproof of his two words with her tone. "When her lord fell at the battle of Ninemarr, she took command of the forces and stopped the rout. She is very shrewd in council and brings years of experience, for she is of middle life and had four sons in your service. Only one remains alive.

"And the fourth and last of your leaders, my lord, is one Shara. I have led my house since we broke out of the fire ring at Tortu and my elder brother covered our retreat.

"These are the ones with whom you will deal mostly, but there are others you must learn to recognize." She continued patiently, and he strove to memorize the details about men and a few women whom, upon meeting in the future, he must be able to greet as old comrades in arms.

Andras discovered that he was more proficient at this study than he would have believed. But he was a little surprised when Shara stopped suddenly and sat looking down at her hands.

"There is one other." Her reluctance was so visible that it was as if she spoke under duress. "That is the Arch Priest Kelemake."

"Kelemake!" Andas was surprised, though why should he be, he thought a moment later. If he, Andas, had had a counterpart here, surely others he knew must also. That he recognized none of the names Shara had recited earlier meant nothing. There had been a vast upheaval here. People who normally might never have come to the Emperor's notice were now in direct contact with him.

"You speak as if you know him—"

"There is a Kelemake in my world, though he is not an arch priest there. He was a court historian and taught me for a while."

She fastened at once on the explanation he had already guessed. "If there was an Andas to match an Andas, perhaps there is a Kelemake to match a Kelemake. Of what manner was the man you knew?" Now that they were alone, she spoke as equal to equal with none of that subtle deference she showed in company. And her directness made him more at ease with her.

"He was a man difficult to know—of deep learning, but little interested in anything beyond his work. He kept apart from the court, staying in the archives. In the end, the Emperor, my grandfather, appointed him keeper of the archives. He was not a man of religion, yet he knew more of its forms than many devoted priests, just as he knew much of other things but never exercised his knowledge. In spite of it all, he was no Magi—he never went through their training. Yet I would have thought that was what would have attracted his temperament the most."

"Knowing the forms of religion and learning rooted

more in the past than the present—both these things could be said of our Kelemake also. He is a man who rules the temple brotherhood with a firm hand and has proved steadfast in support. Yet, I do not like him. And Andas, also, found him such that he could not bring himself to appoint him to the inner council. This I think was resented as a slight, though Kelemake has said nothing. But those who gather about him have tried to change Andas on this matter. My lord said that in him he sensed a flaw he could not put name to. And, let me tell you, there are some men—yes, and women—to whom if the need arose, I would tell our present deception. But Kelemake would be the last. Watch him with care—I cannot honestly tell you why. But in such a life as we lead, shadows can be worse than substance, for substance can be faced bodly and fought, but shadows slip away, only to return, always waiting for our courage to fail and our reason to falter in some time of need and despair."

"I am warned. And never has an emperor had more reason to lean upon his Chosen," he said deliberately, for he was moved again by her inner strength, by the fact that she could so set herself to preparing another to take the place of the man she had loved. That she *had* loved Andas but kept it within her, making no parade of her emotions, he had no doubt.

"As I am Chosen, so were you also," she said quietly.

He held out his hand. "Therefore, let us be handfasted anew."

When they had begun this talk, the last thing in the world Andas would have thought of doing was to offer her his hand so. Yet now the act came very easily and naturally, though there was nothing more in it for them both, he was sure, than the comrade tie existing between good friends—such friends as he had never before had the fortune to know.

"Prince!" Yolyos hailed from the lower level.

Andas stepped back from the girl and went to look down. The Salariki smiled up at him.

"The hunting is good, so good that your foresters need aid. They urge us to go on to the pass and have a message sent for transport, for this meat should get to the smokers as soon as possible. And you should be at your headquarters, also."

So they traveled trails that led them out of the woodlands, no longer haunted, at least for a space, by the obscene creeping horrors the enemy had unleashed there. It had been noon when they began that journey, but the way was easy enough, so they reached the pass before sundown.

The small garrison there greeted them warmly. Shara had privately informed him that none of the men stationed there had been of his close following. They greeted him with a respect he could meet easily.

Ten of them were sent down the back trail to pack in the unexpected bounty of meat.

"Lord, there are rumors of the crawlers out—" the commander had ventured before they left.

"They are out no longer." Andas told him of their own adventure and found the officer staring at him wide-eyed.

"Four—four crawlers killed! Lord, this is almost as good news as learning that the Drak Mount is breached. With the forest free, we can harvest game to push back the black fear of famine. If we but had our old weapons —what we might not do in our own behalf!"

"We have a skimmer also." Andas gave a terse account of their great luck in that encounter. "We dared not fly it in lest we be shot by our own defenses—"

"You need not fear, my lord. Perhaps we no longer possess the coms of the old days, but here we have that which serves us in a like manner, if less speedily. We can send your message, and you can fly back to head-quarters. Marcher"—he spoke to the door sentry—"summon Dullah with his swiftest fliers."

Then he spoke once more to Andas. "Lord, inscribe what message you wish. It will be in the hands of your first captains before moonset, for Dullah is a master breeder of horn hawks, and his messengers have never been bested for speed or accuracy."

"Give me leave, lord," Shara offered. "I will send the message you require, while you gain from this captain knowledge of affairs along the mountains." So swiftly had she taken the matter into her hands that Andas knew he could make no wrong guess.

He admired the horn hawks when their breeder-trainer brought them in, message carriers already clipped to slender legs, two dispatched for safety. They were not as heavy as the birds of that breed he had known in his own world, and they were wider of wing. Their plumage was gray, deepening into black, and would make them invisible at night, while their heads, bearing these "horns" of ridged quills, held bright eyes, used to darkness. In their natural state they were nocturnal.

Shara busied herself with a sheet of tough, light skin the captain produced, printing terse script thereon with a fire pen. As she wrote, Andas turned again to the captain.

"Tell me how it goes along the mountains." He was very ready to add to his information, needed if he were going to continue in the role of commander in chief.

16

The light was bright enough for Andas to study the faces of those seated at the table. Shara had done well. He had known each of them at once from her description and was able to greet them without hesitation. Kwayn Makenagen sat at his left hand in the place of greatest seniority. Beyond him was Patopir Ishan, facing him the Lady Bahyua Banokue, and to his right, Shara.

They had welcomed him earlier with open relief, in which he could detect no sign of consternation. Yet with Shara's warning he was alert. That was why Yolyos sat now at the end of that council table facing Andas. He did not know how much the alien's strange warning sense could do to unmask a traitor, but it was a safe-guard of a sort.

It was Ishan who spoke first, eagerly. "It must be the truth, my lord. This fellow was well-nigh dead when my scouts, found him after his skimmer had crashed. They heard his story and went to the Drak Mount. There are no signs of life to be seen."

"Tricks!" Makenagen returned as forcibly, favoring his colleague with a glare. "Bait to get us into a trap."

"The Arch Priest reports"—it was the Lady Banokue who spoke, in a low, calm voice—"that this prisoner is speaking the truth. He has tested him under hypnosis. The plague has spread widely through the Drak Mount. And what has fought us for the past months have been robots set on auto controls. Now those are going inert for want of tending."

"Inert!" Makenagen snorted. "They were in working order enough to blow a hole through our last land crawler. And that but ten days ago while we were hunting you, my lord." He directed his words to Andas. "I tell you, to venture into the land around the mount is fatal. No, this is a trap. Let the Arch Priest talk of the truth— we all know that in the old days a man could have his memory tampered with, be implanted with a false past. It was against the law, but it was done. They could have implanted this wretch—they still have machines while we are reduced to crossbows and the riding of elklands!"

Andas inclined his head to acknowledge the bitter logic of his captain's reasoning. What he had seen of this barren headquarters did not encourage a man. The spirit of those who held it was far higher than their ability to carry on war against those they admitted still held weapons of so-called civilization. It was as if they expected some of the old hero legends to work in their behalf, letting the "right" win by the favor of some supernatural force. But to depend upon a supernatural force—Suddenly his thoughts turned to what had lain at the back of his mind since their ordeal in the forest.

"Most dead or dying, said this prisoner?" he asked Ishan.

"Many so. There are some among them who appear immune. But those form only a skeleton force, unable now to defend the mount to any purpose. We can move in—"

"And among these dead was Kidaya?" Andas interrupted.

He saw the eager look fade on Ishan's face. "Now. This man was but a squad leader—he had no contact with the superior officers. But he said that a month ago, perhaps a little more—he was so dazed by the trials he had been through that he was vague on time—the lords who had declared for Kidaya and she herself took the last of the cruisers and departed."

"I suppose he did not know where?"

"There could be only one place she would seek," Shara

said in her usual toneless voice. "She would go to the Valley of Bones where there is a power to help her."

They were silent. Ishan stared at the girl, and the Lady Banokue looked down at her folded hands on the table top, hands a little plump, with the rings of her rank cutting into her flesh as if she had worn them so long that they were a part of her. Makenagen plucked at his lower lip. As Yolyos relaxed in his seat, Andas thought he saw the Salariki's nostrils expand as if he tested some scent in the air.

"If the off-world mercenaries are alone and those who hired them have, in a manner of speaking, deserted them"—Andas spoke first—"then perhaps we can persuade them that they are contract broke. And if we offer terms, they may surrender in honor."

"It is a trap!"

"That we have a means of testing. We have the skimmer. Suppose we return this prisoner to the mount by it and then await results? Mercenaries do not take kindly to contract breaking on alien worlds. It will depend upon what promises have been made them."

"Shara nodded. "And do not think that such have not been made. There is good reason to believe that oaths have been taken to hold these men even as they died. The heart of the rebellion is not Drak Mount now—it is the Valley of Bones."

"But to get to the valley, I must have something I am sure lies within the mount."

"You have a plan, my lord?" asked Makenagen.

"I have this." Andas showed his hand on the table top. Across the flat of his palm lay the key.

"But you cannot—the temple is under deadly radiation!" Ishan cried.

"Not deadly if one has a radiation suit. I know what I would seek. I can find it wearing such protection."

"No!" Makenagen brought his fist down on the table with force enough to make the blow audible. "You would die. This is too great a risk, and if we have not you, then Kidaya has won and we might as well all put knives to our own throats and have done with it!"

"What do we then?" Andas asked. "Do we wait here until Kidaya and that demon crew think up another evil to send against us? Have we not slipped down far enough into the dark of barbarism? We need what is in the mount, and we need it now! You all know what this means, what force it is said to unlock." He held the key now between thumb and forefinger as a pointer aiming it down the length of the table.

"The temple is impossible," Makenagen repeated. His eyes were on the key, but his head shook stubbornly back and forth, denying any promise it might have.

Andas wished he could accept that as firmly as did this noble. What he held to as the only plan he could formulate was nothing he wanted to do. He was no hero willing to die to accomplish some task that might or might not save the situation. But it was part of the burden laid on him. Only the rightful emperor or his proclaimed heir could hold the key and set it in the place it was meant to go. And he was not even sure what he would unlock if he could accomplish that much, save that he did believe to the full that it would give him the ultimate answer to the life of the empire. And it would seem that the hour had come when they must have that answer or go down to defeat.

If Drak Mount was the well-equipped fortress they claimed, there must be radiation suits there. Wearing one of those, he could enter the temple or its ruins and then—"Take one step at a time," Andas cautioned himself—these were formidable steps.

"Let the prisoner be brought," he ordered Ishan,

knowing the longer they sat in council, the less they would decide, and to act was important.

In appearance the man proved to be like those from whom they had captured the skimmer, save that he had lost all self-confidence. But his training held, and he came to attention before Andas.

"You have told us a tale of your troubles," the prince began. To him the prisoner seemed broken in spirit. He could well believe that they had pumped out of him all that was to be learned. But perhaps Yolyos could learn more.

"The plague, Your Mightiness—"

"Just so. And I have also heard that your employer or employers broke faith—is this not so?"

The man looked startled, as if that question had penetrated through his own misery.

"Broke faith, Mightiness?"

"Did not the false rebel Kidaya and her lords withdraw, leaving you, whom she had brought hither to fight for her, to die alone? To the mind of an honest man, soldier, that is breaking contract. Have you not thought of it so?"

"Nothing has been said, Mightiness. We hold to duty."

"Needlessly. Now, soldier, there is that you can do, not only in your own behalf, but also for your whole company—what is left of them by now. You can take our terms to whomever remains of your leaders with authority enough to agree to surrender. We shall grant mercenaries' terms with full honors, oath pledge for that. This is now no battle of yours, for you shall see no pay from those who fled."

"Mightiness, no one can return overland to the mount. I came forth on a skimmer, which failed me. The heavy arms are all on auto and locked there, by the Lady Kidaya's orders. There can be no way for me to get in."

"You came by skimmer—you can return by skimmer. Or have the air defenses also been locked on auto?"

The soldier licked his lips, but his eyes did not shift under Andas's level regard.

"No, Mightiness. It was thought that—that those of your command no longer had any air power. And it was also said, Mightiness, that you yourself were dead, or soon to be so!"

"Yet I am not, nor are we lacking in air power. You will be taken to the top of Dark Mount and there dropped with your grav belt—" Andas turned to Ishan. "He was wearing a grav belt?"

At the captain's nod, the prince continued. "You will carry to your commander our terms. We shall give him the space of a day to consider them. If he accepts, he and at least two of the highest ranking officers under him shall signal from the top of the mount. A skimmer will be sent to bring them to me to give truce oath. Do you understand?"

"Yes, Mightiness."

"Have him ready to go," Andas told Ishan.

"They will not yield." But Makenagen did not sound as emphatic as he had earlier.

"I think that they will. The mercenaries sell loyalty, but it must work both ways. If they believe that contract is broken, they will surrender on mercenary terms. Since we cannot ship them off-world, we shall take their paroles until we can."

"You put faith in their oaths?" Makenagen still fought a rear-guard action.

"You know the breed, do you not?"

"Yes. If they will take trust oath."

"One thing waits upon another." Andas fell into the more formal court speech. "The day grows near, my captains—the audience is ended." For the first time he

250

stepped from battle commander to emperor with that dismissal. They went, save for Yolyos, to whom he made a gesture, and Shara.

"What did you learn?" Andas hardly waited before they had gone to ask.

"First, your traitor is not here. Second, you read that prisoner aright. I think he will do exactly as you wish. Let us hope his superiors do likewise. But what you intend to do, Prince—or should it be 'Emperor'?"

"I believe that which this opens"—Andas stowed the key once more within his clothing (he had shed at last the grimed and badly worn coverall and been fitted with tunic, breeches, and boots)—"will give us the answer to Kidaya at long last. It is the mightiest weapon our race ever knew. We are pledged never to call upon it until the last extremity. And to my judging, we have reached that point. We can wait out the fall of the Drak Mount, and that may take centuries with their defenses on auto—those will run until the energy is exhausted.

"But it is not the Drak Mount that matters so much as the Valley of Bones. For as long as the empire has existed, the Old Woman has menaced it. How does the warning go?" He looked to Shara, who replied.

"Dark spawns dark, evil gives root to evil.
What man has wrought, man can destroy.
But that is the way of man.
For the other, it is waiting, watching—
And in the end triumph over all.
Night will fall, day comes not again.
Winter's cold knows no spring.
And the dried bones will lie in rows,
But none shall weep,
For there will be no eyes to hold the tears."

"A mournful enough saying," the Salariki commented.

"This has some meaning beyond its gloomy surface words?"

"The Old Woman negates all we believe is life. She wears many faces. Sometimes she has sunk to become a bogey with which to frighten children; other times we see her followers walk proudly with power. But there was always the warning of an ultimate confrontation between the power invested in him who can use the key and the Old Woman. I think the time has come—here and now."

"And Kidaya was sent into the world to induce that coming?" Shara mused. "Then all the evil she has wrought here falls into a pattern that one can understand, for if it had been the Empress's crown she wanted, she could have gained her ends without wreaking such destruction on friend and foe alike. She has had choices, and always her choice has fallen in a way to bring more chaos. So you take the weapon of the key. And where do you bear it—to the Valley of Bones?"

Andas suddenly felt very weary, like a man pushed to the edge of endurance who must yet stoop and add another burden to a load he already carried. "Where else?" he asked her simply. He had never wanted to do more than what now seemed light and pleasant duty in his own time. But there was no turning back. From the moment he had laid hand on the key, he had chosen the path that led straight here, and he could not turn aside, even if he would.

"But not alone," she protested.

He was too tired to argue. Sometimes when he was alone (which seemed to be very seldom now), he would close his eyes and rub his fingers across the lids, as if to so rub away all the light and sound about. Without Shara he could not have played his part for an hour. Sometimes he wished she would let him blunder into self-betrayal so he could be free.

Now he went to the window of the small room to which the rule of the empire had shrunk. For a space action was out of his hands. All hung now on the surrender of Drak Mount.

"Emperor"—Yolyos gave him the title without any of the accompanying honorifics his own people used—"there is someone coming and"—he had faced around, his nostrils dilated—"this is not right—"

Andas had no chance to ask for explanations, for the door sentry looped back the blanket that served as a curtain.

"Lord, it is the Arch Priest with tidings of urgency."

"Let him enter."

The man whom came in was twin to the Kelemake Andas remembered. He had not followed the universal habit of eradicating his beard, but sprouted a small growth on his chin, trimmed into an aggressive point. His voluminous robe was not as shabby as the garments of the rest of the garrison and was the russet-red of the temple. And he also had the conical, pointed miter of his rank, though this was not jeweled in regal splendor, but merely carried on its front a silver representation of the key. A like replica depended on a long chain about his neck.

Andas had seen him twice since he had come to the fort. But both times it had been a purely formal meeting in company. It seemed to him that the Arch Priest, instead of making a point to welcome his emperor back, had, as unobtrusively as possible, chosen to escape any direct communication with his leader. But he was here now and seemed eager for an interview.

"Pride of Balkis-Candac"—his voice was that of a man who had learned to use it effectively with audiences— "the message is that we move on Drak Mount."

"After a fashion," Andas agreed. "An offer for surrender—"

"These off-worlders, these evil ones—they should not be allowed parole!" There was a glint in the priest's eyes now. How much dared Andas judge this double by the man he had known? Of old such a look meant that Kelemake, the scholar, was preparing to rip to shreds some long-held belief.

"They are mercenaries. We shall offer them the usual peace by oath."

"When such as they have despoiled this world, brought the empire to dust? Pride of Balkis-Candace, those who have passed beyond will not be honored by such mistaken mercy. I pray you think again before you offer terms to drinkers of blood. Let them stay and die in the hole into which they have sealed themselves."

"Much the easier way." Andas hoped that he sounded reasonable. The priest's attitude was a little strange. Theirs was not usually a cry for revenge. "Save that it may take years. And we do not have years to go on starving out our own existence. If this struggle can be brought to an end, then the oaths are worth it."

"There will be no peace with Kidaya!" Kelemake fairly spat. "And she is not at the mount."

"No. She is where we must seek her."

Kelemake showed his teeth in what might be a smile, savoring of contempt. "Doubtless with weapons taken from the mount. Which perhaps might be a worthy plan, save that those with whom she shelters now have such weapons as can put to naught any taken from Drak."

"Not at all." Andas's hand went to his tunic breast beneath which lay the key. "There is this." On some impulse he did not understand, he drew forth his heritage. Again it seemed that the light in the room gathered to it.

The change in Kelemake was astounding. His hand

had been resting on his own silver key, the badge of his office. Now he twisted that up and out as if thus he held a cutting weapon. But whatever he intended was never completed, for Yolyos sprang. The Salariki had been edging to the side, and his sudden attack beat the priest of his knees. A second chop from the alien's hand collapsed him. Yolyos stopped and jerked loose the key, examined it, and a moment later uttered a deep growl.

"A fine toy indeed for a priest, Emperor. Behold!" Holding the key as Kelemake had done, he moved closer to the table. There was a click, and in the wood of its top quivered a tiny dart hardly as long as a cloak pin, which must have been fitted snuggly into the shaft of the key.

"Do not touch it!" Yolyos swept out an arm to keep Andas back. "There is a very suspicious smear on it. But I will tell you something else. This"—he stirred the body of the priest with a boot toe—"was not a man—not as we know men."

"Android?" Andas jumped to the one conclusion ever with him.

"No, he was human once. What he is now, perhaps your followers of the old Woman can best name. But this is your traitor or I never have sniffed one with more of such stink!"

"Kelemake!" breathed Shara. "But the priests, they are armored against the Old Woman. They have to be, or they could not function as priests."

"But how long has it been since there was a temple with protective safeguards to uncover such?" Andas asked. "You smelt his treachery?"

"I picked up a foulness like those woods creepers, enough to know he had kinship with them. And he came here to kill you, which suggests one thing—that those you would face hold you in fear. Perhaps this last plan of yours is what they dislike."

"But how would they know—we have only just discussed it?"

"Did not you show me those eye and ear holes in that palace of yours? If there are not such in the walls hereabouts, then this one had his spies. He must have been worried indeed to risk killing you before witnesses and so betraying himself. Either he planned to kill us also, or else he has served his master—or mistress—as much as he can and was due to be discarded. How better quit the service than in a blaze of glory, removing the chief threat with you?"

Andas knelt beside the priest, turning the body over. He did not expect to find Kelamake dead. Surely Yolyos had not struck that hard. But he was, and Andas searched the man. He did not know what he sought, save that there might be some link between this traitor and the enemy. And he found it at last in the interior of the miter, lying directly behind the key symbol. It was a tiny device, which, when he tried to rip it free, proved to have a whole network of very fine wires buried in the sides of the headgear where they might touch the skull of the wearer.

That skull was shaved as was customary among priests. Yolyos squatted down on the other side, looking first at the cap and then at the skull. Suddenly he put forth a hand, extending the claws on two fingers to their greatest extent, and made a savage pass across the skin, tearing it open. No blood flowed, and they could all see the glint of metal that ripping had uncovered. The priest wore a metal plate as part of his skull.

"More of your Nessi dealings," Yolyos commented. "They appear to temper their magic with science, if one can call it that."

Andas stood up. "The sooner we visit the Valley of Bones, the better," he said between set teeth.

17

Andas paced back and forth. The rooms in this small fort, never meant to serve as more than an outpost, were not intended for pacing. He could cover the space in about four medium strides. But he could not sit still with the thoughts that clawed at his mind, even as the Salariki had clawed free the Arch Priest's secret. How many more of those gathered at this heart of the command were more—or less—than they seemed to be? He had only Yolyos's talent to "smell" out the enemy.

Dark old tales came unbidden to his mind. Once his people had worshiped gods who turned their faces from the light, who were to be appeased only with blood sacrifices. Only the Old Woman existed still from that time. Then kings had kept about their persons "witch doctors," men and women supposedly with the gift of literally sniffing out prospective enemies. The result had depended upon the whim of those doctors. And the innocent must have suffered with the the guilty many times over. Yet Andas could not believe that those of human breed had ever been gifted with Yolyos's talent. And he should be thanking Akmedu that not only had the Salariki followed him into this waking nightmare, but that he was also comrade in arms.

The alien sat now, cross-legged, in a deep window seat, watching Andas. He had refused the clothing of the Imperial forces, save for breeches, boots, and a cape. Apparently to cover his furred upper body caused him discomfort. And he held to his nose a wilted green ball he had clung to ever since they had left the woodland, though the aroma of those herbs and leaves had faded considerably since they had been gathered.

Shara sat in the single chair. Her torn and grimed garments had been changed for male clothing. Only the intricate braiding of her hair betrayed her sex, for otherwise she might have been a boy. She sat quietly enough, her heavy-lidded eyes not turned on Andas at all, but fixed as if she looked inward and not outward.

"How many—" Andas flung around to face both of them. "How many such can there be among us?"

"None, among those I have seen—save that devil-priest," Yolyos replied calmly. "Be sure I would know. He was a puppet jerking to the will of another, like the shadow people of our entertainers. None else I have met are so."

"But where one has entered—"

"In the very ancient days of our people"—Shara spoke from the same memories as Andas had—"such searchers were known. The king would summon all his people to a meeting and send out his witch-finders to run about among them. Those they touched with their wands were killed. But—"

"That was savagery," Andas said. "Disclosure of the king's enemies depended upon the whim of men who had private hates and quarrels to avenge. If there are any here, Yolyos can sniff them out. I think we may be safe for the present. But we must move against the Valley of Bones before it looses worst against us!"

There was a polite scratching at the doorframe outside the curtain. At Andas's call, Ishan entered. He was smiling broadly.

"Lord, your wisdom read aright these sulkers in the Drak Mount. They have agreed to a meeting. The skimmer has been sent to bring them as far as the Tooth Craig, even as you ordered."

Andas felt a small leap of hope. At least this far he had judged the situation aright. In spite of the priest whose body had been dragged out hours earlier, he had made the first move of his complicated game, and it was successful.

"Let us go then." He was already heading for the door. Yolyos swung from his seat, the girl close behind. There were elklands waiting, the smaller, surer-footed breed of the mountains. Their best pace was a raking trot, and they continually bobbed their heavily horned heads up and down. Now and then one voiced a bellow, to be echoed by the rest.

Andas, Shara, Yolyos, Ishan, and a squad of the latter's own shield men made up their swift-riding band. The Tooth Craig was at least two hours' steady riding away. They must travel ever alert as this was wild and broken land. And, after the unmasking of Kelemake, Andas trusted nothing.

They made a rough camp at the craig, Andas and his leaders a little apart. Down before them stretched the raw land of the waste, a northernmost arm of that in which they had landed the drone ship in that other Inyanga. Andas wondered fleetingly if Elys had told her story and what the false emperor had made of it.

"They are coming." Shara touched his arm.

A skimmer showed against the sky like an insect. Ishan spoke, and half of his men vanished on the rocky hillside about their appointed meeting place. Andas was startled at their skill at taking cover. But these had been part of a hard-beleaguered guerrilla force for years. Those who had not learned were long since dead. They had been given orders not to move unless treachery was offered.

There was barely enough level ground for the skimmer to alight on. It moved sluggishly, carrying an overload of passengers. Four men in mercenary uniforms disembarked. They wore their side arms, as by custom they could, but carried no larger weapons. Their heads were concealed with helmets on which the protecto visors were down. But as they exited from the craft, each deliberately snapped that visor up and removed his helmet to stand bareheaded.

Two were young, aides or squad captains. But those they escorted were older, men plainly well established in their business of war. The one in the lead held up his hand in a peace salute to which Andas responded.

"Commander-in-Arms Modan Sullock," he introduced himself brusquely. Then he indicated his followers. "Captains Masquid, Herihor, Samson."

"The Imperial son of Balkis-Candace"—Ishan spoke formally—"his Chosen, the Lady Shara, his comrade in arms, Lord Yolyos."

Sullock's attention for Andas and Shara was fleeting compared to the measuring stare he gave to the Salariki!

"Salariki!" His surprise was unconcealed. But he recovered his aplomb quickly. Once more his hand raised, this time in a fall salute to Andas.

Under the circumstances it was a waste of time to stand on ceremony. Andas came directly to the point.

"You have our terms, Commander-in-Arms, and you must have considered them seriously or you would not be here. They are simple—your contract was broken when she who employed you fled, leaving you to the plague death. We offer you parole with honor. And though we cannot give you off-world withdrawal, since ships no longer fin down here, we offer you the best we can. This has never been any quarrel of yours, save that you used your fighting ability to aid a usurper. You have your choice—stay pent in the Drak Mount and let the plague and time end you. Or surrender the fortress to us on honorable terms. We do not seek you, who are but tools, but her who brought this ruin upon us."

Sullock studied Andas for a long moment before he

answered. "Since you know so much about us, then you must also know that it is beyond our power to surrender the mount entirely. Many of its heavy defenses are on auto, and that has been tampered with so it cannot be shut off again. There is no way to reach the mount safely overlands."

Andas shrugged. "Let it stand, so, a monument to the evil that used it. We have a skimmer. Do you have any?"

"Two, recalled from scout duty. No cruisers—your Lady Kidaya took the last in commission."

"Let those ferry your men out to a place we shall appoint. They will bring with them rations and only the side arms that by law are theirs. There is but one thing you must give me and that as soon as your exodus begins."

"That being?"

"A radiation suit that will fit me. And the best you have at the mount. Those are our terms. Do you wish to confer with your men at Drak before you give us one word or another?"

"You will accept truce oath and parole us then after interplanetary custom?"

"We will," answered Andas promptly. Whether they would believe him after all these years of bitter struggled, he did not know. It must seem that he was utterly confident now.

"I am empowered by custom also," returned Sullock that, "to agree to terms. And we shall accept. Our contract is broken." From his tunic he brought forth a sealed tape, tossed it to the ground, and set his heel upon it, grinding it, case and tape together, into a mass that could never be read again. "When shall we come forth?"

"You can begin as soon as you return to the mount.

But I want that suit at once, so I shall go with you. Your men can stay here."

Andas saw Ishan start forward as if to protest, but he waved him back, giving him no chance to speak.

"Each shuttle taking your men out will bring a selected party of ours in," he continued. "We shall clear out supplies and arms—"

"The plague!" Shara spoke in warning.

Sullock looked to her. "Lady, the plague died four tens of days ago. There have been no new cases since. It went when those we served left."

"But why?" she demanded. "Why should Kidaya seek to kill those who served her?"

"Your suspicion is quick, lady." Sullock grimaced. "Now it took us a little longer to spell out the truth. Well do you say, lord"—he turned to Andas—"that our contract was broken. There came a messenger to that one who hired us. She was in a fury of excitement thereafter, and she left, taking her own with her, and an evil lot they were. As for why she would be rid of us—well, the defenses were on auto in the mount and the food was limited. We cannot lift off-world now, and we had become an embarrassment to her. She relies now on other methods of warfare. And she would have left us to death-haunt that hold, in truth, had not our first medic found the herbs in the water system and removed them. She is a woman in form, but within—she is not human!"

"No plague but poison!" Shara exclaimed. "But she could use plague, the threat of it, to isolate us, keep out any from the stars. In truth, what is she, Andas, who plans so?"

"She serves that other. And, it would seem, well. The more reason to strike to the heart of that dark, and soon."

So they took truce oath with the mercenaries, and the

ferrying of those within the Drak Mount began, moving them to a long valley to the north of the Place of Red Water. There they set up camp with what rations they brought out of the mount. Andas did not mistrust the men who had surrendered. Their custom of standing by their parole was known galaxy-wide.

Since there were no ships now lifting from Inyanga, he wondered whether he might later follow with them an old method of his people, offering them soldier land for settlement. They could so provide the core of a new army, since soldier land could only be inherited in each new generation by service in the forces. But that would come later—a decision for the future. What faced him now was not months away, but in the immediate hours— or days ahead.

It was Sullock who ordered the radiation suits brought out of storage for Andas's inspection. Though they had not been used, perhaps in years, the prince knew them for models he had seen in his own time as adequate for heavy duty. He had no tech among his own force to test them, so he had to depend upon the aid of such among the mercenaries. That expert reported that four were in working condition.

Andas chose the one closest to a good fit, though it was a little large. By the advice of the first medic among Sullock's men, his body, before he dressed in the suit, was given an additional shielding of those plasta bandages used in radiation treatment. The binding made him more clumsy, but it was further insurance against painful death.

To the last, Shara demanded to share his desperate eventure. Andas was adamant in his refusal. Only one man could do this, and by the choice of fate, that one was he. He persuaded her at last that the safeguards in the temple were such that, even if she went with him, she could not accompany him all the way and would only be a burden for him.

The only addition he insisted upon being made was a com unit that would allow his voice to be projected beyond the suit. The lock that he would have to deal with was partly controlled by certain sound waves.

Whether the temple, being in the midst of the ruins, was intact enough so he could enter it, he did not know, since no one had penetrated to it since the blow-up. He wondered whether the destruction had been done deliberately for that reason, not just to wipe out the palace and its defenses. If the Old Woman was as powerful as she seemed, then those who served her might well know of the existence of that which he sought.

It took them a full night of labor to install the com in the suit. Andas willed himself to sleep in the commander's quarters of the Drak Mount, taking what rest he could."

"If I do not return," he said to Shara and Yloyos the next morning, "then to you, Shara, the rule. My lord"— he looked then to the Salariki—"this is not your world, and it may be that you cannot leave it again, nor is it your war. But if you would serve this lady with your talent, as you have aided me, then I shall be content, for no man ever had a better comrade in arms in any undertaking. I know not what form friendship takes among your people, but among mine this feeling is such I name you 'brother.'"

Somewhere in the mount the Salariki had found a small bag of spices, which he kept at hand, sniffing it often. But now he let that drop so it dangled from the cord that bound it to his wrist, and he put out both his hands, claws sheathed, so Andas laid his own in them.

Delicately the claw on each forefinger extended and

266

dug into Andas's brown flesh until a drop of blood showed.

"Lady," said the Salariki then, "since this, my brother, has no nature-given claws to mark me, do you take the knife at your belt and do to my hands as I have done to his."

Shara did so without question, using the point of her belt knife as delicately as Yolyos had his claws.

When drops of blood showed on his hands also, still holding Andas's hands, he raised them to his lips and touched tongue tip to the blood. Then Andas followed his example in a twin gesture that brought Yolyos's blood to his own mouth.

"Blood to blood," said the alien. "We are clan kin now, brother. Go content that I shall stand where protection is needed for your first lady."

So it was that with the salt-sweet taste of Yolyos's blood still on his tongue, Andas pulled on the heavy helmet of the suit and allowed the tech to fasten it. And then he clumped in the thick boots to the skimmer, taking his place in the rear by the harness that would lower him as close to his goal as the craft could get.

As they neared the site of the ruins, Andas was appalled by the task of identification here. All those towers and buildings that should have served as landmarks had been leveled, toppled, or had disappeared in craters. The skimmer circled as the pilot waited for Andas's choice of landing site. In this awkward suit he could not climb far among the debris below. He would have to be put down only a short distance away from his goal. But where was the temple?

Then he was able to trace what he thought was the Gate of Nine Victories. He waved the pilot eastward. There he saw the broken pillars of what could only be the colonnade of the temple terrace. Andas signaled, hooking the descent line to the belt already buckled about him. The hatch in the belly of the skimmer opened as the machine went on hover, and Andas clambered through.

The lowering cord played out slowly and evenly, and it continued to reel on as, twisting and turning, he descended to what had once been the entrance to the temple. As he went, Andas studied what lay below, trying to locate the points of reference he needed. The closer he approached, the more the temple showed its hurts. Walls had collapsed, but there seemed to be open spaces enough to enter.

His boots touched pavement, and he moved his gloved fingers to free the belt hooks. Then the line snaked speedily aloft, to descend again, this time weighted with the one other thing he had taken from the mount, a blaster. With that he hoped to open any blocked way.

From ground level the mounded mass of the temple was almost threatening. If it had been congealed with the fire of the blast, he could never have made the attempt to enter. But now he started toward a promising opening.

Luckily he did not have to penetrate the main part, but rather work north to the other end of the terrace. There was the Emperor's Gate through which even he would have passed on only two occasions in his life, when he went for his crowning and when the urn of his ashes on a cart, which would run of its own volition, would pass after his death ceremony.

The barrier of carved metal was a crumble of broken bits. Andas used the blaster with care, cutting a passage until he stood on the block he sought, where the Emperor's death carriage would halt for a long moment coming and going. There was no chance in this welter of ruin to hunt for the spring that would release what lay beneath.

He applied the blaster on half voltage, cutting around the block. Then putting aside the tool, he used a bar of twisted metal to lever out the freed stone.

Below was a dark opening into which he flashed his torch. Steps showed, seemingly uninjured in spite of the wreckage above. But his suit was too bulky to pass through the hole. He used the blaster again to nibble around the edges and enlarge the space. Then he started down.

There were ten steps, steeper than those of a normal stair. The whir of his radiation counter was a constant buzz, but he tried to forget that warning. There was no way he could help it, so he must not let it alarm him into carelessness. The freeing of the blocked passage was only the beginning.

There was a passage leading on from the foot of the stairs, running in toward the heart of the temple. What he sought had been placed directly below the throne whereon the Emperor sat at all state services.

Andas's torch showed him only blank walls of stone, nothing to suggest the importance of this crypt. Now—a door. But before him was only another blank wall putting an end to the way. He had expected this. Now, if only—

Andas ran his tongue across his lips. He raised his gloved hand but did not quite touch the com. It had been adjusted as well as the tech could do it. He could not alter it any.

He spoke. The words were very old, in a language he did not understand. He doubted if any, even like Kelemake, who had made a study of the ancient records, could translate them. Nor did he know their meaning, only that they must be intoned slowly, with pauses between their groupings, in this place.

There was no answer. No door opened—the wall did

not fall. He tried a second time, sure that he gave the right accents in the proper places, without result.

It must be the com at fault. That probably distorted some tonal quality that was of major importance. He would have to unhelm to recite the words properly or fail. But with the radiation counter buzzing—unhelm here?

When there is only one answer you accept it—or retreat. And he had come too far; this was too important to retreat. Nor could he ruthlessly burn through the wall. It was provided with safeguards against that. What he sought would be destroyed at the first alarm.

Andas placed the blaster against the wall, and his gloved hands loosened the face plate of his helmet. The air was dead, with an acrid, burning smell that filled his nose. Yet he could not hold his breath and recite at the same time. He spoke the formula for the third time and knew that this must be his last try.

He closed the plate of the helmet, coughing. Then, the wall split down the center, the halves slipping back into the corridor. It had worked!

He was still coughing as he faced, a couple of paces farther on, a grill of metal that glistened in his torchlight as if it had been recently polished. The center of that grill was worked into a design he knew, the legendary "lion"—a fabulous beast sacred to the Emperor. The open mouth of the creature was his keyhole.

Now, would the key from one world fit the lock of another? This was no time to lose confidence. It slid in easily enough.

Turn to the left—it opened! The lock was the same. At his push the grill swung in, and he shuffled on. There was a pedestal in the very center and on it a box. This also showed a keyhole, but Andas did not wait to try his key. He had plucked that out of the grill and fastened it to his belt. Now he slid his hands under the box and lifted it.

He had expected it to be heavy, but it was lighter than the blaster, and he could carry it easily under one arm as he turned to retrace his way, making the best speed he could.

Though he no longer coughed, his throat was dry and his eyes smarted. Whether he had taken such a dose of radiation as would doom him, he dared not think. He must take what he had found to those who might be able to use it, even if he brought his own death with it.

Up the steps he went, back into the open where the skimmer had dropped him. Though it was very hard, encased in such armor, to tilt his head back, Andas managed it far enough to see the skimmer on hover. He raised his arm in signal.

The ascent rope came tumbling down. Andas pitched the blaster from him. He needed that no longer. Still holding the box close, he made fast the hoist cord and gave the signal to rise.

The hoist jerked as it took the strain of his weight. He was hauled up, hoping that the pilot had taken the precautions in which they had drilled him, erecting a force screen between him and his passenger. No one would dare to approach Andas now until they had used every method of decontamination. But he had done it. He had their greatest weapon now in his two hands!

18

Having gone through the most rigid decontamination processes the medico and techs of the mercenaries could devise, Andas sat alone before the box. He thought only of what must be done now, rather than of the results of the tests they had forced on him. He had known that his quest might well be fatal, though it is hard for any man to face directly the fact of death, of ending all that he knows, feels, is—They had told him the truth, that the tests had showed a higher degree of radiation than the body could survive.

So, he had made his payment in advance. What he bought must be worth it. Andas inserted the key and turned it.

Surprisingly, though it must have been locked for centuries of time, the lid arose easily. And in the interior, bedded down in a thick layer of spongy material, were two things, one a roll of what seemed to be thin leather, the other a length of metal links, the metal dark and dull, studded with small bosses in no decorative pattern. He drew that out and straightened it to full length on the table. Disappointment choked him.

Indifferently he took up the roll, slipped off the ring that kept it tight, and flattened it out. The inner side was printed with signs and drawings, meaningless to him at first.

To have bought so little with his life! Then the promises of legends were worthless. Perhaps they had never intended to do more than to give a prop to the emperors, a confidence in knowing that if the worst came, there awaited a way out. And they were expected to find their own solutions first, not to fall back upon this deception.

Yet all the precautions—would such have been taken to preserve a fake? Yes, if the fact that it was a fake was never to be unmasked, that the belief in it was its only power.

Andas looked down at the script he could not read, at the diagrams that blurred as he stared at them. Unless—

It was a moment or two before, sunk in his despair and disappointment, Andas realized that he was able to read a word here and there. Those long hours with Kelemake, when the archivist had been so immersed in his own studies that, needing a sounding board, he had expounded them to a boy, were paying off. Intently Andas shaped the archaic symbols with his lips and traced diagrams by fingertip. There was much he did not understand, but enough—perhaps just enough—that he could!

He drew the length of metal links to him and let it slip through his fingers as if counting them. But what he quested for were those bosses that had a meaning. An hour later he leaned back in his chair. Around his waist those links made a belt. He had done what he could without fully understanding the preparations. But the old tale had not failed him.

There was only one reason for life left, to carry what he held—or rather take what he now was—to the Valley of Bones and there fight the last battle, which would decide the fate of the empire one way or the other.

Andas came out of the room. Shara sat on a stool against the wall. Beyond her Yolyos lounged, inspecting the inner workings of one of the hand weapons from the mount. They turned to him, but he raised his hand to warn them off. How deadly he himself might be now was a matter of some concern. There was that in their faces which warmed him, even through the ice that had encased him since he had heard those test readings.

"No. I have now what may be the salvation of the

empire," he said hurriedly. How long did he have before the final illness began? "You have the skimmer ready?"

"Andas." Shara spoke only his name and reached out her hand to him.

"No," he repeated. "This thing was laid to me. He gave his life to begin it and bound upon me the oath to finish it."

He looked then to Yolyos. "It has been good," he said simply. "I never had a brother, nor anyone save my father whom I could trust. It has been good to know such a one, even for a short time."

Yolyos nodded. "It has been good," he answered, his voice a low purr. "Go, brother, knowing that one stands to do here what must be done."

At his orders they cleared the short hall between the room and the outer courtyard where the skimmer waited —the craft already contaminated by his flight to the temple. But there was the garrison drawn up, and, as he went, for the first time in his life he heard the full-throat roar of those hailing him as the Emperor.

"Lion, Pride of Balkis-Candace, Lord of Spears—hail!"

Andas dared not look either right or left to see those who shouted, knowing that pride alone would help him to finish that march with dignity. Somehow he reached the hatch of the skimmer and climbed into the pilot's seat. Still he could not allow himself to look back. He touched the rise and was above them in a leap, the force of which made him breathless for an instant. Then the flier was on course, heading toward the last battle of all.

Andas had only one guide to the Valley of Bones (save the general directions he had been able to piece together from old accounts), and that was the ring, for it was united, he was sure, to the source of its power. He had it wired to the control board of the skimmer and watched it for any variation in the set.

His course was not a straight one after he topped the mountains, but a zigzag to pick up a trail for the ring. And before midday it had proven to be a guide, for the dull set glowed, took on rippling life, and grew the brighter as he flew on in the direction it indicated.

There were more heights ahead, the sere spur range of the Ualloga, once a chain of volcanoes making a blazing girdle for the continent. Their broken cones now were sided by such cliffs as not even the wild cam sheep knew, a riven and waterless land that repelled man and animal alike. In his own Inyanga the range had seldom been penetrated and many of the peaks never explored.

The stone glowed, flashed as he had never seen it do before. It pointed directly into this land. How much longer did he have, Andas wondered, before death attacked his body? The thought made him shift to top speed.

Thus he overshot his goal and was aware of it only when the gem signaled it. He circled about, also intent on what the visa-screen showed of the land below.

It was no true valley the ring brought him to, but the hollow of a giant crater. And, as he went on hover, Andas was aware of something else. About him the linked belt was warming, rousing in answer to some energy, while through his body he began to feel a vibration, almost as painful as the one that had accompanied the crawlers.

He put the skimmer on descend. There was no need to take any precaution over his arrival. Andas did not in the least doubt that those who sheltered in this hole knew of his coming. But he watched the screen carefully.

The very heart of the crater was a lake, though the waters there did not mirror the sky above, but were a dead slate gray. Around its shores there was vegetation. It had a withered, dead look, lacking the brilliant color and shadow one saw in normal plants.

Farther away from the water were heaps of some graywhite material set in loose order. And while they resembled no buildings he had ever seen, Andas believed them to be shelters for those who made this dismal mountain cup their home.

He brought the skimmer down on the only nearly level space he sighted. The visa-screen showed him that and a portion of sand and gravel beyond, as well as scraps of blighted vegetation—but no one moved. If there was a reception party, it was in hiding.

With care he unwired the ring, being careful not to touch the band itself. That he dared not do while he wore the belt, for their powers were so opposed, one to the other, that he believed such a connection might be fatal to him. Into the ring he inserted the end of an officer's baton, which Yolyos had smoothed down to serve that purpose. And holding this before him, he left the skimmer.

The nearest of the shelters was close enough to see clearly, and he was startled at its material. There was no mistaking the nature of the loglike objects piled to form its walls—bones—huge bones! He had never heard of an animal large enough to yield such. But why not—was not this the Valley of Bones—though that was a literal statement he had not known.

Andas's right hand hovered about his belt but did not quite touch it. With his left he held the baton well away from his body. The glow of the ring was torch-like through the gloom of the valley.

Again he looked about for some sign his arrival was known—that they were prepared to move against him. Nothing stirred. There were no sounds. If bird or insect lived in this gloom, it was silent now. There was a feeling of waiting that made him want to linger by the open hatch of the skimmer as his only refuge.

Perhaps all his race was conditioned to expect the worst here. There were too many old terror tales about the ruler of this pocket—and of much more when she wished to reach out and touch this one or that to be her follower. But the fact that he knew he was a walking dead man was armor. Fear of dissolution was now longer hers to threaten.

So Andas walked away from the skimmer, from all the world that he knew, carrying the ring as a torch. And since the huts of bones seemed the logical place to start searching for whoever dwelt here, he went to those.

Sometime later he reached the end of that line of weird dwellings, having found each empty, though there was good evidence that they were occupied. But where were those he sought? That sense of expectancy, of being on the brink of action, had never left him. Yet no movement, no sound, indicated that he was not alone in the valley.

Would the ring continue to lead him? He could try an experiment. Andas loosed his grasp on the baton until he held it by only the lightest of grips. Then he spoke for the first time. Though he purposely kept his voice low, yet his words rang unusually loud in his own ears.

"To thy mistress, go!"

The baton quivered, moved. He tried not to hold it too tightly lest he hinder that movement, yet he must not drop it. It turned at a sharp angle left. And he pivoted to face that way. The baton stiffened to point, and he found he could not make it waver.

Away from the bone-walled huts it led him, from the lake, from the skimmer. It was like a spear aimed at the steep side of the crater.

Then he saw that he walked a marked way, sided by stumpy pillars, first knee high, then waist, and finally topping his shoulders, and these were also bones.

So walled in, Andas came to an opening in the cliff. As he paused, there was a flash within, a leap of greenish flame. He smelled a stench that was worse than the odor of the crawlers.

Then a voice called, "You have sought us out, Emperor. Have you then come to seek your crown? But your hour is past—even as the crown has passed to one who can better wear it!"

In the green of the flames he saw the gathered company. Back against the wall on either side were a sprinkling of men, who stood, staring in a kind of despair and complete surrender, as if all their strength had been drained. But in the center was a group of women, and behind them another, enthroned.

Andas raised his eyes to the face of that one. On her head was the Imperial crown, the sacred one worn only when the ruler took his oath of allegiance. It was death for a lesser man to touch it. At the sight of that in this place, anger blazed hot in him.

The head on which it rested was held high with an arrogance he thought not even an empress in her own right could have shown. Her face had the perfection of a soulless, emotionless statue, with only the eyes and a cruel curl of mouth betraying life.

Her body was bare of any robe, but she held on her knees, so that it covered her to the base of her throat, a huge mask. That mask was demonic, yet not ugly. Rather it seemed great beauty had been twisted to serve great evil, so that it was degraded and debased.

"Andas." He saw the cruel smile grows as she spoke. "Emperor that wished to be. Behold your empress! Give homage as it is due!"

As she spoke, the mask before her looked at him also with a compelling stare. He shivered, knowing that it, too, had life—or was in some way an extension of a life force that had no human connection, more to be feared than merely alien.

"Homage, Andas, humble homage—" She made a chant of the words. And that chant was taken up by the women gathered at the foot of the throne until it beat in his head. But he stood erect and did not answer.

It appeared that she was not expecting such defiance, for now she ran tongue tip across her lips and ceased that chant. But a moment later she spoke again.

"You cannot stand against me any longer, Emperor of rags and tatters, of a ruined empire. If you have come to surrender—"

"I have not come to surrender, witch." Andas spoke for the first time, and his words cut across hers as swords might clang blade on blade in a duel.

"Yet you bear our emblem as a banner!" She laughed, pointing with her chin to the ring.

"Not as a truce flag, Kidaya, but as a torch to show me your path."

"And you have walked it—to your end, Emperor of ashes and dead men!"

"Not yet!" From whence came that flash of inspiration he never afterward knew. It was like an order sent ringing through his head by the will of a power beyond his own knowledge.

He readied the baton as if it were a throwing spear, such as a man uses for skill hunting. And he hurled it, so that the ring at its tip entered straight into the mouth of the mask.

Then he saw the lips move, close upon the wand and snap it. The portion bearing the ring, with the ring, vanished.

"To like fares like!" he cried, and the words also came from somewhere outside his own mind.

There was a moan running through the company. But Andas was no longer aware of them—he saw only Kidaya. Now, as her mask of confidence broke and she allowed emotion to show fleetingly upon her face—consuming hate—he traced a likeness to the Princess Abena, faint though it was. The princess was at the beginning of a crooked and shadowed road. This woman had walked the full way to stand at its end.

She laughed. "My poor littling! Now you have thrown away what small protection you ever had. As the Old Woman has eaten your safeguard, so shall she now eat you." She fell then to crooning, rubbing her hands caressingly along the sides of the mask, so that Andas could see that she did not need to steady the thing on her knees, but that it rested there of itself.

Kidaya crooned, and the mask began to grow larger and larger until it hid all of her, save her slender feet and the hands that still gentled it. If this was illusion, the hallucinatory power behind it was very great.

The eyes were alive, and they looked upon him with a stare as if to draw him forward to death, while the mouth opened and a great tongue used its tip to beckon him.

Andas could feel the urge, the need to reach that mouth. But what he wore about him kept him steady, though the pull was nigh unbearable. And all the time the mask grew.

Still Andas waited for the signal he was sure would come. Move too soon and that which manifested itself in the mask would not be drawn far enough into this plane of existence to be destroyed. Wait! But the need to go to it— He swayed as he stood, torn between the witchery of the mask and the counter force about his body.

He could not stand it much longer—he would be torn apart!

The signal he waited for came with a flash of energy filling his whole body. Andas raised his hands and began to trace in the air the contours of the mask. From his lips poured the ancient chant he had learned at the fort. It was the sound and tone of those words that should release the energy now filling his entire being and aim it as he made of himself a vessel of destruction.

His whole body quivered and shook with what filled it. Andas believed he could actually see faint threads of light shooting from the tips of his fingers. And then he obeyed the call of the mask, leaping up to meet it as if he were its prisoner at last.

There was—

But no man could—would—be allowed to remember what came then. There was nothingness and the dark.

He was cold. He had never been so cold in his life. Life? No, this was death, which had been his burden and finally finished him. But could one smell in death? Could one feel? If so, then old speculations were at fault. Smell, feel, hear—for there was moaning he could hear.

See? Andas opened his eyes. He lay on rock, looking at blasted, blackened stone, so stained it might have been worked upon by blaster fire.

Stone? Memory came back. So, he was not dead. He levered himself to his knees and swung his head slowly from side to side. And what he saw sickened him somewhat but did not pierce far, for it was as if the cold he felt created an ice barrier between him and the world.

He could not get to his feet, but he crawled out of that hollow until he crouched in the open between the bone walls of the pathway. He was no sooner in the open than there was a resounding crash from within. A great billow of gritty dust puffed out, so he cried aloud and threw up his arms to cover his face. But afterward there was no moaning in the dark.

284

Andas crawled on, and the stones and gravel cut his hands and knees. He felt no pain, for the cold kept him in its hold, and no other sensation could pass it. Finally he came to the skimmer.

It took the last of his strength to crawl within and tumble into the pilot's seat. He had to raise two bleeding hands to set the controls, nor was he fully aware as the craft raised from the valley and swung around on the recorded tape that would take it home.

For a while he was limp, inert, preserved from all feeling. That he had accomplished what he had gone to do, that what occupied the mask had been destroyed in this world, at least for a space, and with it those who had served it, he knew. But he felt no triumph. It was like watching a taped story in which one was not personally involved.

He had hoped to die swiftly and cleanly in that final moment when he made of himself the ultimate weapon. But it seemed that the very power he had invoked had preserved him, to die more horribly and lingeringly. That, too, he was able to face with detachment, which he dimly hoped would continue to hold. If the energy had burned out of him all fear and emotion, so much the better.

At last he either lapsed into a stupor or slept while the skimmer bore him away from those ominous mountains toward a land waiting to be reborn.

When Andas awoke, he was not in the skimmer, but lying on a cot bed, and around him were the walls of the fort. So he had made it back after all—or the skimmer had made it for him on tape command. But again there was no feeling of triumph in him, only a vast weariness. He wanted to close his eyes and sleep. Perhaps this was the first symptom he must endure before the end.

Someone moved into his line of vision. Shara stood there—but with a difference about her. Those tight braids were gone. Her hair made a soft halo about a face that was still far too thin and drawn. Again the years had fallen from her. She was young, and in her burned a light that made her far different from the woman who had wept over the dying emperor. But though she did not weep for him, she would watch a second emperor die. Suddenly feeling broke through the cold that encased him. There was no one to weep for him. And the desolate loneliness was more than he could bear. Andas closed his eyes. But it seemed she would spare him nothing.

"Andas! Andas!"

Reluctantly he looked at her once more. She was on her knees beside his bed so her face was close. There were tears in her eyes after all. One spilled over to form a clear droplet on her brown cheek.

"Andas—"

"It is done," he told her. "The Old Woman—is destroyed—perhaps forever. Rule in safety, Empress!"

"Only with an emperor!" she replied. "Andas, the medic—he could not find any radiation deterioration. You will not die, not now!"

He continued to stare at her. She was telling the truth. He could read it in her face. Not die? With radiation readings such as they had told him? It was impossible that any human being could survive.

Any human being! Did he have at last the answer to his one moving question? Was he Andas—the *false* emperor, the android? This was the proof.

"I am not what you think—no emperor, not even a real Andas." He must tell her now, before she went on building on something which did not exist. She would perhaps have some kindness in her, but being human, she could

ANDROID AT ARMS

not but repudiate him for what he truly was.

"You *are* Andas!" she told him firmly. Her hands closed upon his with a grip he could not find the will to fight. She held them, imprisoned in hers, against her breast. "You are Emperor Andas, of that there is no question."

How could he make her understand? There was only the stark truth left.

"I am an android—made to look like the other Andas in my own world. But I thought that I was real!"

"You are real! You are Andas—"

"No!" His energy seemed to grow with his need to deny, to make her realize what he was. "This proves it. I am an android. A human being could not have survived such radiation. Don't you understand? I am *not* human!"

"Brother." A hand with fur growing down its back came out of nowhere to rest lightly on his shoulder. Andas turned his head to see Yolyos.

"Tell her," he appealed to the Salariki. "Tell her the whole story. She must not go on believing—"

"He has told me, Andas! When you went as we thought to your death, he told me. Do you think the medics would not have known that you were android? They believe that you were healed by the force you used to destroy the Old Woman, that it might have killed you instead if you had not been already exposed to the radiation, but that one balanced the other, to your saving."

"Yet neither would have affected an android—"

"No one could make so human an android. You are a man. Believe—accept it—" she entreated him.

But he looked to Yolyos. The Salariki smiled. "If you are android, so am I, but we are near enough human, it seems, to be human. Why should it then matter, brother? If it has saved your life twice over, be glad for it."

287

"Be glad—" Shara leaned closer. Her lips were warm and comforting on his.

He surrendered. Near enough human to *be* human. He would believe—he had to now.